MURDER
ON THE
MISSISSIPPI

MURDER
ON THE
MISSISSIPPI

A SALLY WITHERSPOON MYSTERY

ERIK S. MEYERS

To my mother, my sister and my late stepfather for their love and support.

Praise for Murder on the Mississippi

"An enjoyable, but deadly cruise down the Mississippi that will keep you in suspense from start to finish! A relaxing trip down the river that turns into a nightmare for main character Sally Witherspoon is a delightful mystery for readers. There's a lot going on aboard The River Queen."—Ivanka Fear, author of the Blue Water Mysteries and Jake and Mallory Thrillers

Chapter One

Oh, wonder of wonders, the day had finally arrived.

Sally Witherspoon leaned back and inhaled the scents of nature, her greying chestnut ponytail swaying in the wind. The bright sun on her bare arms felt glorious.

Ever since she had been a child in Savannah, she had dreamed of taking a paddlewheel boat trip down the Mississippi, just like Mark Twain. But the Mississippi was a very long way from the Atlantic coast of Georgia.

Now that she lived in northwestern Arkansas, the river was much closer, and she could finally make her dream come true. Being an independent adult with money certainly helped as well.

It was not a moment too soon.

Six months had passed since the terrible events surrounding the murder of her best friend and business partner, Bill Arnold, and several others in her adopted town of Berry Springs.

After she and Detective Finnegan had solved the multiple deaths, she had put her nose to the grindstone to try and forget. Luckily, her employee Magda had been kind enough to stay on and help run her biker bar, Sally's Smasher. Otherwise, she didn't know how she would have managed. And Annette, who had unexpectedly gotten a share of the bar in Bill's will, had suddenly decided she wanted to learn the bar business, though she allowed Sally to buy her out first.

It had been an emotional, but satisfying six months.

Now it was time for a break.

When Sally first started planning the trip, she had thought she might want to bring someone along for company. The more she had thought about it, the more she had realized she really needed time to herself.

In her typical meticulous way (though maybe this really meant her occasional inability to make a decision), she spent a month researching tour operators, boats, sights, and cities along the way and the history of the Mississippi River itself.

Weighing length of time away, cost and things she wanted to do and see during the trip, including having a large room with a balcony, she chose The Royal Barge boat tour company. Or maybe she chose it just because of the name. That would make her feel like royalty. Even better, the name of the boat was "The River Queen."

She also appreciated that it wasn't a typical tour. Entitled "Hidden History," they would be visiting special historic sites related to the peoples that the United States had caused so much pain. This included several Native American places as well as a World War II Japanese Internment Camp. Sally's own family history in Savannah had included slave owners. She was ready to face this past and perhaps help to try and atone for it in the future.

It was an exclusive boat tour with only eight other passengers. The intimacy and quiet would be restful, considering she spent most nights with tons of people at her bar in Berry Springs.

Best of all, the tour started in Hannibal, Missouri, the birthplace of Mark Twain. She had read all his books growing up and had always wanted to see where he was born. And Hannibal was a lot closer than Hartford, Connecticut, where Twain lived for years as a famous adult.

It would be a magnificent ten days sailing all the way to New Orleans, and Sally couldn't believe the adventure was about to begin.

She opened her backpack and pulled out the info on the trip she had printed out, including a list of the passengers. She was definitely a people (and paper) person, so she wanted to try and get a sense of them before she actually met them in a couple of hours. They would get a guided tour of Hannibal in the afternoon, then board the ship in time for dinner.

Glancing down at the list of names, she was excited to see that it was quite an international group. She had been in such a hurry to get everything ready at the bar for Magda and Annette to handle for ten days on their own, she had just quickly printed out the tour info and stuffed it in her backpack before heading out to drive the six hours to Hannibal. Realizing on the way that this was too long to drive all at once, considering she left the bar at five pm, she had stopped at a motel in Jefferson City around nine pm to rest up for the last part of the journey.

She had rolled into Hannibal that Thursday around ten am after a quick breakfast and was now enjoying the sun on a bench on the river in Nippers Park at River Point.

The bright sun was starting to get to her, but she loved the warmth. She pulled her water bottle out of her backpack and took a long swig. Then she rifled in her bag for a baseball cap. She always had one with her featuring the Sally's Smasher bar logo on it. It always got a lot of attention and questions. She did love to talk about her bar and her adopted town of Berry Springs.

Looking back at the list, she counted seven countries represented.

There was the U.S., China, Australia, Israel, Spain, Italy, and South Africa.

Sally liked that it was a mix of couples and singles. She hated being the odd person out if all the rest of the travel group were couples. She had traveled a lot around the US and had been to Europe a few times and South America once, so she was eager to learn more about where all these probably fascinating people came from.

Jason and Amy Wong (Beijing, China/Cape Town, South Africa)

Dr. Lilian Wilcox (Alice Springs, Australia)

Jim O'Sullivan (Boston, Massachusetts)

Aharon Cohen and Niv Peretz (Tel Aviv, Israel)

Brin Clarkson (Valencia, Spain)

That is an odd name for a Spaniard, she thought.

Brother Francesco (Assisi, Italy)

Wow, sounded like a colorful group. And included a monk. As a Catholic, Sally had always dreamed of going to Assisi, where St. Francis had lived, but she didn't think that would be happening any time soon. She would definitely be pumping the monk for all the information he would give her on the holy city.

She looked up from the list and across the river. The mighty Mississippi was rolling along, not too high for this time of year. It lulled Sally into quiet reflection, something she hadn't been able to do for a while.

She drifted back to daydreaming about going to Italy. Maybe she could even go to Rome and meet the Pope.

Sally wondered what Italy was like. Would it be as colorful and crazy as she had read about? A couple of her friends in Berry Springs had been to Rome and had loved it.

She was awakened from her reverie by the alarm on her phone.

Glancing down, she saw it was time to head to the meeting point for the Hannibal tour. Her dreaming would have to wait until she was on the boat. It seemed like she had just sat down on the bench, but actually, three hours had passed. She would have to hurry if she was going to meet the rest of the passengers on time. And she hated being late.

Sally stuffed the printouts in her backpack and jumped up.

She headed down Main St. to the Mark Twain Home, the beginning of the afternoon tour.

Chapter Two

When Sally arrived at the Twain boyhood home, it was easy to spot her group. They were the obvious tourists milling about on the front lawn awkwardly trying to take up a conversation with people they didn't know.

She also heard a few languages being spoken.

Sally strode right up to the group.

"HI, I'm Sally Witherspoon," she said a bit too loudly.

Not only did her tour group turn toward the voice, but so did everyone on the porch waiting to get into the house.

She turned a mild shade of red.

A short, fit, and tanned woman spoke first.

"G'day. I'm Hoppy Wilcox," the woman said, pumping Sally's hand.

"Nice to meet you, Hoppy. The list said Lilian Wilcox, though. Was that a mistake?" Sally replied.

The woman coughed.

"Um, well, I hate that name. Everyone calls me Hoppy."

Wilcox brushed her brown hair out of her eyes.

"Okay, cool. Welcome to America," Sally said, realizing immediately that was a pretty dumb thing to say.

Maybe she was more nervous than she was letting on.

Hoppy laughed, and this brought the rest of the group over.

Everyone shook hands and introduced themselves.

Sally was already trying to scan them for personality traits and place them all into some kind of pattern, as she did nightly at the bar. She pinched herself subtly to remind herself that first impressions could be deceiving and that she wasn't on bar duty for once. And how much could you get to know people over just a few days, even if they were going to be confined to a boat together for much of the time?

She spontaneously decided that she liked Hoppy, Aharon, and Niv from Israel, and Brin Clarkson, a Canadian living in Valencia, Spain, the best. She hoped they could become good friends. Well, at least for the trip. There was nothing more annoying for a tour group when no one got along or worse, disliked each other.

Walking into the Twain boyhood home with the group, she noticed that Jim O' Sullivan, the retiree from Boston, didn't seem so happy to have a male couple on the trip. But Sally wasn't going to let his homophobia spoil the trip. And if he tried anything, she would be telling him where to stuff it.

She didn't know where that aggression was coming from, but it was the 21st century. She couldn't understand, or tolerate intolerant people.

And if he really reacted this way, why did he choose this tour, which was all about diversity & inclusion?

She would definitely have to find out more about Jim from Boston.

The people she couldn't read, at least not right away, were Jason and Amy Wong from China and Brother Francesco, the Benedictine monk from Italy.

"Welcome, everyone," a tall blond young man with a British accent said, "I'm Martin Sandworth, first officer on the River Queen and your tour guide during your trip with us."

Everyone in the group murmured 'hello.'

Sally swooned, well, at least in her mind.

Sandworth led them into the first room on the tour, the family dining room. Like most old house tours, the table was set with the best china and fake food to look like the family was about to sit down to dinner.

The group stood at the rope, while Sandworth easily climbed over and stood close to the table.

"Welcome to the home of Mark Twain, who lived here with his family from 1840. He was..."

A cough stopped him. Eyes all turned to the person who coughed.

It was Jim O' Sullivan, a short, rotund gentleman with thinning grey hair and a bushy beard.

"Um, well, he was born Samuel Clemens to be sure," Sullivan said.

Sally detected what sounded like a slight Irish accent, but she wasn't one hundred percent certain.

He was definitely going to be the most annoying on the trip. There was always someone in every tour group trying to show off their knowledge and one-up the guide.

Usually men, she also noted.

Sandworth just smiled.

"Well, yes, that is correct, but of course, he is much better known as Mark Twain."

Gotcha, Sally thought.

Sullivan shrugged, and the tour continued throughout the house. Sullivan only interrupted Sandworth twice more, and everyone seemed relieved of that.

Sally had been impressed how much Martin Sandworth knew about Mark Twain, and while she had read most of his books and several biographies, she also learned a thing or two.

The tour ended as always in the small gift shop, which was mainly Twain's books. The group split up and they all browsed the store, many feeling obligated to purchase something.

Sally found a display of leather bookmarks, something she tried to collect on every trip. She chose a navy blue bookmark with a "Mark Twain" signature on it and the words "Hannibal, Missouri." It was simple and would easily remind her of the trip.

"Sally?" a voice behind her inquired.

Sally turned.

"Hi, I was wondering if you wanted to join me for a walk?" Brin asked, smiling.

Sally had taken an instant liking to her. She was just over five feet tall, bright red hair, in a brilliant blue dress. She had leather boots on with straps up to her knee. Sally loved funky, fun people.

"Sure, that would be great Brin," Sally replied, "I really only wanted to see the Mark Twain house, to be honest, not all of Hannibal."

Brin beamed, leaning over and whispering, "Perfect. Me too!"

The two strolled out of the house and down the steps.

Martin came running after them.

"We still have more of the town to see," he pleaded.

Sally turned back to him and put on her friendliest smile.

"Is it okay if we skip the rest? We wanted to take a walk on our own," she explained.

Martin didn't reply immediately.

This wasn't a kindergarten, she thought, but kept that thought to herself.

Finally, he said, "Well, okay. Just be on the ship latest by six, darlings."

Gosh, Sally loved his accent.

They waved to him as they headed away from the house.

Sally looked at her phone.

"Well, we still have about two hours until we have to board the ship for dinner. How about a walk down Main Street and along the waterfront?" Sally suggested.

"Sounds perfect. If you don't mind, I'd like to smoke my pipe."

"Wow, yes, of course."

Sally tried to keep a neutral face as Brin pulled a large black pipe out of her humongous purse, almost as big as Brin herself.

She lit it and puffed away, trying to blow the smoke away from Sally.

"I don't know too many people that smoke pipes," Sally began.

Brin laughed.

"You mean, you don't know too many women that smoke pipes. I love it. It gives me a mysterious feel and helps to keep difficult guests at bay if they think they will try anything on me. Makes me look unique, you know."

"Guests?" Sally asked.

"Yes, I run a small boutique hotel in Valencia, The Brass Monkey. I inherited it from my mother, who fled Canada when I was a child."

"Wow, a hotel. That is so cool. I run a biker bar, so I can understand the point about difficult guests. We get our fair share of fights, but my partner

Bill always…"

She choked up. Sally didn't know where that came from. She was talking about Bill as if he were still there to help with the bar and the bar fights. It had been six months, but Sally had a hard time admitting to herself she wasn't over his death yet.

"Sally?" Brin asked, placing a hand on Sally's arm.

Sally took a deep breath and smiled.

"Oh, nothing. The bar fights in the bar unnerve me a bit. Sometimes I wonder why I bother," Sally said, trying to change the subject.

"Well, though we only just met, you seem like a caring, supportive person who wants to provide a nice experience for your guests, but you don't really like violence. Though if not, a biker bar might not have been the right choice."

She laughed at the last part.

Sally didn't reply and just looked out at the water. Brin took the hint and puffed away at her pipe in silence. The smell was sweet and soothing, but Sally tried not to inhale too much.

They continued down Main Street and through the historic district. It was a beautiful spring day, and Sally had to keep her arms tight to navigate through the packed streets. She frowned every time she bumped into someone. Hannibal was more popular than she had anticipated. Mark Twain was known the world over; Hannibal, Missouri, on the other hand, wasn't exactly on the main tourist drag.

They stopped and looked in at a bakery with delicious-looking chocolate cupcakes in the window. Sally heard her stomach growl, but she didn't want to spoil her appetite.

She looked over at Brin.

They quickly walked away before either of them was tempted.

Reaching the end of the historic district, they strolled the short distance to the river and found a bench in the sun to enjoy. Coincidentally, it was the same bench Sally had been sitting on earlier.

"So what brings you to Missouri and the Mississippi? It isn't exactly a typical tourist attraction," Sally asked.

Brin didn't respond, but got up and took a selfie of her, her pipe, and the river. She sat back down and began tapping rapidly on her screen. Sally waited a couple of minutes as Brin did whatever she was doing.

"Yay," Brin screamed. "I already got a like."

Sally was on social media, only because they had a bar page there, but she didn't have too much time for it. Brin seemed to know more about it.

Brin looked up from her phone.

"Sorry, I didn't mean to be rude. I'm here visiting my sister in New York. She's a tax lawyer, and I used to live there. I've loved the Mark Twain books for years and always wanted to visit, so I decided to take an extended vacation and come here."

"What about the photo?" Sally asked, curious why she had spent so much time on her phone.

"Oh, I'm quite the influencer in Valencia and make some money on the side doing it. I promised my fans I would document the whole trip here for them. I should really be taking more pictures to post."

Sally smiled, "Go right ahead. I'm happy just sitting here in the sun."

She pulled out a novel from her backpack.

"I think I'll just read and let the world go by."

"Thanks," Brin said, quickly jumping up and running down the path.

Sally laughed, shook her head, and put her head down in the latest murder mystery she was reading, "Death Has Windows."

Chapter Three

"Welcome to ze River Queen. I am Matilda Kramer, your captain. I hope you will have a very pleasant and enjoyable stay on board."

The captain had met them at the gangway as they boarded.

Sally immediately fell in love with her accent. German, she thought.

She was also impressed with her stature. Captain Kramer was at least six foot tall with tight steel-wool hair and long, bony fingers. Sally thought she fit the part perfectly.

"My first officer, who you've already met, vill check you in. Ve vill all be dining together at 7:30 p.m. at ze front of the ship."

With that Captain Kramer, smiled widely then spun around and marched away.

Martin Sandworth came forward to read their names out and hand them their key cards, which gave them access to their room and also allowed them to pay for whatever they needed on board.

Sally had pushed herself toward the front of the line so she would have more time to relax and freshen up before dinner. Or maybe it was just her competitive nature.

"Dr. Lilian Wilcox," he began.

Sally heard a sigh behind her.

"That's me. But please call me Hoppy, like I said on the tour."

Hoppy moved around Sally and took her key.

"Sally Witherspoon," Sandworth continued.

"Thanks," she said, grabbing her key card and heading straight to her cabin for a quick shower.

Walking quickly down the hallway, she caught sight of Hoppy heading into her cabin on the right. When Sally got to hers, number two, she saw she was right next door to Hoppy.

Holding her key at the lock, it beeped, and she turned the handle and headed inside.

The room took her breath away.

Looking right out onto the river, she saw two comfy chairs with bright cushions on a small balcony. The cabin was decorated in cheery colors with floral prints. She had a large bed, a sofa, a coffee table, and a small desk and chair. The latter was right at the window, so you could sit there and look out at life going by, or just water.

She dropped her suitcase on the bed, opened it, and began getting ready for dinner.

The shower was glorious. Her house in Berry Springs was older ("charming" as the real estate agent had put it), and the hot water never quite got as hot as she wanted it. The large shower in her room on the ship was wonderfully hot, and she spent much too long enjoying the luxury.

She had set an alarm to leave for dinner on time, and she was dismayed to hear it just as she shut off the faucet. So much for relaxing before dinner.

She decided to forgo drying her long hair and quickly dressed. She rarely wore makeup, but decided for a light shade of pink lipstick. She was on vacation, and dinners on cruises were supposed to be elegant. She had even brought one of her few dresses on the trip. Stepping into the dress, she zipped it up, slipped on her red flats, and did a final check in the mirror.

She took a deep breath, reminding herself she was finally on vacation, and headed down the hall to dinner. She hoped she wasn't going to be the last one there.

Walking into the dining room, she quickly saw that there was one person still not there, Hoppy.

She checked the seating chart at the front of the restaurant and saw she even had her own table. She had lucked out and gotten one right at the back of the restaurant, facing out to the river.

Smiling at everyone as she passed, she slid into her seat and was just blown away by the view. The sun was setting, and the river was shimmering with color. What a treat.

She was staring out the huge windows at the river when there was a slight cough behind her.

She turned to see the waiter with two bottles of wine.

He was beautiful, at least six feet tall with very dark skin, the blackest of eyes, and perfectly manicured nails.

"I am Kwame, your server this evening," he said. "Would you like red or white wine with dinner?"

"Oh, right, one sec," Sally responded quickly, glancing at the menu booklet on her table. While she ran a biker bar that mostly served beer, she loved wine and always wanted to make sure the wine fit with the meal. She saw it was a set three-course menu for everyone, with a vegetarian option for the main course. She decided to go with the meat.

Looking up, she said, "I'll have red, please. What red wine is it?"

Kwame turned to show her the label.

It was American, from Virginia, she was quite impressed. One of her favorite labels.

"Oh, wonderful."

Kwame smiled brightly and poured her first glass.

He walked over to the next table.

Reaching down to smell the bouquet, she knew this would not be her last glass. This was vacation.

Tasting her first sip, she was overjoyed. Nutmeg, spice, and a hint of dried fruit were just perfect.

As she was savoring the delicious Virginian wine, Hoppy came over to her table.

"Mind if I join you? I hate eating alone. I don't know why they do this on these trips. We're such a small group, we should all be sitting together at one table."

Her voice rose as she said this, and all heads turned to her.

Hoppy turned red and sat down quickly.

Sally didn't have time to respond, but she decided she wouldn't mind the company.

She did a short sweep around the room. On one side of her, she saw Jason and Amy Wong, on the other, Aharon Cohen and Niv Peretz. Brin Clarkson was sitting alone just behind her. Brother Francesco and Jim O'Sullivan were at the last table on the side of the ship at the edge of the big windows. Sally wondered if they knew each other. Jim O'Sullivan was most assuredly Catholic.

Oh, stop it, Sally, not every Catholic knows each other. She realized she didn't know either of the men, and she was Catholic. She stopped trying to get to know everyone in her mind in three seconds and turned back to Hoppy. They would all be on the boat for ten days together, 24/7, so there would be time enough.

"So, what made you choose this trip?" Sally asked.

"Exhaustion," Hoppy admitted.

Sally furrowed her brow.

"Um, excuse me?"

"Oh, sorry, I meant that's the reason I needed a holiday. I'm a doctor in the outback near Alice Springs in Australia, and I've been married to my work for far too long. I could see the symptoms of burnout long ago, but I had my patients to attend to."

"Sorry to hear. That sounds harsh," Sally offered.

Hoppy smiled, "Yeah, I'm too tough on myself. It wasn't until my assistant found me collapsed on the floor that I finally admitted I needed a break. I've never been to America, and I only speak English, so I thought this was a good choice."

"Wow, that's a long way to come for a vacation. And you didn't choose one of the normal vacation spots for foreigners, like New York or Florida."

"I definitely wanted somewhere quiet to recover, but also something to do, so I wasn't completely by myself. I loved the thought of the river tour and like most of the guests here, well, probably everyone, I've read all the Mark Twain books and I fell in love with the Mississippi through him."

"Well, I hope you find the relaxation you're hoping for. It's been a crazy time for me, too."

Sally started telling Hoppy about her biker bar, though she decided to leave out the part about Bill's murder, at least for now.

At that point, the first course came, a bowl of creamy tomato soup. Sally realized when she saw it she was starving. Maybe she and Brin should have gotten something at that bakery in Hannibal.

Hoppy and Sally stopped talking and dug into the soup. It was served with lovely warm crusty bread and creamy salted butter. Sally was really going to enjoy this trip. No cooking or cleaning up! That was the bar owner talking.

They had just finished the soup when there was a tap on the microphone.

Everyone turned their heads toward the small stage in the corner.

Captain Kramer was standing there holding the microphone.

"Good evenink, I would like to welcome you, my guests, to the River Queen. It is a pleasure to have you all here on board zis ship. I have been captain of the River Queen for five years now, and I always enjoy welcoming new people. This group is small, so please do take the time to get to know each other a bit. We will all be here on this ship together for the next ten days. And there's no getting away from zat." She ended the last sentence with a deep chuckle.

Everyone tried to laugh, but Sally felt no one really thought it was funny, herself included.

"So in this spirit, I will tell you a little about myself. As you can probably tell from my accent, I am not from the U.S.

I am originally from Vienna, in Austria, but I've lived here for years and years. My family has been running a restaurant in Vienna for one hundred and fifty years, so hospitality is in my blood. I came here and fell in love with the waterways of your country. Somehow, this river we are on reminds me of the beautiful Danube flowing through my home city. I hope you will enjoy the river as much as I do. Thank you, and enjoy the rest of your evening. During your stay, please don't hesitate to come to me with any questions."

Sally noticed that besides herself, Francesco and Amy Wong were the ones paying the most attention to what the captain said.

As she finished, her eyes swept the room with the hint of a smile. She put down the microphone and walked back to her table. She was eating with Martin Sandworth, her first officer.

Sally was glad the captain hadn't asked them to change seats after each course. That had been one of the weird things her old boss in Atlanta had done during department workshops. He never got it that people can't be forced to like each other.

She turned back to Hoppy just as the main course arrived. They seemed to be serving at a fast clip. Sally hoped this wasn't going to be the pace every evening, but maybe they were just trying to impress with efficient service the first night. She would have to try and have a word with the captain. The bar owner in her always had ideas for improvements in service whenever she ate or drank somewhere. And she usually brought them up to the manager or owner right away. Annoying as that probably was for them.

Kwame placed their dishes in front of them, steaming as they should be.

"Mmmm, this steak looks delicious," Hoppy said.

"Yummy! And those lovely crisp potatoes with it. I'm definitely going to enjoy this trip. I'm usually the one serving people."

Hoppy laughed.

"Yeah, I can imagine. I hope no one gets hurt on this trip. The ship people always jump with joy when they know a doctor is on board if something happens."

Sally shuddered. She prayed this would be a quiet voyage.

The rest of the evening went smoothly. Afterwards, Sally drifted toward Aharon and Niv's table. Hoppy had jumped up right after dessert and apparently headed back to her room.

"Hey, I'm Sally," she said smiling down at the two Israelis.

"Uh, hi. Yeah, we know your name," Aharon replied, grinning.

"Oh, right, sorry. New people jitters, I guess," she said, not knowing where that came from.

"No worries. So, how did you like the dinner?" Niv asked.

"It was great. So nice to not have to serve anyone, but get served."

"Not serve anyone?" Aharon asked, his forehead full of wrinkles.

"Oh yeah, I can tell you all about it. How about a drink in the lounge?"

Sally offered, pointing to the doors at the far end of the room.

Aharon and Niv looked at each other.

"Um, maybe another night, Sally," Aharon replied, "We're still exhausted from the flight."

Sally waved it off, "No problem. Some other night."

She turned and walked over to enter the guest lounge at the edge of the restaurant.

She entered and felt like she had walked into her dream bar. Everywhere there were comfy brown leather chairs and sofas with throws to keep you warm. There was a small fire going in the fireplace, which luckily only gave off a calming light rather than heat. It was a warm time of year, and no one needed a hot fire, even with the chill of the air conditioning.

She dropped onto the comfy sofa in the corner.

She had thought to bring the mystery she had been reading. She had just settled into the cushions when Kwame came over.

"I hoped you enjoyed dinner," he said, smiling.

"Oh yes, it was delicious. What a lovely start to the trip," she replied.

"What can I get you?"

"I would love a glass of the red wine you served at dinner. That lovely Virginian one. Perfect."

Kwame walked over to the bar.

As he did, Sally saw Amy and Jason Wong enter the room. She looked down at her book but decided learning all she could about the other guests was more important.

Sally waved to them, hoping they would join her. Amy saw her and directed her husband over to the corner where Sally was relaxing.

Amy towered over her husband, and her bright blond hair and blue eyes made her look like a model.

Sally deviously wondered how someone like Jason had ended up with someone like Amy. He reminded her of her bean-counter accounting colleagues back in Atlanta: rat-like and nervous.

"Would you like to join me?" she asked.

"Oh, thank you," Amy said. Sally caught some kind of twang in her voice, then she remembered the passenger list had indicated Amy was from South Africa.

Amy and Jason sat on the two comfy chairs across from the sofa Sally was lounging on.

Kwame came over with Sally's wine.

"Oh, that looks lovely. Is that the same wine we had at dinner?" Amy asked.

"Yes, ma'am," Kwame replied.

"You loved it too?" Sally inquired.

Both of them nodded.

"We'll have two glasses of the red Sally has," Jason ordered.

"So, what brings you to the U.S.? I saw on the list that you are from China and South Africa."

Sally loved jumping right in.

"Well, yes. I've gotten an important post at the Chinese embassy in Washington, and we have a few weeks before I start. We thought we'd use it to relax a bit before the politics commence," Jason explained, smiling.

"You know you love that, dear," Amy replied.

"Wow, that sounds like an incredible opportunity," Sally replied.

"I'm so proud of him. Even if it means giving up my work, for a while. Maybe I'll open a restaurant in DC."

"Oh, you have a restaurant in China?" Sally asked.

She leaned forward, excited to meet another person in her industry.

Or maybe it was wine. She looked down at her glass and realized she had already downed half of it.

"Yes, actually, Amy is one of the most famous chefs in China. You mean you've never heard of Amy Wong?" Jason said, looking at his wife.

Sally wasn't sure she was going to like either of them. She had a biker bar in a small town in Arkansas and loved down-to-earth people. She had mostly been like that in Atlanta. These two sounded like they were gracing the world with their presence from on high.

"Well, I've never been to China, and I don't really follow the luxury restaurant scene," Sally replied.

Amy winced when Sally said that. Oops, she hadn't meant to make that come out as harshly as it probably did.

Maybe the two of them were lovely people.

"Yes, I have the only three-star Michelin restaurant in Beijing," Amy explained as if that meant anything to Sally. She had heard of Michelin stars, but three didn't sound like that many. She'd have to do her research.

"Wow, impressive," Sally offered, hoping to move on. Hopefully, they had something else to chat about.

"So, how did you go from South Africa to China?" Sally continued, hoping to change the subject.

Jason turned to Amy and said something in what Sally thought must be some form of Chinese.

Amy ignored him and looked at Sally. Jason clenched his fists and sipped his wine.

"Well, I'm from South Africa, yes, but moved to China as a child, after a couple of years in Australia. My father was a diplomat, and we moved a lot. But when we got to China, we all decided to stay. Though we still keep a home there. I'm proud to say I'm fluent in Mandarin and Cantonese," Amy said, her cheeks brightening.

Sally almost blurted out 'well la-di-da' but didn't want to sound like an ass.

Kwame luckily came over at that point.

"Anything else I can get you?" he asked.

Sally replied, "Oh yes, another glass of the red, please, and some mixed nuts."

"Nothing for us, we're heading back to our room soon," Jason replied.

"Well, sounds like you both have such an exciting life. I run a biker bar in a small town in Arkansas. I can't keep up with you two," Sally said smiling hoping it hadn't come out too bitchy.

"Oh, a biker bar, how interesting," Amy replied, sneering.

Sally ignored her.

"I worked in Atlanta and got sick of city life. My ex-husband and I went on vacation in the Ozarks, and I fell in love with the little town of Berry

Springs," Sally continued.

"How quaint," Amy said.

Sally wasn't sure if it was the wine or her attitude, but she wished she hadn't asked them over to sit with her.

Luckily, Amy and Jason got up to leave.

"Lovely speaking with you, Sally. Have a nice evening," Jason said as they turned and hustled out of the lounge back to their cabin.

Sally fell back on the sofa and breathed a sigh of relief. That had been exhausting.

Chapter Four

Lying in bed the next morning, Sally spontaneously concluded Brin was the most fun person in the group. She decided to tag along with her the rest of the trip as much as possible. Sally had never met a real influencer before, and maybe Brin had some tips for her bar's social media page.

Well, maybe for the tourists. Berry Springs was a popular destination in the Ozarks during the summer, though things started to die down by the middle of September.

Ugh, she needed to find a better comparison. Ever since the murders six months ago, anything referring to death or dying just made her ill.

She checked her phone and saw it was only seven am. The first stop on the boat tour was St. Louis, which they would reach around nine. She still had time for a quick breakfast and shower.

She lay back in bed, enjoying the luxury and the quiet before reaching for the phone and ordering a room service breakfast for eight a.m.

Before jumping in the shower, she decided to first make herself a coffee in the room and sit on the balcony.

Glorious, Sally thought as she sipped her coffee and felt the gentle movement of the boat against the river. The bank she looked at was covered in vines and trees, almost like being in the jungle, or what Sally thought it would look like. She checked the map on her phone to try and figure out where they were. Just turning a deep bend where the Illinois River flows into the Mississippi. Not far from St. Louis.

She saw a stork on the riverbank and tried to get a picture. Squinting at the photo on the phone, she just saw grey and white against green. She really needed to get some tips from Brin, or just a newer phone. She had bought it a few years ago when the phone had been brand-new on the market. At the time, she had felt so cool and exclusive owning one of the fancy phones, now it was outdated.

A knock at the door made her jump. Already eight? She'd have to wolf down the breakfast to have enough time to shower and get dressed. They were all supposed to meet Martin Sandworth at the gangway at nine am for their day tour of the city.

* * *

Promptly at 9:10 am, Sally jogged down the hallway toward the entrance to the ship. She turned the corner and saw the rest of the group already standing there, ready to go.

"Sorry," she muttered as she tried to catch her breath.

"Okay, well, let's go and explore St. Louis," Martin said, a slight undertone of annoyance in his voice.

Sally followed the group out of the ship and onto the river quay. There was a small van waiting to take them all to their first destination, the Gateway Arch, which they could already see in the distance. At over six hundred feet in height, it couldn't be missed. Even from their distance, it looked gigantic. Sally couldn't wait to take a closer look.

Climbing into the van, Martin slammed the sliding door shut, and they were off.

Sally slid into a spot next to Brin.

"Hi Brin, how are you doing?" Sally asked.

Brin nodded but said nothing. Her face, and her phone, were pointed at the Arch.

Sally let her do her influencer thing.

At the Arch, they took the tram to the top.

Sally's breath was taken away at the view.

Brin squealed and began running around snapping photo after photo.

Sally decided not to try and keep up.

"Oh, the world of social media," a deep voice behind her said.

She turned to find Brother Francesco standing behind her.

Sally laughed. "Yeah, she really seems into it. I feel like I could learn a thing or two from her."

"Yes, she seems the expert. We are trying social media at my monastery, for the many visitors we get, but when you spend most of the day praying, gardening, or eating, there isn't much time left for other pursuits," he explained.

Sally looked him up and down and felt he belonged more in a 1950s Italian movie than in a monastery. He had thick black hair with a movie-star wave. His brilliant blue eyes were quite the contrast. To top it off, he had full, sensuous lips.

Sally had to shake the thoughts of his looks. She decided to distract herself.

"So you are in Assisi, I read?"

"Yes, St. Killian's Monastery, not too far from the St. Francis church. We are a small brethren of Benedictine monks in a monastery that has been there since 1610."

"Wow, sounds wonderful. I've always wanted to go to Assisi."

He raised his eyebrows, "So you are Catholic, I assume."

"Yes, how did you guess?" Sally said, grinning.

"I am a monk. We can always tell a Catholic when we see them."

He bellowed.

Sally looked at him, wondering if he was joking or actually meant it. She wasn't sure.

"What made you become a monk?" Sally asked, turning the conversation back to him.

Francesco stared at her and turned red.

Oops, wrong question?

"To be honest, it was to get away from my family, well, parts of it. I guess I sort of felt a calling, but I'm from a small village in the Alto Adige region of northern Italy. I was going stir crazy there and had to get out. My family drove me up the wall," he said, his voice louder by the end.

Sally was surprised to see the monk had a temper, though he was only human. She seemed to have hit a sore spot.

"I can understand getting away," Sally said, thinking of her ex-husband Bart.

The monk nodded sagely.

"I'm sorry for my outburst, it's just…well, forget about it."

"So did you find what you were looking for there?" she asked.

"I'm not sure yet," Francesco replied.

"Well, enough of the past, I was going to look at the exhibit, would you like to join me?" Francesco asked.

"Sure."

The two walked in silence over to the interactive screens, explaining the history and architecture of one of America's most iconic structures.

"So what brought you on this boat tour, Brother Francesco. It seems an odd place for a monk from Italy to vacation."

He laughed.

"Well, we really don't get vacation like you do, but I was asked to visit a Benedictine Monastery, St. Simeon's Abbey, near New Orleans, so my brothers decided I should have a short rest before, outside of monastic life. I've been quite ill over the past year and only recently recovered."

"Oh, I'm glad to hear you are feeling better. Rest is so important after an illness or trauma. I've had a rough six months myself," Sally admitted.

"Oh, you have been ill too?" the monk asked.

"Well, not exactly."

Maybe because he was a monk, but Sally felt something cathartic in explaining what had happened in Berry Springs just a few short months ago. Every time Sally mentioned a murder, the monk's eyes went wide. She didn't know why she decided to pour it all out, but it felt like a confession to her. Not that she had killed anyone herself, but she needed to get it all out.

When she finished, the monk smiled at her.

"Wow, you really have had a terrible time. I want to thank you for sharing it with me."

He placed his hand on her shoulder, and she felt a weight lifting.

"Thank you, Francesco. It was such an awful experience."

"There is always something good that comes with the bad. Think about what that could be," he replied.

Maybe God was watching over her in the guise of an Italian monk. She was Catholic, though she never felt that religious, but at that moment, she was at peace.

Their quiet reverie was broken as Martin came over to tell them it was time to head back down and continue the tour of St. Louis.

As they moved toward the ride down, Sally heard what sounded like loud Chinese behind her. This time it was a man's voice.

Chapter Five

Sally turned to see Jason Wong jabbing his finger at his wife. Amy was ignoring him and stepping up her pace to get ahead of him to the ride down.

Sally had no idea what they were saying to each other, but it didn't seem good.

Martin walked over to both of them and tried to calm them down. Sally heard snippets of the conversation "other guests here," "public place," "just started the trip."

This seemed to work, and Jason stopped yelling. They made it to the ride down, and Amy deliberately got in the first car with a clear look that she did not want Jason to follow her.

Sally's curiosity got the better of her, and she followed Amy and sat down across from her. Amy scowled at Sally but remained quiet.

Brin jumped in next to Sally, and now Amy went black.

"Hey, wasn't that an amazing view?" Brin asked, enthusiasm seeming to be her drug.

"I got some great pictures for my followers. I hope they love them. Oh, wait, I know they will. I'm a top influencer," she laughed.

"Could you please be quiet," Amy said between gritted teeth.

"Geez, lighten up, honey," Brin retorted, raising a middle finger at the same time.

Sally burst out laughing in spite of herself.

Amy turned to look out the window, ignoring them the rest of the way down.

Sally was fascinated by Amy Wong for some reason. She really would like to understand her better. Sally's first thought was that perhaps Amy was more upset about giving up her restaurant than she was excited about her husband's big appointment in Washington.

She didn't want to only dwell on that, so she turned to Brin.

"Brin, you must give me some social media tips. I'd love to try and spice up my bar's page, you know, trying to get more tourists to visit us when they come to Berry Springs."

Brin nodded vigorously, and her bright red hair flailed about.

"Of course. I love to help people with their accounts. Social media is my life, well besides my hotel. Sometimes I'm not sure which should come first," she giggled.

They reached the bottom of the arch and climbed out.

"Everyone, our next stop is the beautiful Botanical Gardens. We will be taking our van, it's about five miles from here," Martin explained, pointing them to the exit.

They followed him outside. The sun was glaring, and Sally regretted leaving her sunglasses in her cabin.

Oh well.

The van was waiting at the edge of the walkway, and they climbed in.

Everyone got in randomly, so Sally ended up seated next to Niv. He gave her a big grin.

"So sorry about last night. We didn't mean to be rude, but Aharon was tired," as he said the last words, he whispered, "and I needed to get in a walk around the ship. I wanted to work out, but that wouldn't have been a good idea on a full stomach."

He flexed his arm for her, as if that would impress her.

She did admire his huge biceps. He had beautifully dark curly hair on his head and, Sally noted, on his chest. His deep V t-shirt left little to the imagination.

"No worries. I understand. We still have plenty of time for a drink together and a chat," she replied.

"Of course," he said.

Aharon tapped him on the shoulder and said something to him in what she guessed was Hebrew.

Sally really wished she knew more languages. She loved the international flair of the group, but as a bartender, she was desperate to understand what they were saying.

Oh, Sally, that would be eavesdropping, she told herself, but wasn't that what made a good bartender?

At the Botanical Garden, they started with a sandwich lunch at the café. Sally's stomach growled as if she hadn't had a big dinner the night before or the sumptuous breakfast.

As a group, they were served a selection of sandwiches, bottles of water, and carafes of coffee and tea.

Sally grabbed what looked like a cheese sandwich and planted herself in a middle seat, ready to take in the conversations around her. She really was itching to get to know her fellow passengers better. She had yet to say more than two words with Aharon or Jim.

Chewing away, she was glad to see Jim sit down next to her.

"'Mind if I sit here?" he asked in greeting.

"Of course," she replied in between bites.

"How did you enjoy the Gateway Arch?" he asked.

"What a view," she said.

"Oh yes, but I was most interested in how that thing stays where it is. I don't know much about math or engineering, but it seems like a miracle it hasn't collapsed," he said, his eyes twinkling.

"Is that why you came on the trip?" she asked.

Jim shook his head.

"No, just came for the river really. I didn't know we would be seeing all this diversity nonsense," he replied.

Sally frowned.

"Well, isn't it part of our history that we sometimes try to forget?" she offered.

"Whatever. I'm first-generation American from Dublin. I only really care about Irish history. I'm going to focus on the river and enjoy that as much as I can."

Sally decided to change the subject.

"Do you like to fish?" she asked.

"What's that?" he yelled, turning one ear toward him.

The rest of the group turned their heads toward him.

Jim turned red.

"Damn hearing aids, never work the way they're supposed to. What was that you were saying? Am I rich?"

Sally laughed.

"No, fish as in the things that swim in water. Do-you-like-to-fish?" she said slowly and slightly louder.

"Oh, fish. Yes, I do. I'm not sure there will be much fishing on the river, but sure as gold, I'd love to try. I'll have to ask Martin about that."

"There has to be some place you can try during the trip," Sally suggested.

Jim just shrugged his shoulders and ate his sandwich.

She would have a lot to tell Magda, her employee and friend, when she got back to Berry Springs. The events six months ago had brought them closer together. And Sally wouldn't have been able to manage the bar without Magda and Annette.

Oh Annette. Bill's will leaving Annette a part of the bar still made her twinge. Even if Annette had suggested Sally buy her share a few weeks after Bill's death.

Luckily, Hoppy came over and got her out of reverie.

"Sally, Sally?" Hoppy said, snapping her fingers.

"Huh, what?" Sally replied.

"I was asking if you wanted to walk around the Botanical Garden with me."

"Oh, sorry, I was miles away, wool gathering."

"What a quaint phrase," Hoppy said.

"Yes, from my Savannah grandmother."

"You must tell me all about her. Come on. We don't have all day here, and I want to see some of the really exotic plants, you know, the ones that are poisonous."

Sally shivered. Poison. Oh well, life must go on. She pushed Bill's murder out of her mind and followed Hoppy into the greenhouse.

Chapter Six

The heat and humidity hit Sally like a wall. She quickly peeled off the light jacket she was wearing.

Hoppy seemed not to notice, even if she was wearing a scarf and leather jacket.

"Oooh," Hoppy squealed.

Sally liked plants, but she didn't get quite as excited as Hoppy seemed to.

She walked over to where Hoppy was pointing.

"Oh, I love the flesh-eating plants," Hoppy said.

"That's a bit morbid," Sally replied.

Hoppy shook her head.

"Honey, it's life. Eat or be eaten, I say. These are nothing compared to some of the poisonous plants and animals we have in Australia."

Sally had always thought of going to Australia, but she wasn't sure she wanted to be dodging something poisonous every two seconds.

"Can we move on to something a bit less carnivorous?" Sally asked.

"Spoil sport," Hoppy replied with a giggle.

They walked through the rest of the greenhouse and found large palm trees reaching to the ceiling. These reminded Sally of a lonely, relaxing beach somewhere in the Caribbean.

Maybe she should have gone somewhere further away.

They finally got to the greenhouse exit, and Sally breathed a sigh of relief when the temperature and humidity dropped rapidly as they left.

"Oh look," Sally pointed to the sign that said "Rose Garden."

"My favorite flower. Let's go there next."

"Sure, why not? Though I hope my allergies don't act up. Those flowers can be deadly for my sinuses."

Sally replied, "Don't worry. If your allergies act up, we can leave, or you can wait for me at the edge of the garden."

"Sure."

The two women made their way down the hallway and outside. The outdoor space was surrounded by a high stone wall and was bursting with color and fragrance. The rose garden was right where they walked out, and Sally saw several other flower gardens in the distance.

Ha-chew.

"Oh, Sally. I'm not going to make it. I'm sorry."

Sally turned and checked her phone.

"That's okay. I don't want you to be sniffling and sneezing all day. Why don't we meet back at the cafe in an hour for coffee?"

"Sounds good. You enjoy the roses while I find something that I won't sneeze at. I saw a sign for Australia, so maybe they have something here I'm familiar with," Hoppy replied.

At that, Hoppy turned and walked back inside.

Sally watched her go and then turned and closed her eyes. She took a deep breath and sighed with relief.

The smell of old English roses relaxed her like nothing else. That's why she always liked to buy rose bath gel for her long baths.

Sally strolled through row after row of roses, looking down at the signs to try and make out which rose was which. She loved roses and had even tried to grow a couple of them in her backyard, but somehow they never took.

As she came up on the end of the second row, she found Jason Wong sitting by himself with his hands in his face.

Sally coughed, and he looked up, quickly wiping tears from his eyes.

"Oh, hi Sally. Sorry."

"Are you okay, Jason?"

He stiffened.

"Yes, of course. Why wouldn't I be?" he asked.

"May I join you? It's a lovely place to sit."

Jason motioned for her to sit down, but he didn't look like he wanted to talk.

Sally sat there with him, enjoying the fragrance and the peacefulness.

After a few minutes, Jason's voice broke the silence.

"Um, I want to apologize for our scene at the Arch."

Sally's mouth went wide, not expecting his openness.

"I don't like public displays of emotion, and I'm sorry we made you witness that."

Sally waved it off.

"Don't worry. We're human, and emotions are what make us human. You don't have to apologize."

Jason turned red.

"Well, I was brought up that emotions are evil and that we should suppress them. Perhaps I should have been Vulcan."

"You're a Trekkie?" she asked.

Jason nodded, "Well, a silent Trekkie. My wife doesn't approve."

"I love Star Trek. The thought of space exploration sounds so exciting."

"Yes, yes. But we are only able to explore one planet, this planet, at the moment. I'm excited I got this important post in Washington. I've always wanted to live in America. And I hope our daughter will want to study here. She is now seventeen, and she has been exploring different options."

Sally wanted to pat herself on the back at that moment. Somehow, her bartender skills always got people to open up and blurt out the inside words.

"Oh, I love Washington. You will have a fantastic time," Sally replied. "Is your daughter looking at universities there?"

Jason shook his head.

"No, unfortunately, Bai is not looking there," he said quietly.

"Oh, that's too bad."

Jason brightened slightly.

"Well, you know kids. They never want to be seen with their parents."

Sally didn't have kids, but she had seen plenty in Berry Springs.

"What about South Africa? Your wife must still have some family there," Sally asked.

Jason looked frozen, "No, not South Africa either."

Sally decided to quickly change the subject.

"So what made you choose this trip?" Sally asked.

Her standard question to all the out-of-town guests.

Jason looked relieved they had stopped talking about his family.

"Well, as my wife told you last night, we have some time before I start my appointment in Washington. We thought a river cruise would be a lot of fun. And the Mississippi River is known the world over. Oh, and of course, we both love Mark Twain's books."

Sally nodded.

"Me too. I've always dreamed of doing a trip like this," she replied, "And I liked that it was combined with a look at a side of American history that most people try to ignore or forget."

"China has its own history it tries to forget, but people always remember," Jason replied a bit mysteriously.

Sally quietly checked her phone and saw she only had fifteen minutes left before she was to meet Hoppy again. The time seemed to fly by when chatting with Jason.

"So great talking to you, Jason, but I promised to meet Hoppy soon for coffee before we head back to the ship. I hope you don't mind."

"No problem. I will stay here and enjoy the peace and quiet."

With that, Sally got up and walked toward the rest of the outdoor flower garden. She hoped to see and smell at least a few more interesting flowers before heading back inside to meet Hoppy.

As she walked away, she glimpsed Jason staring into space.

Chapter Seven

Sally went warp speed through several gardens outside and then strolled back in toward the café.

At the entrance to the greenhouse, she found Aharon and Niv talking.

They both smiled when they saw her.

"Hi, Sally," Aharon said, "Enjoying the garden?"

Sally nodded.

"Oh, it is just lovely here. I've just been sitting in the rose garden, breathing in the heavenly fragrances."

Niv turned green.

"Oh, that would make me ill. Those smells really make me nauseous. And I have terrible hay fever. We haven't been to see much," he explained.

Aharon added, "Which is really too bad, but oh well."

As he said this, he looked at Sally.

He had the same dark, curly hair and eyes that Niv had, but was shorter with a bit of a belly.

Sally thought he looked like he really enjoyed life.

"What are you doing now?" Niv asked.

"I'm headed back to the café for coffee with Hoppy want to join me?"

"Oh, that would be nice. Not much more to see here for us anyway," Aharon said, glancing at Niv.

Niv smiled, "Sure."

As they walked the rest of the way to the café, Niv took a turn into the men's room, so Sally and Aharon strolled along by themselves.

"So what made you decide to come on this trip?" she asked.

Aharon sighed.

"Well, it was my idea, Niv wasn't too happy about it. We usually go somewhere gay on vacation…"

Sally looked at him.

"Yes, I know a bit cliché, but we like the camaraderie and most of the places are in the sun with a beach, which reminds us of Tel Aviv."

"No judgment here," she replied.

"Well, we both love Mark Twain, and I always wanted to do a river cruise. We've been to America before, but only to New York and Key West. The middle of America is a bit far for us, but here we are. We also both liked the idea that it wasn't just a cruise, but also a tour of relatively unknown parts of American history."

"That's what I loved about the tour. That it combined the river with history. There's too much of our history that we try to forget," she admitted.

"Yes, but history always seems to repeat itself."

She felt a bit uncomfortable talking to someone Jewish about history. She had had a few Jewish friends in Atlanta, but most didn't want to talk about parts of Jewish history, like the Holocaust.

"I agree. It is sad that so many forget and just pretend everything will always be better in the future, when it often isn't. Maybe tours like this can help that," she replied.

"Oh, well, enough about history. Tell me about you." Aharon said.

As he said this, they reached the café and Sally scanned for Hoppy, but she was nowhere in sight.

They found a quiet table in the corner to wait for Hoppy and Niv.

Aharon got up.

Sally thought she had said something wrong, but they hadn't exchanged that many words, so she didn't know what was going on.

"What would you like?" he asked.

Sally laughed.

"What's so funny?"

"Oh, that's my quirky brain. I thought you were getting up to leave," she explained.

"Oh god no. You're one of the few people I feel like talking to on this trip."

"Oh, thank you! I'll have a cappuccino with an extra shot."

Aharon went off to get the drinks, while Sally sat and wondered where Hoppy was. She checked her phone. Niv also seemed to be taking his time. And they only had just over a half hour to get to the van and back to the ship.

Relax, Sally, you're on vacation. If they're not back to the ship on time, that's not your problem.

She took a deep breath and looked out the window of the café.

As she did, she saw Hoppy walking in the garden, chatting with Brin. Both women waved when they saw Sally, but they didn't look like they were coming into the café. They sat down on a bench in the garden and continued their chat.

Oh well. Sally smiled in spite of herself. Maybe it was a good thing, giving her more time alone with Aharon and Niv.

Aharon returned with the coffees.

Glancing around, he frowned.

"I hope Niv is okay. His stomach has been a bit wobbly."

"Oh, that's too bad," Sally said.

As she said this, Niv came into the coffee shop and quickly found them sitting in the corner.

"Everything okay?" Aharon asked.

Niv smiled.

"Yes, dear," Niv replied quietly

Turning to Sally, Niv explained, "I sometimes have a sensitive stomach, though I love to eat."

"I hope you're feeling better," Sally replied, patting his arm.

"Yes, thanks," Niv replied.

"Do you want something to drink?" Aharon asked.

"Peppermint tea would be good, if they have it," Niv replied.

Aharon nodded, got up, and went off again to get the hot drink.

"Aharon really treats me like his son sometimes. I'm thirty-eight, an accomplished author, not twelve."

Sally decided the best thing was not to comment on that and let Niv vent.

"Wow, you're an author. That's amazing."

Niv beamed.

"Thank you. Yes, I write biographies of famous Jewish people. My first was on Sigmund Freud. I've published five books and I'm now working on a biography of Golda Meir."

Niv was clearly proud of his work.

"Fascinating," Sally replied.

Aharon came back with Niv's tea and they sat in silence for a few minutes.

Both men seemed to be thinking about something.

She decided to break the silence.

"So Aharon, you were wondering about me," she said.

Aharon looked up.

"Ah, yes, right."

"Well, I run a biker bar in a small town in the Ozark Mountains in Arkansas."

"Wow, that sounds rough," Aharon responded.

"Oh, I love it. I used to be a boring accountant in Atlanta and decided I needed a change. My now ex-husband and I had gone there on vacation and loved it. When we got back to Atlanta, I decided to leave him and make my own way. And to be honest, I hated accounting. Who knows why I even got into it in the first place?"

Aharon laughed, "Well, I'm a lawyer, and I think that's because my mother kept pushing me into the law, but who knows?"

"Parents," Sally said, shrugging.

Both men nodded in agreement.

"I love running my bar and meeting so many interesting people. I'm glad I pursued my dream. Too many people realize too late that life is short. I'm in my late fifties. I can't imagine spending the last fifteen years in that bland office in Atlanta."

Niv spoke up.

"I agree. Aharon and I try to make the most of life. I'm glad I've been able to write full-time, with Aharon's help."

Aharon took his hand, and Sally blushed, being part of the moment.

"Okay„ everyone, let's go," Martin said from behind them, startling all three.

"Where did you come from?" Niv asked, winking at Martin.

Martin blushed and just gestured them all out.

Sally had thought she would be the one to know the time and leave the café, but apparently the conversation with the Israelis had been more engrossing than she thought.

That meant she really was starting to relax.

She followed Martin, Aharon, and Niv out of the café. When they got to the van, Hoppy and Brin were already inside, along with the rest of the group.

Sally slid into a seat next to Hoppy.

"Sorry, Darl," Hoppy apologized, "Brin and I got chatting and we lost track of time."

Sally smiled.

"No worries. We're all here to enjoy ourselves. We shouldn't have too many obligations, right?"

Hoppy turned back to Brin as Sally listened in. It seemed Brin wanted to do a story on Hoppy, the Outback doctor.

"It will definitely go viral," Brin said proudly.

"Whatever that means," Hoppy replied.

Brin's mouth fell open.

"Just kidding, I know what that means. Just teasing the influencer," Hoppy replied, winking.

Sally loved the group atmosphere. It really was an interesting mixture of personalities and people. All seemed nice and fun. And it was only day two. Who knew what the rest of the week would bring?

Chapter Eight

Back on the ship, Sally decided to tackle the captain, well, figuratively. She was dying to find out more about Vienna.

Sally left her cabin and walked down the hallway and up the stairs to the deck area. They hadn't had much time to sit outside up to that point. But Sally was going to make sure she planned some downtime up there with a cocktail and a good book.

Walking to the front of the ship, she saw the captain with Martin Sandworth. As she reached the door, she saw Brin coming out.

"Oh, Sally, hi. I've just had the most amazing interview with the crew. An exclusive for all my fans in Spain and around the world," Brin squealed.

Sally felt all she did was shriek and squeal, but she was certainly enthusiastic about life.

"That sounds great. I was just going to talk to the captain and found out a bit more about the ship," Sally explained.

"You mean, found out more about her. You don't lie very well," Brin was nothing if not direct.

Sally laughed.

"Well, I guess that too. She seems so mysterious, such a cool person who has had an adventurous life."

Brin agreed, "Definitely! Well, I'm heading back to my room for a snooze on the balcony before dinner."

"Enjoy," Sally called after her as Brin headed for the stairs.

Sally opened the door to the bridge and stepped inside.

The captain and Martin Sandworth stopped their conversation and smiled at Sally.

"Um, hello Sally, can ve help you?" Captain Kramer asked.

Sally looked at the floor.

"Um, well, I just wanted to have a chat. Do you mind?"

"With me?" Captain Kramer asked.

"Yes, if you don't mind."

Captain Kramer seemed to consider whether it was worth it.

"Okay. Martin, you have the bridge. I will only be gone a few minutes."

"Yes, Ma'am," Sandworth replied a bit too militarily for Sally's taste. Though that accent got her every time.

He looked so fit and trim in his uniform with his blond hair and blue eyes.

"We can talk outside, ya?" Captain Kramer suggested.

Sally followed her out to the deck. The sun was still shining, and it was wonderfully warm up there.

Kwame happened to be up there serving drinks to Niv and Aharon.

The captain waved him over.

She looked at Sally.

"Um, I'll have an iced tea, extra sweet," Sally ordered.

"Two, Kwame. Thank you," the captain added.

When Kwame had left, the captain turned to Sally.

"Thank you for your time, Captain Kramer."

Kramer managed a smile.

"Please, call me Matilda."

"Okay, Matilda. I just am so fascinated about the ship and what you told us about your background last night, I thought we could have a chat."

"Are you a reporter, Sally? I feel like I'm being interviewed."

Captain Kramer winked at Sally.

"Just kidding. I love to get to know my guests. We are such a small group each time, so we should all get to know each other a bit."

"I love traveling, though I haven't seen as many places in the world as I would like. I always wanted to go to Vienna."

Kramer looked off in the distance.

"Ah, Vienna. I love that city," she said.

"But you've been in the U.S. for years," Sally added.

"Well, true, but Vienna will always be in my heart. If you get there, you must try my family's restaurant, *Die Goldene Gabel.* For me, it is the best restaurant in the world."

"Um, could you spell that?" Sally asked, tapping the name of the restaurant in her phone as the captain spoke.

"It means the golden fork, by the way,"

"And what made you leave Vienna and come to the U.S.?" Sally asked.

At that, the captain frowned.

"To be honest, it was a mistake at first, but I soon got over it. And then I found the riverways and here I am," Kramer explained, sort of.

Sally felt like the conversation was over before it had really started, but at least she had gotten some of what she was hoping.

Maybe tackling the captain like that hadn't been such a great idea.

"Well, thank you, Captain. I don't want to keep you any longer," Sally said.

Captain Kramer sighed loudly, as is if Sally had relieved her of duty for the night.

"No problem. Sank you for ze talk," the captain replied, smiling.

The German accent seemed to come and go.

Captain Kramer got up and walked back to the bridge, just as Kwame brought the two iced teas.

He put them down on the table while looking at the captain re-enter the bridge.

"She really is a unique creature," he said.

Sally wanted to get more out of him, but Hoppy called him over to her table.

"Yes, she is," Sally said as he walked away.

* * *

Dinner that Friday evening was a buffet. Sally was looking forward to that because it meant they could sit anywhere they wanted.

She decided her focus that evening was cozying up to the monk.

Relax, Sally, you are on vacation, not investigating a murder.

Back in her room, she had a little time to check her emails before getting ready for dinner. She had told Magda, her bartender, if she had any questions, she should email. Text messages were to be only used in an emergency.

Sally really wanted to relax, and she knew if Magda was texting her, she would be right back at work behind the bar.

There were a couple emails from her accountant with the monthly reporting. And only one from Magda, asking her how she was enjoying her trip.

Phew, when she saw Magda's email address, she tensed, thinking there might be some kind of problem.

Relax, Sally, Magda has been working with you for years.

She laughed to herself and went to take a shower for dinner.

They had been told to dress casually. The formal dinner was the next night, Saturday night.

Sally decided to not go too casually. It was a luxury boat tour after all.

She pulled on black trousers and a cream blouse. She had brought one of the few pieces of jewelry she owned, a pearl necklace she had inherited from her grandmother. It came with matching pearl earrings, and she really felt fancy.

Sparkly blue flats completed the outfit.

She checked herself in the mirror and decided to brush her hair again. She usually kept it in a ponytail, but that seemed too casual, even for a casual dinner, but she hadn't done a good job of tidying her hair.

She went into the bathroom and grabbed her brush.

She had done two strokes when there was a knock at the door.

Sally put down the brush and walked to the door.

Through the peephole, she saw Brin smiling.

She opened the door.

"What's up, Brin?" Sally asked.

"Oh well, I wanted to have a quiet chat with you before we headed to dinner."

Brin moved to enter the cabin, but Sally blocked her way.

"Well, I was still getting ready. Can't it wait?"

Sally put her hands on her hips. She didn't like being interrupted. Brin's visit seemed very mysterious. She liked her, but maybe there was much more to her than meets the eye.

"Oh, you are way too uptight, girl. I just wanted to have a bit of a gossip. You seem like someone who notices stuff," Brin explained.

"Gossip?"

Brin nodded.

"Yeah, I wanted to get your take on our fellow passengers. You know, who they are, what they are like. I have no one else here to gossip with. The others seem a bit uptight, well, except for the Israelis, and Hoppy of course."

Now she shrieked with laughter.

Sally wasn't sure if she was really amused or just a bit off her rocker.

"Oh, all right, come on in."

They sat down on the couch.

The clock on the wall said 7:15, so they didn't have much time before dinner.

"So what do you think of everyone?"

Sally was a bit annoyed at having let Brin in.

"Why does that matter?" she asked.

"Oh, honey, chatting about people behind their backs is the only fun thing in life," Brin explained.

Sally frowned. She didn't think that was true.

"Oh lighten up," Brin pleaded, "How do you think I became such an influencer? Gossip, hon."

Sally felt like a grandmother sitting with her irreverent granddaughter. Maybe she really did need to lighten up.

"Well, I like the group. I really like that we are all a bit different, a bit quirky. And from many different countries."

Brin stared at her intensely.

"Anyone you don't like?" Brin asked.

Sally was about to answer 'Amy Wong' or 'Jim O'Sullivan', but they had only been on the ship a day, and she didn't want to jump to conclusions. Or add fuel to Brin's gossip fire.

Diplomatically, Sally responded, "Well, I haven't really gotten to know anybody well yet, so I wouldn't want to answer that now."

"Oh, how touching," Brin responded, clucking her tongue.

"Well, how about you?"

"I hate Jim. And Amy Wong. He is prejudiced against anyone not white, straight, male, and American. And Amy Wong is just a bitch with her hoity-toity 'I'm a Michelin star chef' attitude.' I feel sorry for her husband. Though he seems tough enough to handle her arrogance. I guess he'd have to be to be married to her."

"Wow, a day here and you already 'know' all this?" Sally said, using air quotes.

"Honey, when you run a hotel and see everything I've seen, you would be quick too."

"Well, I do run a bar, but I hate jumping to conclusions. Maybe you will be proven wrong," Sally replied, pointing her finger at Brin.

Brin just laughed.

Her phone pinged multiple times. Ignoring Sally, she grabbed it and high-fived the air.

"Ooh, one of my posts from the Arch got a thousand likes and fifty comments already. My stardom continues."

Sally got up from the couch.

"Come on, Ms. Influencer, it's time for dinner."

Brin kept staring at her phone. Sally tapped her shoulder.

"What, oh, right, dinner. Time to find out more gossip about our fellow passengers. Keep your eyes and ears open, Sally. I will be questioning you again tomorrow."

She laughed.

They walked down the hall to dinner, and Sally was glad she had decided to try and sit with Brother Francesco. She didn't think she would be able to handle a whole evening of laughing and shrieking. And getting the gossip third-degree.

Chapter Nine

Sally walked into the dining room, while Brin bounced in.

Sally sped up to get to the table, where she saw Brother Francesco sitting alone, and slid into the seat opposite him without asking.

He smiled when she sat down, but said nothing and kept staring out the panoramic windows.

Sally decided to join him in his reverie, and her breath was taken away by the river.

They were just pulling away from St. Louis, and the lights of the city and surrounding towns looked like a fairytale.

Looking starboard, she watched St. Louis fade away into the distance.

The riverbank quickly turned to trees and sand, and she felt as if they had entered another world.

"Ahh, isn't this just Heaven?" she said.

"Well, I have a different idea of heaven, Sally," Brother Francesco replied, grinning.

"Oops, yes, of course. I meant that it was like paradise on earth," she said, her cheeks burning.

Her fellow Catholics at home would not be pleased. She tried, but sometimes words just slipped out.

"Oh, don't worry. I'm not a pedantic monk. And who knows how long I will be a monk?" the monk replied wistfully.

Sally wanted to get all the details immediately. Then she remembered that it was what had annoyed her a bit about Brin's interrogation. Then again, she was a bartender and a good listener.

And if she were honest with herself, she was the one doing the interrogating, trying to get to know people in more depth in three seconds. Maybe she should step on the brake a bit. There was a fine line between trying to get to know people and being intrusive.

She decided to wait a few moments before speaking and let the monk open up himself if he felt like it.

Kwame came by right at that moment.

"Good evening, Sally. Good evening, Brother Francesco. What would you like to drink tonight?" Kwame asked.

"Hi, Kwame," Sally said.

"I would just like a Coke," Brother Francesco said.

Kwame raised his eyebrows. Coke for dinner on a luxury cruise, he must have been thinking.

"Yes, a Coke," he replied.

His English seemed excellent, without much of an accent. She wondered where he had learned it.

"And you, Sally?" Kwame said, turning to her.

"I would like a glass of South African red, if you have it."

"Of course, we have wines of the world on board," he said, smiling.

Kwame left to get their drinks.

"So you were saying you might not be a monk for long. Why is that? If I may ask," Sally said, relapsing into her probably too direct mode.

Brother Francesco ran his hand through his wavy black hair several times, then he arranged the flatware neatly next to his plate.

Still looking down, he said, "Well, I just don't know if it is the right thing for me."

"But you seem to enjoy the life, well as far as I can tell," she replied.

Brother Francesco did what Sally would term half nod, half shake his head.

"That's the point. While I was ill and couldn't do much around the monastery, I really started to think about my life and what might be in front of me. I'm already forty-four, but no one is too old for a change, right?" he said.

Kwame came over with their drinks. He placed them delicately at their places and walked over to the next table, where Brin had cornered Jim O'Sullivan. Jim did not look very happy.

Sally still didn't know why he had chosen this tour. He probably didn't know himself.

"Cheers," Sally said, raising her glass.

"Salute," the monk replied.

They clinked glasses.

"Oh, I wish I knew more languages. But when would I find the time?" Sally wondered out loud.

"Then, you must come to Italy and visit me in Assisi. I can teach you Italian."

Sally laughed. "Yeah, I would love that, but I'm kind of stuck in my small town running my bar. Though it's better than accounting."

Francesco looked grave for a second.

"Accounting? You were an accountant?" he asked, "That's what I've been thinking about."

Sally raised her eyebrows at the last statement. Monk to accountant?

"Yes, for way too many years, in Atlanta, in Georgia. I hated it. And to be honest, I wasn't very good at it. I somehow fell into it after college. And it allowed me to stay close to my parents. I'm from Savannah."

"Midnight in the Garden of Good and Evil," the monk replied.

Sally laughed.

"Yes, there is that. But Savannah is so much more. Such a wonderful place to grow up. Like yesteryear."

"Yesteryear?" the monk asked, his brow furrowed.

"You know, like from a different time, a time in the past."

"Ah okay. My English is not always that good," he replied.

The last word came out like "good-e."

"Well, I would say it is excellent. You speak English so well, almost like you were born in America."

"I wish. No, one of our monks is American, and I try to speak English with him whenever I can. And he tries his Italian. He's been with us for many years, but his Italian still needs work. At least he can get through the prayers, though many are in Latin anyway," Francesco explained.

Sally was glad he was finally opening up to her.

"Oh, that is wonderful, you have someone to practice with. Where in the U.S. is the American monk from?"

"Boston. I was mentioning that to Jim, but he didn't seem to know him. Well, I guess not every Catholic knows every other Catholic in Boston."

Sally grinned, "True."

Kwame brought the first course of Vitello Tonnato. After that, they would be allowed to attack the buffet set up in the center of the room.

Luckily, the menu explained the first course. Sally had never heard of it. Slices of veal with a tuna fish sauce didn't really sound so appetizing when she had read about it, but as she tucked in, she decided it was divine.

"Wow, this is delicious," Sally said.

The monk replied, "Yes, it is one of my favorite dishes. And they actually made it authentically. I didn't think that was possible in this country. Wonderful service onboard."

At that, the monk put down his fork and looked around the room. Sally followed his gaze and saw that he glanced at each table.

All the passengers were there, as well as the captain and Martin Sandworth, at a table tucked into a corner near the lounge.

Francesco seemed as curious about everyone as she was.

Turning back to his food, he scooped up another bit and chewed.

Sally decided enough time had passed since the monk had mentioned accounting.

"So you said you wanted to be an accountant," Sally said.

"Yes, I love numbers. I help the abbot with the monastery finances. And one day I realized I enjoyed doing that more than praying, contemplating life and God, and following the rule of St. Benedict."

Sally nodded as she took a bite of veal dipped in sauce.

"Have you spoken to the abbot about this?" she inquired.

Francesco couldn't answer as he had just taken a sip of Coke, but he shook his head.

Swallowing, he replied, "No, I couldn't. The abbot has been very good to me. I wouldn't want to disappoint him."

"Well, if he has been so good to you, wouldn't you think he would want to help you be the person you want to be?"

At that, Francesco said nothing, but just kept eating.

Sally decided not to press her luck. She wanted him to tell her more about Italy and living in Assisi, and not scare him away with her questioning or unwanted advice.

Kwame came and took their plates away, and they headed to the buffet.

Sally decided to use this opportunity to try and sit with the Wongs. She really wanted to, well, subtly, find out what was going on with them.

Six months ago, she was investigating multiple murders, now she felt like a psychiatrist trying to get to the root of all the relationships on board.

Though she would have to constantly be reminding herself to not take it too far.

* * *

Since the group was so small, there was no line at the buffet, which Sally appreciated.

She slid in behind Hoppy, who was busy piling salad on her plate. Sally was astounded as she watched Hoppy pile more and more lettuce and vegetables on one small plate.

"Wow, Hoppy, you seem to be a master in getting your money's worth," Sally said.

"I hate going up several times, and I only eat salad if I can. After last night's meal, I'm ready for a huge vegetable feast," Hoppy explained.

Sally was definitely going to get her money's worth, with everything available, even if that meant she put on a few pounds. The stress of running around at the bar would soon take that off fast enough when she got home to Berry Springs.

Sally took a salad plate and placed a few vegetables and salad leaves on it. There was a huge spread, even if it was only for nine passengers.

Next to the salad, there was a basket of still-steaming bread rolls.

Sally inhaled the wondrous smell and was taken back to her mother's kitchen in Savannah. Fresh bread was a family thing, and as Sally remembered it, her mother was always either kneading or baking. She wondered how her mother found the time to do that with raising Sally and working full-time as a nurse at the local hospital. She smiled as she thought of her mother.

She grabbed two rolls and several pats of butter and turned to see where the Wongs were sitting.

They had smartly chosen a larger table near the window, with a chair left for Sally, just as if they had planned it.

She popped into the seat without asking.

"Hi Sally," Amy said not too brightly.

"Sorry, mind if I sit with you? I think your table has the best view. So smart to choose it," she mumbled as she settled in.

Flattery usually got her everywhere.

"Um, well, I guess," Jason replied, looking at his wife. Amy shrugged her shoulders, and they all started in on the salad course.

Sally looked to her left and saw Aharon and Niv now sitting with Brother Francesco. The three of them looked like something out of a 1950s film. Niv was leaning over toward the monk, who was obviously uncomfortable with the attention. Aharon shoveled salad in, winking at Sally, who quickly turned away.

"So did you enjoy the Botanical Garden?" Amy asked.

"Well, yes, I did. The gardens were beautiful. I love the smell of roses," Sally replied.

"Ugh, can't stand them. I have terrible allergies, so I decided to walk around the area of town where the garden was," Amy said.

Ah, that explains why Jason was sitting by himself. Or does it?

"That's too bad. So much there to see. I'm really looking forward to tomorrow's tour of the Trail of Tears State Park. A sad time in our country's history, but important to never forget," Sally said.

At that, Amy looked worried.

"Trail of Tears?" she asked.

"Um, yeah, haven't you read the itinerary?" Sally asked.

Amy shook her head.

"Jason did, but I'm just interested in Mark Twain and enjoying the river. What's the Trail of Tears?"

Sally shifted to her explaining voice, "Well, I don't know all the details, but in the mid-1800s, Native Americans were forced to leave their land so the settlers could take it. They crossed the Mississippi, where the park is. America was founded on land stolen from the peoples already here. Terrible. I know there is no going back, but maybe we can try and make some kind of amends. Your country must deal with that too, you know, apartheid."

Amy turned dark, "I am well aware of what apartheid is."

She looked like she might hit someone.

"Oh, I'm sorry, I just…"

Jason waved her away, "Don't worry. South Africa is not my wife's favorite subject. Let's just enjoy the evening."

Amy remained quiet and finished the rest of her salad.

Sally really couldn't get the couple. There was something strange about them, but she couldn't quite put her finger on it.

The rest of the dinner was uneventful, but Sally was glad when Brin came over at the end of the meal, even if she knew what Brin wanted.

"Hi, you two."

They both smiled at her.

Turning to Sally, "Hey, what about an after-dinner drink?" she asked, "Niv and Aharon said they would join us."

"Oh, that would be great," she replied and quickly got up, almost knocking over the chair.

"Have a lovely evening. And thanks for the company," Sally said to Amy and Jason.

"Thanks for joining us," Amy replied, though Sally didn't feel she really meant it.

Chapter Ten

Sally had stumbled to her room past midnight, not sure how the evening had passed so quickly with Brin, Aharon, and Niv in the bar. They had each had at least three gin and tonics, but Sally had gotten some social media tips from Brin, so there was that. If she could remember them.

And she had been fascinated by Niv talking about his writing. She felt so cool spending the evening with an author.

The alarm on her phone rang Saturday morning, and she was now lying in bed with a terrible headache. She was glad she had packed her super-strength headache pills. They always got rid of the pain within an hour or so.

Since they would be spending the day exploring the Trail of Tears State Park and the river nearby, they didn't have to be ready until eleven am. It was an all-day tour that included lunch.

Sally was glad she had some time to recover.

Though she wasn't 'on-duty' as it were, nor was she solving a murder, she was still trying to sort the people and their quirks in her mind. The group certainly made for a motley crew.

It was already the third day of the tour, and she felt she really had gotten to know Hoppy, Brin, and the monk.

The Wongs were a mystery to her. She wasn't even sure they were really married.

Where did that thought come from?

Aharon and Niv seemed lovely.

That left Jim, who was nice enough, though Sally was a bit disturbed by his bigoted comments. She hoped he wasn't going to make a scene today at the park. Just what they needed. Though Martin Sandworth could probably take care of him.

Ah, yes, Martin and the rest of the crew. She would love to find out more about them.

That night was the formal dinner, and she hoped to get another word with the captain. Vienna sounded divine, and Sally wanted to learn more about how Captain Kramer ended up with her own boat on the Mississippi.

She also wanted to meet Mary Rogers, the maid. She had only seen her from a distance as she came out of one of the cabins after cleaning it. And she definitely wanted to corner Kwame. The mysterious waiter had a past that Sally was dying to discover.

But first, the nosey parker had to deal with her headache.

She pushed herself up in bed and grabbed her forehead.

Argh, she wasn't sure she was going to make it to the bathroom to get a pill.

Grabbing the phone, she called room service.

"Hi, could you send a full breakfast with your strongest coffee to my room?" Sally asked.

Kwame burst out laughing.

Was he supposed to do that?

"Ah, good morning, Sally. Have a late night?" he said.

She grimaced.

Of course, he knew exactly what kind of night she had had, since he had been serving them the drinks.

"Um, well, yes. I need breakfast fast," she pleaded.

"We'll have your order to you in fifteen minutes," he said and hung up.

Thank goodness.

She slowly swung her legs over the bed and got up an inch at a time.

She swayed back and forth as she made her way to the bathroom.

The walk had taken a lot out of her, and she was breathing heavily and sweating when she finally made it and grabbed hold of the sink.

Sally fumbled in her toiletry bag for her pills and quickly popped one in her mouth, washing it down with a glass of water.

She made a mental note to lay off the gin and tonic at that night's dinner.

Although the pill took an hour or so to work, the wetness of the water helped quench her thirst and begin to wake her up. She debated having a quick shower, but it would have had to be like a five-minute one, so she decided to wait until after breakfast. And she wanted to wait until the pill started working before she had to move around too much. She didn't want to fall in the shower and hit her head.

She slinked out of the bathroom and over to the couch at the same pace as before.

Looking out, the sun was shining and she decided to eat on the balcony.

Hopefully, she wouldn't fall overboard.

Sally closed her eyes and took deep breaths. That helped.

There was a knock at the door, and she called, "Come in."

The staff all had access keys, which Sally was glad of at that moment because it meant she didn't have to get up.

The door opened, and Mary Rogers came in.

"Oh, I was expecting Kwame," Sally said.

"I bet you were," Mary replied with a wink. Sally noticed an Irish lilt in her voice.

"He's busy taking orders for breakfast, so I'm the delivery girl this morning," she explained.

"Nice to meet you. I'm Sally," Sally replied.

Mary laughed, "Yes, um, we know all our guests."

Sally pointed to the balcony. "Could you put the tray out there? I'd love to eat in the sun."

"Tough night?" Mary asked.

Sally just smiled, but didn't want to admit anything.

Mary placed the tray outside and walked back toward the door.

"Thank you," Sally called after her.

Mary turned and smiled, then left Sally alone with her thoughts and her slowly receding headache.

* * *

By the time Sally managed to leave her cabin, her headache was almost gone. As she pulled her door closed, Aharon and Niv were just coming out of their cabin diagonally across from Sally's.

"Good morning, Sally. Sleep well?" Aharon asked as they walked together toward the gangway to start their tour.

Sally put her hand on her head.

"Well, sort of. I can't believe I had so many gin & tonics. To be honest, I can't remember exactly how many I had."

Niv laughed, "Um, Sally, it's called a holiday. You're supposed to have fun."

"Exactly," Aharon added.

Sally just shrugged her shoulders. She liked to have fun, but she didn't want to wake up every day with a splitting headache.

She had booked this tour for the relaxation, but also to learn about the hidden history. She wanted to be alert for that. Today was their first tour of an historical site, the Trail of Tears Park.

Her family had been in the U.S. since the late 17th century, which she was proud of. On the other hand, the more she thought about how the country had been founded, the more uneasy she got about her family's past.

There had been native peoples across the country, and the U.S. had swept them away. Many died of disease, others were slaughtered, and the rest were bundled onto dry pieces of land euphemistically called "reservations."

Sally wondered if there could ever be atonement.

One way in which she tried to be more aware of her own family's past was to learn about what happened to these peoples and others the U.S. had treated literally like slaves.

At the gangway, the rest of the group was already waiting.

"Well, so you're all here. Thanks, everyone, for being on time. Cheers," Martin began.

"Today is our first historical visit. And it's a sad, but important one. As you saw on your itinerary, we are now at Cape Girardeau, Missouri. Across the river is Illinois, and we are not too far from Arkansas. Cape Girardeau is the site of part of the Trail of Tears. During the winter of 1838/1839, 13 Cherokee Indian groups were forcibly relocated to Oklahoma. Crossing the Mississippi River in these conditions was harsh, to put it mildly. Thousands of the native peoples died that winter. And the park is there to talk about what happened and remember the dead. I think this is an important reminder of what the U.S. did to build the country. And none of you, none of us, should ever forget it," Martin explained.

Sally noticed a tear in his left eye.

"Oh please, I'm not from the U.S.," Amy Wong said, her arms crossed.

Brin burst out laughing, her red hair jumping with each bounce of her head.

"What the hell is so funny?" Amy asked.

"Um, you're a white from South Africa. Do the math," she shrieked.

Amy turned red and didn't say another word.

"Well, now that that is settled," Martin said a bit harshly, "Let's go. It is just a short walk to the park."

As they began to walk toward the gangway, Captain Kramer came into view.

"Enjoy your tour today, everyone. And please let me know if you need anything. We're here to please," the captain said as she walked by.

Sally felt she had learned that on an infomercial, but maybe she was just trying to be friendly. As a bar owner, Sally knew the importance of keeping your guests happy.

The group continued single file across the gangway and onto the dirt path.

They were immediately greeted with a huge sign that read "Trail of Tears State Park: Never Forget."

Sally didn't want to forget, but she didn't want to feel the hammer of the past at every turn.

This was not going to be an easy trip. Though maybe that's why she chose it.

They reached the main entrance, where Martin waited for all of them to gather.

"Before we begin, I wanted to give you a little history of Cape Girardeau, where this park is located. The name of the town comes from a French soldier, Jean Baptiste de Girardot. He came here when this was part of the French colony of La Louisiane. And later, he established a trading post here in 1733. The town itself was incorporated in 1808, and it grew to become the largest port on the river for some time between St. Louis and Memphis. In 1927, the great flood of the Mississippi hit the town as the river rose to up to forty feet above normal. We will be visiting the town later for a short coffee break before we head back to the ship."

"Get on with it," Sally heard Hoppy mutter under her breath.

Martin led them first to the visitor center, where there was a twenty-five-minute introductory film.

As the film started, Sally looked around at the rest of the group. She was glad to see everyone seemed uncomfortable at what they were being told.

Except for Jim. After five minutes, he yelled "bullshit" and walked out.

"Bigot," Brin yelled after him.

He ignored her and kept walking.

Everyone else pretended that hadn't just happened and turned back to the film.

Sally just couldn't believe what she was hearing. How could a government do this to people? As the film explained in black-and-white language, the U.S. government treated them like property, just like slaves.

I guess that's how they convinced themselves it was okay, Sally thought, getting more nauseous.

As the film ended, she heard weeping behind her. She turned slightly to not make it so obvious, and she saw Amy Wong and Brin in tears.

Sally had wondered what Amy thought of apartheid. At least she knew that Amy had some feelings. Though would she want to watch a similar film about South Africa? Sally wasn't so sure.

But why was Brin weeping? Well, Sally had to admit to herself that her eyes were not dry herself, but she didn't burst into tears.

The lights came on, and most of the group got up to walk through the visitor center exhibit.

Sally noticed, though, that Brin was still sitting in her seat, her head in her hands.

What was going on?

Sally walked over to Brin.

"Are you okay?" she asked, sitting down and patting Brin's knee.

Brin looked up, her mascara running every which way.

She sniffled.

"I'm sorry, Sally," she began.

"It's okay, Brin. This is a terrible piece of history to face," Sally replied, pulling Brin into a hug.

Brin didn't pull away.

Finally, Sally leaned back and waited for Brin to speak, but only if she wanted to.

"I know, I'm always the bouncy, happy person, or I try to be, but this place has really gotten to me," Brin confessed, pulling a tissue out of her pocket and blowing her nose.

Sally wasn't going to tell her that often, the happiest people on the outside are the saddest on the inside.

"I know, I can't believe what happened here," Sally said in sympathy.

Brin shook her head.

"No, it's not just that."

Sally's forehead wrinkled.

"What do you mean, Brin?" Sally asked.

Brin blew her nose again and wrung her hands in her lap.

Sally waited for her to speak whenever she was ready.

Finally, Brin looked up at Sally.

"Well, I told you I'm from Canada, right?" Brin began.

"Yes, and you now live in Spain," Sally responded.

Brin nodded.

"Well, what I failed to mention, and maybe the main reason I came on the tour….ugh self-torture Sally," Brin whispered.

Sally leaned forward but remained silent.

After what seemed like eternity, Brin spoke again.

"I'm not one hundred percent clear about this, so I'm not sure why I'm so upset, but from what my mother tells me, we have some First Nations blood in us."

Sally's hand went to her mouth.

"Oh, Brin, I am so sorry you had to hear all this today."

"Well, yeah, I thought I'll put my brave face on, and again it's just a family story, which even my mother admits may not be true, but anyway. What the settlers did to my people was awful and terrible, and I just feel devastated," Brin exclaimed, showing a side of her that Sally didn't think existed.

Brin was really opening up to Sally, though Sally wasn't sure how much comfort she could give Brin.

Reluctantly, she admitted to herself that it could easily be one of her ancestors who was involved in driving the native peoples along the Trail of Tears.

"You know what, let's get up and look for some spiritual comfort," Sally suggested, the Catholic part of her coming to the fore.

"What, what do you mean?" Brin asked.

"Brother Francesco. I find it so cathartic speaking to him," Sally explained.

"Oh, I don't believe in that mumbo jumbo," Brin said, "but he is a nice person to talk to."

They both got up and found Brother Francesco standing just outside the video room.

Somehow, he knew he was needed.

"May we walk through with you, Brother Francesco?" Sally asked.

The monk nodded, "Of course, and please just call me Francesco."

"Thank you. That film was so heartbreaking, I didn't want to walk through here on my own. What terrible things my government has done."

Turning to Brin, she nodded, encouraging her to speak up.

Brin stopped.

"What is it?" the monk asked in his soothing monk's voice.

"I was just telling Sally that my mother has said we have First Nations blood in us. I thought the place wouldn't affect me, but it has," Brin explained.

The monk hugged her.

"Many governments have done terrible things over the centuries. The worst thing is forgetting them. I'm glad this park is here to remind people of what happened, even if some just want to forget," he said.

Sally responded, "Oh yes. I wondered why Jim walked out. His family came from Ireland, and I don't think life was great for them."

"Yes, Sally, but he is white. The white man always thinks themselves superior. Bad for them is not as bad for those seen as 'other'," Brother Francesco explained, using air quotes at the end.

Brin remained silent, and Sally hoped the walk and talk with the monk would help her process what she was feeling at the moment.

They wandered through the rest of the visitor center in silence. There were more explanations, including an exhibit of people, looking terrified and alone. Sally thought she might be sick, but she forced herself to look at it.

Brin stopped there.

"Sally, thank you so much for your help. And Francesco. I'm just going to go outside and sit in the sun. It's just too much for me," Brin explained, turning before either had a chance to respond.

Sally was close to following her out.

The information and heartbreaking scenes she had witnessed in the film and throughout the visitor center made her angry, but she wasn't sure what she could do.

Sally shuddered. She was definitely a person to take responsibility, but she now felt the burden of humanity on her shoulders.

She felt a hand on her shoulder.

"Are you okay, Sally?" the monk asked.

"It's just so much to deal with. I feel so helpless, like I should have done something to help them. Brin, my family…slaveowners," she broke down in tears. Gosh, this place was making everyone weep.

Francesco gave her a hug.

"The past can be difficult to deal with. And families can be terrible, can't they?" Francesco said.

Sally pulled away and wiped her eyes.

"Thank you, Francesco," she said, "I'm going to head outside to find Brin. Would you come with me?"

"Of course," he replied, smiling saintly.

As they walked outside, her head ached. Was it from the drinking bout the night before or the difficult subject here?

Ugh, why was she torturing herself with this trip? For that is what it felt like.

Brother Francesco quickly led her out of the visitor center to a bench a way's away where they could sit in quiet. Brin was sitting nearby.

Sally put her head down and took deep breaths.

"Are you okay?" a voice asked. It was Brin. Now, who was comforting whom?

"Um, well, not really," Sally responded.

"May I sit?" Brin asked.

The three of them sat on the bench together. Brin between Sally and Francesco.

"Shall we take a walk through the woods. It might help us all," Francesco suggested.

As they got up from the bench, Aharon and Niv walked over.

"Sally, are you okay?" Niv asked.

Sally nodded, "Thank you, I'm feeling better. I just got a bit overwhelmed in there."

"Yeah, being reminded of your country's past deeds can be tough. We get hit by it all the time in Israel," Aharon said, a bit defensively.

Sally felt like deflecting from her own pain by bringing up the Palestinians, but decided that would be a childish idea.

"Would you like to join us? We were about to take a walk through the woods," Sally offered.

Brin and Francesco began to move off.

"Oh, wait, I'm coming," Sally said.

"Um, well, we will walk back to the ship. The exhibit was enough for us, and I'm tired," Aharon explained, not too convincingly.

Niv laughed, "What he means to tell you is we are sick of this place, and I need to get to the gym."

Aharon said something harshly to Niv in Hebrew.

Niv threw up his arms and walked toward the ship.

Aharon waved to Sally, then followed him.

Sally ran to catch up with Brin and Francesco.

"Sorry, I guess they didn't want to come with us," Sally said.

Francesco shrugged, "To be honest, who cares. Let them do their thing."

Brin agreed, "Yeah, let's just enjoy nature. There's been enough to think about and deal with here."

The three walked single file down a path covered in cedar chips. The air was fragrant and relaxing. Sally definitely needed that to decompress after the visitor center. But she was glad she had been there, and she really was looking forward to the rest of the tour. Even if it meant more memories of U.S. deeds, many in the country would love to erase from history.

She was glad Brin wanted to join them. Being alone with your thoughts, especially in moments like this, can be so difficult.

They came to a fork in the path and found Jim O'Sullivan sitting on a bench, sipping a bottle of water.

"Oh, hi, Jim," Francesco said.

At the voice of the monk, Jim raised his head.

"Oh, Brother Francesco. Hi."

He nodded at Sally and Brin.

"Are you okay?" the monk asked.

Sally and Brin walked down one of the paths to give the two some room for conversation. But they were still in earshot.

"Yes, I'm fine. I just didn't like what the film at that visitor center was saying," Jim explained.

"But every country has its past. Its dark past," Francesco said in a quiet voice that Sally could only term his 'holy voice.'

"Oh, I know, Father, but it felt like the film was blaming all white people for the tragedy. I had nothing to do with it," Jim explained, rubbing his bushy beard.

Sally felt his Irish brogue was turned up at the emotions.

Francesco nodded in a saintly way but said nothing.

Jim looked up.

"That's why I walked out. I'm sorry I swore. My Irish blood, you know," he chuckled.

"Well, we'll just let you sit here by yourself and contemplate your thoughts. How does that sound?" Francesco asked.

"Sure," he replied, sounding like he had just been admonished.

"Will you join us later in town at the coffee stop before we head back to the ship?" Sally asked. She had walked back over to invite him.

Jim looked at Sally, "I'm not sure. You kids go ahead without me, I think."

"Okay," Sally responded and walked back over to Brin.

Francesco rejoined them, and they finished the walk back to the visitor center.

Chapter Eleven

Seated at the café, Sally was alone with her thoughts.

She wasn't sure that was a good or bad thing. The rest of the group had decided to walk around the town before heading back to the ship.

She realized that while she loved the small group and the ship, there never was really any 'me' time. She was either eating on the ship, getting ready to eat on the ship, getting ready for the day's tour, or on the tour. Any downtime she had was brief. She needed to somehow figure out a way to have a nap, a luxury she rarely if ever got at home.

In spite of herself, she pulled out her phone to send Magda a short text to see how everything was going at the bar. And wish her luck for that Saturday night. Those nights could get brutal. She knew Magda could handle it, but she wanted to encourage her anyway.

Okay, and maybe she was a bit of a micromanager. Sometimes, even after all those years, she still couldn't believe she owned her own biker bar in the Ozarks. And she wanted everything to be just right.

Sally was glad to hear the beep only a couple minutes later.

"Thanks, Sally. All good here. Have a great trip!" Sally read from Magda.

Sally took a sip of coffee and sat back.

She pulled the latest mystery she was reading out of her backpack and was quickly absorbed in it.

She heard a ding indicating someone had entered, but she didn't look up.

The voice at the counter ordering a coffee sounded familiar, so she put down her book to find Jim standing there. He caught her glance and waved.

Now she really was glad she had come here. Jim all to herself.

Besides being a bar owner, she was a busybody, she admitted to herself.

She motioned Jim over.

When he had picked up his coffee, he joined her in the corner.

"Hi Jim, have a seat," she said.

"Thanks much. Where is the rest of the crew?" he asked.

"Oh, no one wanted coffee, just me. They preferred to walk around town and get some fresh air. I'm all fresh-aired out," she explained.

"Yeah, that tour really got to me, too," Jim admitted.

Sally decided not to touch that subject.

"So, you're from Ireland?" Sally asked, jumping right in.

Jim's steel-blue eyes twinkled.

"I wish. No, me dad was from Ireland," he explained, turning up the accent, "I do have Irish citizenship though."

"Did you ever think of retiring there?" Sally asked. Ireland was one of the dream places she had only been to once, years ago on her honeymoon.

Jim shook his head.

"No, I love Boston. I've lived there all my life. Got my friends there. I do have a house in Ireland, the cottage where me dad grew up. I try to get there every couple of years. It's a gorgeous spot in County Cork overlooking Baltimore harbor."

Sally had no idea where that was.

"Sounds wonderful. I was in Ireland once. For my honeymoon many years ago. We toured around the country. I loved Dublin and Galway the most, oh, and of course, the Cliffs of Moher."

"So you have a husband?" Jim asked.

Sally looked away, "Um, no, we're...divorced. Well, actually, the marriage was annulled."

"You're a Catholic lass?" Jim asked.

"Yes, not a very good Catholic, though. The Catholic in me was torn apart by the annulment," Sally explained, though she wasn't sure Jim really believed her.

"Well, divorce is not an option, right. So good thing you got that annulment."

He stroked his bushy beard, and Sally thought he looked a bit like Santa Claus, the St. Patrick version.

"So Boston. I've always wanted to go there. It sounds wonderful," Sally said.

"Yes, reminds me of Europe, which is what a lot of people say, I guess. There's a large Irish population, which is how me dad came to be there. His cousin had left just after World War II, and Dad just decided to follow. He met me mother just after he got to Boston. And my brother was born nine months after that. I'm the middle child. We are a true Irish Catholic family, so in total I have ten brothers and sisters. Though unfortunately, I don't really see them much these days. They live all over the place."

He was beaming, though there was a twang of disappointment in the last statement, Sally felt.

"What an amazing family story. I wish I knew more about my family background," she said, her stomach twisting. This reminded her of the tour that day at the Trail of Tears. She did want to know more about her family, she thought, still she wasn't quite sure she would like what she found.

Her phone buzzed.

"Oh, time to head back to the ship. Don't want to be late for Captain Kramer," Sally said.

Jim laughed, "No, she and Martin have us on a tight schedule."

Chapter Twelve

The best part of any vacation was realizing you had days and days stretching in front of you, where you didn't have to think about real life, you were away from home, and you could just kick up your heels and enjoy yourself.

At the café that afternoon, she had been worrying that there was little me-time on the trip. But then she realized the trip itself was time away from the reality of life. Sally decided to make the most of it.

Sally had quickly showered and dressed for the formal dinner that Saturday evening, which gave her thirty relaxing minutes on her balcony. The air was sweet and warm, but Sally kicked herself for not thinking of the ship's direction when she had booked the vacation. Her cabin was on the side where the sun rose, not set. She couldn't imagine what the sunsets must be from these balconies.

Brin's cabin was just across from hers, and Sally decided she would ask her if she could enjoy the rest of the sunsets there.

She could have gone up to the open-air deck above, but she enjoyed the few minutes of peace and quiet alone.

Thinking back to the trip to the Trail of Tears State Park and her emotions, she managed a laugh.

Wherever she went, something was always going on: whether a bar fight, a whirlwind vacation, or well, the last example she put out of her mind.

She sipped her water and raised her glass.

"To you, Bill, wherever you are," she cried.

She swept her eyes over the river and riverbank, now covered in trees, only a cabin or shack breaking up the monotony of the view. The River Queen had left Cape Girardeau the minute everyone was on board. The boat had a bit of ground to cover for the next day's tour at Wickliffe, Kentucky. That's where the Ohio River flows into the Mississippi. Wickliffe is the site of a thousand-year-old Native American site on the river.

Glancing down at her phone, she realized it was time to go to dinner.

Sally enjoyed the quiet hum of the engine and the river lapping against the boat before finally pushing herself up and heading to the restaurant.

In the hallway, she met Brin coming out of her cabin.

"Wow, you look stunning. What beautiful cloth," Sally exclaimed, admiring Brin's colorful caftan.

"Why, thank you. My mother made this for me," Brin said, twirling around, "You must take a few photos of me for my fans."

"Sure, why not?" Sally said as they headed down the hall to dinner, taking a detour to the upper deck to get some snaps.

Heading back downstairs, they entered the restaurant and stopped, their mouths wide open.

"Wow, I must get pictures," Brin screamed, running around snapping away.

Sally was frozen and couldn't move. She let her eyes wander around the room, and she was almost crying.

The crew had turned the dining room into a 1930s night club. The lights had been dimmed, the one large table set up in the center of the room was glowing with silvery pieces and candles. And there was even a jazz band in what looked like period suits playing softly in the corner.

"Welcome to ze River Queen night club," Captain Kramer said, greeting Sally near the door.

The captain was decked out in a tuxedo with a crisp, white shirt. She could have been a gangster.

Sally expected her to pull out a machine gun at any moment.

Martin was standing next to her in a similar suit, well-fitted to his muscular body.

"Wow, this is just amazing. I don't know what to say. I feel like we've gone back in time," Sally said, her mouth wide in awe.

Captain Kramer grinned wildly. The first time she had seen the captain really smile.

"I'm glad you like it. It's our little thing we do for our guests," she explained.

The door opened behind them, and there were several gasps.

They turned to see the Wongs and Hoppy entering.

"Wowee," Hoppy cried.

Even Jason and Amy Wong were speechless.

"This is just beautiful," Amy said, turning to the captain and Martin.

Martin winked at her.

"Thank you. I hope you all have a wonderful evening!" the captain said, moving toward the table.

The table was set for them all to sit together in a large circle.

Sally followed her and saw Aharon and Niv, Brother Francesco, and now Brin sitting there. Only Jim was missing now.

It wasn't quite eight p.m., so he still had a few minutes to show up.

She took a seat between Aharon and Brother Francesco. Brin was sitting next to the monk, while Niv was next to Aharon. The Wongs sat down across from Sally. Amy Wong was sitting next to Martin Sandworth while her husband was next to the captain. Hoppy grabbed the open seat between the captain and Niv, leaving the seat between Martin and Brin free for Jim.

Jim walked in a few minutes later, out of breath.

"So sorry, everyone. I took a short nap and overslept," he said as he sat down.

Then he jumped up.

"Wow, this place is amazing," he yelled.

He stared all around like the others had, then sat down.

"I can't believe I missed this all when I came in. Well me eyesight isn't what it used to be," he chuckled.

"It's fantastic, isn't it?" Sally replied.

Now that everyone was seated, Kwame came over.

"Good evening everyone and welcome to the River Queen Night Club. I hope you enjoy your trip back in time to 1930s New York," he said, his eyes sweeping the table.

"Tonight's dinner includes fish, in the main course. Is anyone allergic to fish?"

Jason and Jim raised their hands.

"Great thanks," Kwame said, smiling. "We, of course, have a fish-less option for you."

Kwame started the drink service.

Everyone chose white wine, except for Jim.

"Red, please, or if you have a stout beer, that would be even better," he said.

"Of course," Kwame said, going over to the bar to get Jim's beer.

"So how did everyone enjoy today's trip?" the captain began.

Her stature, long fingers, and serious demeanor stopped everyone else talking at the table to look at her.

"Uh, well, it was certainly informative," Hoppy began.

Sally's voice was caught in her throat for a moment before she got the words out.

"Well, actually, I was a bit upset by it. What a terrible thing to happen," she said.

"Many countries have done terrible things. We must never forget," the captain replied.

Francesco looked over and nodded as the captain spoke

"That is true," Francesco agreed.

Sally noticed Amy flinch when Captain Kramer spoke. South Africa had as much if not more to answer for, Sally thought.

"Well, I'm glad we came on this trip. It makes you appreciative of the life we all have and the better times we all live in now," Aharon said.

He looked at Niv as he said this, smiling. Niv took his hand.

Sally felt like she was watching a private moment.

The table went uncomfortably silent, which was broken by Kwame bringing Jim's beer.

"Thanks, sir," Jim said, downing half of it in one gulp.

The table broke into small conversations and Sally turned to the monk.

"Thank you, Francesco, for your help today. I really appreciate it," she began.

The monk shook his head. "That is what we spiritual folk are here for," he said smiling. "I hope you are feeling better," he added, glancing at the captain.

Sally replied, "Yes, looking back, I feel a bit silly at my reaction. But sitting in my room just now, I felt like that was a good thing. My reaction, I mean."

Francesco took a sip of wine.

The first course came, which was a Caesar's salad topped with mounds of croutons and parmesan cheese. Each plate had a swirl of balsamic creme topping it off. Though apparently they had not given anyone anchovies, a traditional topping. Cost savings or just a nod to Jason and Jim, who were allergic to fish.

Sally was glad. She hated the taste of anchovies.

"Wow, I'm starving," Hoppy said, diving in before anyone else had a chance to think.

Sally, and the rest of the table, watched as she shoveled in the food in no time.

Kwame brought the rest of the dishes, and everyone else dug in.

The creamy cheese and lettuce made a perfect combination, and Sally enjoyed every bite. Washing it down with a good slug of chardonnay, Sally felt like she was in heaven, or paradise, or something like that. She would love to be served dinner like this, in this atmosphere, every night.

Her bar was for bikers, so she didn't think she could turn it into a 1930s night club, but maybe she could make some changes. She'd have to talk to Magda about that when she got home, which seemed weeks away.

Most of the table was almost as hungry as Hoppy, and the plates were soon emptied.

"Delicious," Amy Wong exclaimed, which to Sally seemed like the ultimate compliment to the kitchen, coming from a famous chef like Amy.

Captain Kramer beamed, "Thank you. We only serve excellent food."

The last sentence came out a bit haughty for Sally's taste, but Amy just nodded in appreciation.

Kwame removed the plates and left them a short break between courses.

Sally decided to get some fresh air before the main course arrived.

"Excuse me, I'm just going to enjoy a few minutes of sunset outside," she said as she got up.

"Great idea," Brin said, getting up to join her.

The rest of the group stayed at the table chatting.

Outside on the restaurant balcony, Brin pulled out her Meerschaum pipe.

"You're going to smoke that now?" Sally asked.

Brin explained, "Well, just a little. And doesn't it fit with the atmosphere tonight?"

Sally agreed, "This is true. Though I'm not sure how many 1930s gangsters smoked a pipe."

"Oh, you fuddy-duddy. I just love to inhale the pipe power. You should try it sometime," Brin replied.

Sally shook her head, her graying ponytail swinging in the wind.

"No way. I will occasionally smoke a cigarette, but a pipe or cigar, never."

"Suit yourself," Brin said, puffing away.

The two stood there in silence for a few minutes. Sally stared at the dying sun, almost below the horizon.

Sally finally decided to ask her a question.

"So, Brin, have you recovered from today's Trail of Tears tour?" Sally asked.

Brin looked at her.

"Are you trying to ruin my evening?" Brin said.

Sally turned red.

"Oh, I'm sorry," Sally replied.

Brin laughed.

"I was as shocked and sad as you were. But if I thought about that all the time, I would have to kill myself. Instead, I try to look to the future and enjoy the life I have in Spain."

Apparently, she had conveniently forgotten her breakdown that afternoon. Or maybe that was Brin's way of trying to deal with the pain.

Sally's stomach twisted again. She felt the guilt her ancestors, the slave owners, should have felt, but she didn't know why she should carry that burden.

Luckily, at that moment, the door opened.

"Dinner's on," Hoppy said, motioning them both to follow her inside.

Brin put out her pipe and walked behind Sally back into the restaurant.

The main course was already on the table, steaming hot.

It smelled delicious. For those eating fish, the main course was grilled salmon with an herb crust, served with roasted rosemary potatoes and grilled vegetables. Just like Sally liked it. Anything grilled was bound to be delicious.

She looked over at the other plates. The non-fish-eaters, Jason and Jim, had gotten spaghetti carbonara.

"Well, I am impressed. I didn't think Americans knew how to make traditional Italian carbonara," Brother Francesco said.

Sally thought it looked like he had wished he had ordered it.

Everyone dug in and oohed and aahed at the tastes. Even Amy Wong seemed to be enjoying it.

"Mmmm, I love salmon," Niv said, in between bites.

"My favorite fish," Sally replied.

Sally turned her head toward Aharon and Niv and saw Aharon shoveling it in, almost as fast as Hoppy. She was still amazed how a small person like Hoppy could eat so much, and so fast.

The rest of the table looked over at Hoppy. It was like the evening entertainment.

Sally glanced at the jazz band. The music blended into the background so well, she almost forgot they were there.

What a perfect evening.

Sally had just taken another bite of salmon when she heard a noise. She looked up and saw Jason coughing.

Amy patted his back, her eyes narrowed.

"Sorry, just something caught in my throat. I'm fine," he said, taking a sip of water and going back to his spaghetti.

Amy smiled at him and went back to her food.

Sally was really enjoying the food, and it seemed everyone else was as well.

Not much was being said, just a lot of eating going on.

Sounds of forks and knives scraping plates were punctuated by a groan.

They all turned to see Jim standing up, his face red.

"Can't breathe," he whispered faintly, pointing to his throat.

Hoppy jumped up to help. Jim grabbed his throat, his eyes wide with terror. Sally was frozen in place, like the rest of the table.

Jim grunted weakly. His face was going blue.

"Do something," Brin screamed.

Martin jumped up to help.

He and Hoppy laid Jim down on the ground as Hoppy began to examine him.

"He's in anaphylactic shock. His throat is closing," she said.

"I have an anti-allergy pen in my medical bag in my room," Hoppy yelled, jumping up and running out.

Martin began CPR, but Jim stopped moving.

Martin pumped his chest and breathed air into his mouth as much as he could get in the mostly closed throat, but Jim lay motionless.

Hoppy was back in less than a minute and jabbed the pen into Jim's thigh.

Martin continued CPR throughout. Everyone was frozen in their seats watching the drama unfold.

Sally thought she was going to be sick, but she took deep breaths to calm herself.

Everyone else at the table was frozen in fear, their eyes wide.

Sally noticed Brother Francesco begin to pray.

Then Amy Wong screamed.

"Honey, it's okay," Jason tried to comfort her.

"It's not okay," Amy cried.

Hoppy jumped up and looked at Captain Kramer.

"Do you have a defibrillator?" Hoppy asked.

Captain Kramer ran to get it, ripping it off the wall near the kitchen.

Running back, she almost threw it at Hoppy.

"Stand back, everyone," Hoppy yelled.

Martin stopped CPR and jumped back.

Hoppy ripped Jim's shirt open and attached the leads. She punched the button on the device to charge it.

"Come on, come on," she urged the device as if that would make it charge faster.

"Clear," she yelled, activating the device.

Jim's chest jumped and fell. Hoppy felt for a pulse.

She charged the device again and activated it.

Nothing.

Hoppy began CPR herself, but Martin came over.

"Hoppy, Dr. Wilcox. I think it's over."

"No, we have to get him to a hospital," she yelled.

Captain Kramer ran to the bridge.

"Do you think that will help?" Martin said, "I was a medic in the British army. He's gone."

"No, he isn't," Hoppy yelled, continuing CPR.

The ship suddenly lurched to a stop. No one fell down, but several were flailing their arms to balance themselves.

Hoppy rolled away from Jim, but she jumped right back and continued her resuscitation efforts.

Brin collapsed in tears. Sally went to comfort her. As she walked over, she did a cursory examination of his plate.

He had said he was allergic to fish, but he had had spaghetti carbonara. It just didn't add up.

Chapter Thirteen

The emergency call Captain Kramer had sent had been quickly responded to by paramedics and police from nearby Klondike, IL, just at the tip of Illinois on the tri-cornered boundary with Missouri and Kentucky. Luckily, the ship had been near a town, even if it was a small one.

The paramedics rushed in. They quickly conferred with Martin and Hoppy before beginning their own efforts. They almost had to pull Hoppy off him to do their job.

Martin led Hoppy to a chair nearby. She sat frozen, watching the paramedics.

Kwame and Mary had set up tables away from the body, so everyone could sit and comfort each other.

Waiting near them but staying at an appropriate distance were two police.

One was about thirty, with dark hair and eyes and a goatee. Sally thought he looked like something out of a country movie. Next to him was a woman about the same age as the man. To Sally, she looked Japanese, but she didn't want to jump to conclusions.

Sally and the rest stared at the paramedics as they worked and finally stood up. Both shook their heads. Kwame handed them Jim's plate to take a food sample from. Then they put Jim on a stretcher and got him out quickly.

Brin began sobbing. Hoppy went white and started shaking.

Sally quickly got up, went over to her, and gave her a big hug. Hoppy stiffened but then pulled Sally in tightly and sobbed.

"I hate losing a patient," Hoppy said between sniffles.

"You and Martin did what you could," Sally replied, looking at the rest of the group.

"Hoppy, you are a hero for trying to help," Francesco added, "Bless you."

"Terrible, terrible," Aharon said.

Yes, their trip would now not quite be as they had planned it.

Sally and Hoppy separated, and Sally pulled her chair over to sit next to Hoppy and hold her hand.

"What will happen now?" Sally asked.

"Well, Hoppy and I aren't registered as doctors in America, so we can't officially sign off on the death. It has to be done by an American medical professional. The paramedics will take Jim to the hospital for the final call. Though there will most likely be an autopsy," Martin explained.

"So much for the rest of the trip," Brin said, wiping the tears from her face.

Sally thought that was a bit callous, considering one of the passengers had just died in front of them during what should have been a wonderful evening.

"Oh, I wish I could have done something," Hoppy cried.

No one knew what to say. They let her sob.

At that moment, the two cops came over to the group.

"Hi, I'm Detective Minori Watkins. This here is my partner, Officer Lance Burnham. Please use they/them for me," the detective explained.

Sally raised her eyebrows at the bravery of the petite detective with the short black hair. This was quite open for what seemed like a small-town sheriff's department. Berry Springs was a very open and welcoming community, very unusual in small towns in the south, and there were a few non-binary people. She didn't expect to find that openness in this area, though.

"I like to get that out of the way right away. Oh, and I'm sorry for your loss," Detective Watkins said.

Officer Burnham added a nod and a smile.

Sally thought he looked a bit like her Sergeant Soder back home, well maybe it was just the muscled arms they had in common. And both were around six feet with smoldering looks.

Boy, Jim would have 'loved' this, Sally thought.

"I will need to question all of you to find out what happened here tonight. I know this must be difficult, but it will be helpful to get the information now, while it is still fresh in your minds," Watkins explained to the group.

Martin Sandworth joined them and handed over a piece of paper.

"Here's the seating chart at dinner. Sorry, it's not cleaner."

"Thank you, Mr. Sandworth," Detective Watkins replied. "Very helpful."

"Please call me Martin. Detective, you can use our lounge to question people if you want," he said, pointing to the doors near where they were sitting.

"Thank you. Well, I would like to start with…" They looked down at the seating chart, "you, sir," they said, pointing to Martin Sandworth.

"Sure, of course," Martin replied, rubbing his arm.

She wished this were Berry Springs, where Detective Finnegan would almost definitely allow her to be part of the interrogation after the help she gave him solving the murders six months ago.

She debated asking the Klondike officers if she could join them in the lounge, but she didn't have any basis to do so. She decided to keep her mouth shut and do her own sleuthing. They probably wouldn't be going anywhere for a while, so she would have plenty of time to 'interrogate the suspects' as it were.

Kwame came over to the group, in tears.

"I'm so sorry," he said.

Several people gasped.

"Sorry?" Sally asked, thinking the murder had just solved itself. That would have been easy.

"Terrible to lose a guest," he said.

"Oh," Sally replied, a tad disappointed.

"Do you know how this could have happened?" Jason Wong demanded.

No one had seemed to like Jim and his bigoted ways, but somehow his death had brought out sympathy in all of them.

Kwame shook his head.

"He said he was allergic to fish, so he got the spaghetti carbonara. We don't put fish in the carbonara, if that's what killed him," Kwame surmised.

"Well, there are a lot of other things that people can be allergic to," Hoppy said, "I've seen it all."

"Maybe it was his heart?" Brin asked, "He was, um, getting on in age."

Hoppy threw up her hands, "Until I see the autopsy, I don't want to guess. His throat was definitely closed, but it could have also included a heart attack."

Sally's first thought was to run to the table and try and take a sample of the food on Jim's plate. Even though she had no idea what she would be doing with it.

"Well, the paramedics took that sample from his plate to test it. Oh, I hope there was no fish accidentally added to it," Kwame cried, collapsing on a chair.

Amy Wong went to comfort him.

Sally sat in silence. She had hoped she would never have to deal with death, um murder, again. She assumed he was murdered. Well, unless the chef had accidentally added fish to Jim's carbonara, or used the same pan as the fish.

She began rubbing her knuckles and looking over to the lounge. She would love to be a fly on the wall there.

"We should have gone to Key West," Niv cried.

Aharon ignored him.

Brother Francesco came over to Sally.

"Are you okay?" he asked, touching her arm.

She wondered why he had singled her out. She seemed to be the calmest person in the room at the moment.

"Yeah, sure, why?" she asked.

"Well, you keep looking over at the door to the lounge as if you are worried someone might say something," he explained.

"Well, no, it's well, I told you what happened to me a few months ago in Berry Springs."

He nodded, "But what does that have to do with this? You seemed very upset about that," the monk replied.

"Well, yes, but I loved solving the puzzle, um, I mean the crime. I feel like maybe I can help here. But the cops don't know me from Adam," she said, "And you told me at the Arch that something good always comes with something bad."

"Yes, I did. So what is the good?" he asked.

"That, as macabre as it sounds, I love solving murders."

The monk looked at her with a mixture of surprise and disdain.

"That doesn't sound very healthy," Francesco said.

"My gut tells me I'm right," Sally replied.

Maybe this was her mission in life. Well, besides running a bar and enjoying a glorious life in Berry Springs.

The door opened, and Martin came out looking a bit shaken. Sally wasn't sure if it was because he had tried to save Jim's life or whether he was worried about the questioning he had just had with the police.

Sally couldn't see why Martin would kill Jim.

But then again, she had only known the people on the ship for three days.

"Okay, we'd like to talk to you, Brother Francesco, next," Officer Burnham said, motioning for the monk to follow them.

Brin jumped up.

"Wait, I was sitting next to Jim. Don't you want to talk to me next?" she asked.

Sally loved her enthusiasm. She wished she could somehow get part of it and take it back with her to Berry Springs.

"Sorry, ma'am. We want to talk to the monk next. You can be right after him. That okay for you?" Officer Burnham asked.

"Sure, sorry," Brin replied, dropping back into her chair and sighing.

Brother Francesco got up and walked into the lounge, glancing back at Sally as he followed Officer Burnham into the lounge.

Sally contemplated when she would be called in for questioning. And whether she could persuade the cops to let her in on their investigation. She wondered if her Detective Finnegan in Berry Springs could somehow help her out here.

Chapter Fourteen

"So, ma'am. What can you tell us about what happened here tonight?" Detective Watkins asked.

Brin had looked crestfallen at not being called in for questioning after Brother Francesco, but the monk had apparently told the police to talk to Sally next.

"Not much, Detective. We were all seated at the table for dinner when Jim got up, red in the face, apparently choking."

"What happened then?" Officer Burnham asked.

Sally related the medical attention Hoppy and Martin had given, as best she could since she was not a medical professional herself.

"What do you think caused his death?" Watkins asked when Sally had finished.

She paused a moment before responding.

"Well, he had declined the fish main course, saying he was allergic to fish," she explained.

Burnham asked, "So what did he have?"

"Spaghetti carbonara. There isn't fish in spaghetti carbonara. Well, there shouldn't be," she said, wondering when they would get the results of the food testing.

"And Brother Francesco told us it looked quite authentic. You know, the traditional Italian way," she added.

Detective Watkins scribbled something in their notebook.

"Do you know who might have wanted to kill Mr. O'Sullivan?" Watkins asked, putting down the pen.

Sally shook her head, then stopped.

"Well, we hadn't known each other that long. It's just the third day of the tour. He kept to himself and didn't really interact with any of the other passengers that much, well, except maybe Francesco. Jim was Irish Catholic, you see," Sally explained, rubbing her hands together.

Somehow, she was nervous, or maybe it was just the awkwardness of relating the events of the evening or the last three days.

"But did anyone seem outwardly aggressive toward him, or the other way around?" Officer Burnham asked.

Sally debated whether she should say anything else. She didn't want to assume anything or point the finger without any real evidence.

She looked at the detective, then the officer. They waited patiently for her to continue.

"Well, he wasn't too happy about the tour stops, that's for sure," Sally said, relating what had happened at the Trail of Tears movie showing.

"But is that a reason to kill him?" Burnham asked.

"Well, he also seemed to dislike Aharon and Niv being a gay couple," she added cautiously.

"Well, I know what that's like," Officer Burnham said, not smiling.

Sally looked confused, and Burnham noticed it.

"Oh, sorry. I don't hate Mr. O'Sullivan, but my husband, Ben, and I get a lot of dirty looks in town, even if I'm a member of the police force."

This seemed like the most diverse small town she had ever come across.

"Ah, okay, well, yeah, he didn't seem to really like what they were. But he was never overtly hateful," Sally explained.

Then she had a thought.

"What about his family in Boston? Shouldn't they be notified? He said he had a big family, so there must be someone there to tell you about how he was as a person."

Sally leaned forward.

"Well, he didn't list an emergency contact for the trip, but we're trying to trace a next of kin to notify," Watkins replied.

Sally had a tear in her eye thinking about what his family would go through when they found out Jim had died.

Though he had told her that they didn't see much of each other, whatever that meant.

This reminded her of the terrible time a few months back when she went with the police to notify Bill Arnold's family about Bill's death after she found his body in the dumpster behind her bar.

As she was considering this, Detective Watkins coughed.

"So, you can apparently help us solve the death," Detective Watkins stated a bit too matter-of-factly for Sally.

That swept away the bad memories quickly. She wiped her eyes and looked across the table.

"Um, what were you saying?" Sally said.

"Brother Francesco told us about your time a few months ago and how you seemed eager to be a part of this investigation," Detective Watkins explained.

"Wow, he said that. I, well, I just learned those few months ago that I love solving crimes. I was fire-tested by helping to solve the murders of my best friend and my priest. I just thought maybe I could help you. You know, be your eyes and ears on the ship. I might be able to get information out of the passengers and crew that they might be reluctant to share with you," Sally was rambling on and finally stopped.

"Well, you certainly seem enthusiastic about it," Officer Burnham said, his brown eyes twinkling.

"Yes, you could say that."

"Well, I guess you could be of help to us. We don't usually have suspicious deaths to solve in our small town, just petty theft and the occasional domestic violence incident, so any help we could get would be great," Watkins admitted.

"Um, isn't it murder?" Sally asked, somehow hoping it was, in a gruesome sort of way.

"Well, we are calling it a suspicious death for the moment. We want to get the results of the autopsy first before we definitely call it murder," the detective explained.

"If you want a police reference, you can call Detective Finnegan in my town of Berry Springs. He can vouch for my assistance last year," Sally offered.

"Good idea. What's the number?" Officer Burnham asked.

***

Unpredictably, Finnegan had given her a glowing recommendation. Apparently, he did not seem surprised that she was caught up in another murder, well, a suspicious death it was being called at the moment.

Sally went back to her cabin while the police were searching the dining room and Jim's room for clues and evidence. They had asked the passengers to return to their staterooms and told them they would be questioning the rest of the passengers and crew in the morning. The boat wasn't moving, so no one was going anywhere.

Sally was excited about being allowed to be part of the investigation, but on the other hand, she now knew her vacation was pretty much over. Though Captain Kramer hadn't officially announced it, Sally didn't think they would be continuing to New Orleans. A murder, um, suspicious death, wasn't solved overnight.

Something Sally knew all too well.

She pulled out the list of passengers to begin thinking about who would want to kill Jim.

Well, as she had told the Klondike police, he had certainly made it known that he didn't like Aharon and Niv, a gay couple, being on board and he was upset at the stops the tour would make at the different sites remembering Native Americans, Japanese internment, and the Civil Rights movement.

Jim seemed to be a cliché and traditional straight old white man, only caring about his own kind.

But as far as Sally knew, no one had met Jim before this trip. If it was murder, that was a fast decision considering it was only the third day of the tour.

And if Jim did die from allergic shock, how did that happen? He hadn't eaten the fish for dinner. Unless he was allergic to something else that he didn't know about. Though that would seem weird, as he is a retiree, and while allergies can crop up, he probably would have known about any other allergies he had.

The first thing that popped into Sally's mind was eggs. Traditional carbonara included egg. And Michael, a good friend of hers in college, had been allergic to eggs.

She sipped the green tea she had made herself in the room.

Then there was a knock at the door.

Looking at her phone, she saw it was 11:30 p.m. Who would be knocking at her door at this time of night?

Sally pushed herself up off the couch. She had changed into sweats and a t-shirt, but didn't bother throwing on anything else for whoever was calling at this late hour.

She walked over to the door and looked through the peephole. She saw Hoppy and Brin standing there.

She opened the door.

"What are you two doing here?" she asked a bit accusingly.

"Um, sorry. Are we bothering you?" Hoppy asked.

Brin was already moving into the room, the bundle of energy that she was. Sally sighed and moved aside, and both entered.

"I couldn't sleep," Brin explained, "so I knocked on Hoppy's door and she was up too. We thought you might be our little detective."

Wow, word spread quickly on a small ship.

"So, have you solved it yet?" Hoppy asked, pouring herself a glass of water.

"Of course not," Sally snapped, dropping into the armchair.

"Well, aren't we sensitive?" Brin said, giggling.

Their enthusiasm quickly melted away her annoyance at their unannounced visit.

"All right. I'm sorry. I just didn't expect visitors now. And I was going through the list of suspects," Sally said.

"Oooh, exciting!" Brin shrieked.

"Shh, the Wongs are next door," Sally shushed.

"Oh, please, those two need a good shaking up," Brin said.

"So whodunit?" Hoppy asked, sipping her water.

Brin jumped up, opened the minibar, grabbed a bottle of tonic and a mini bottle of gin.

"This calls for a drink," Brin explained, pouring herself a generous G&T.

Sally decided that was a good idea and found a small bottle of chardonnay in the fridge. She poured herself a glass and sat back down. She didn't really like green tea anyway and wasn't sure why she had made it in the first place.

"Well, of course, I don't know who did it. The police are still treating this as a suspicious death until the autopsy results are in," Sally explained.

Brin looked disappointed.

"What about his family?" Hoppy asked.

"Well, I did ask the police about that, but apparently he didn't name an emergency contact, and they're trying to get a hold of someone in Boston. He had told me had a big family, but had little contact these days."

"Maybe he lied," Brin added.

Sally shrugged her shoulders.

"Who knows what's going on?" Sally said.

"Oh, it must be murder," Brin replied.

"Hoppy, what do you think? You're a doctor and you tried to save him," Sally said.

Remembering that, Hoppy's enthusiasm suddenly left her face.

"Ugh, don't remind me. I'm feeling a bit better, but I really wish I had been able to save him," she said, rubbing her weather-beaten cheeks.

"Do you think it was a heart attack?" Sally asked.

"Well, he could have had a heart attack from the lack of air, but I still think he died of an allergic shock to something he ate. His throat was closed, and as you all heard, he was desperately trying to breathe," she replied.

"Maybe he was choking on something," Brin offered. She had already downed half her drink.

Hoppy shook her head. "His throat was closed," she said.

Sally thought she sounded determined and definitive, but doctors have been known to be wrong. Sally wasn't going to mention that right now.

She was just trying to get all the facts, not that there were many available at the moment.

"If you need any help, Sally, we're there to help," Brin said, her hair bobbing as she shook her head vigorously.

"Thanks, you two. Hoppy, I could definitely use your medical eye when, I mean if, I see the autopsy results. And Brin, you've been snapping away the whole trip. Maybe your camera picked up something, or maybe you can find Jim's family online," Sally said, glad to have them on her side.

"Ooh, we're like the detective trio. This is going to be a great story for my influencers. It might even land me a book or movie contract," Brin shrieked.

"Well, let's solve the murder first," Sally said, like a teacher talking to a student.

"Yes, ma'am," Brin replied, obviously getting the hint.

"So what's next?" Hoppy asked.

"Well, I think we all need some sleep first to be fresh and ready to go in the morning," Sally replied.

Brin and Hoppy both got up at the same time and saluted.

Sally laughed as she let them out and shut the door.

Chapter Fifteen

Sally woke with the sun streaming through her windows. She had forgotten to pull the blinds closed the night before.

Checking her phone, she groaned. It was only 5:30 a.m., which meant she had not even gotten six hours sleep.

She yawned, and then the memory of the night before hit her like a bolt of lightning, and she jerked up in bed.

Jim O'Sullivan. Dead. Probably murdered.

As she contemplated whether to get up or try and fall back asleep, she realized the sun was moving. And then she felt the vibration.

The boat was underway. But how? They definitely shouldn't be continuing on the tour with a suspicious death on board.

Now she was wide awake. She decided to get to the bottom of this and head to the bridge. She assumed either Captain Kramer or Martin Sandworth would be there on duty, even at that early hour.

She threw on a worn sweatshirt over her t-shirt and shorts and slipped into her walking shoes.

Quietly opening and closing her door, she tiptoed down the corridor. She was mainly worried about alerting Brin that something was amiss. Sally knew she would be tagging along if she did.

She walked onto the deck and up the stairs to the bridge.

She found both the captain and first officer there.

As she walked in, they had been whispering, but they stopped when they saw her. Both looked grim.

"Good morning, Sally. Vat can we do for you?" the captain asked, her arms crossed in the most Teutonic fashion.

Martin Sandworth managed a smile.

"Well, good morning. Sorry for bothering you so early. I was wondering why the boat is moving. I thought we were stuck here until Jim's death was solved. Are we continuing the tour?"

Sally's questions came out in rapid-fire. The bluntness seemed to take the captain by surprise, but she just let Sally shoot the questions at her.

Martin looked at the captain, who seemed to be considering what she should say.

The captain dropped her crossed arms and walked toward Sally, who took a step back. The tall captain had a very authoritative air about her and seemed a bit menacing at times, Sally thought. Definitely the right profession to keep everything and everyone in line.

"Well, yes, we are continuing the tour, with a few provisions," the captain began, obviously deciding to tell Sally everything, as she added, "You will all find out everything anyway."

Sally raised her eyebrows, "Really?! How?!"

The captain coughed before continuing.

"As you know, Mr. Wong is a Chinese diplomat…" the captain began.

"It seems after the death last night and with the police on board, Mr. Wong called his Embassy in Washington. We got a call from a gentleman at the Department of State explaining we were to treat the Wongs with kid gloves, being diplomats and all. Neither the Chinese government nor the U.S. government wanted a scandal or international incident, so we were told to continue the tour. We are meeting several FBI agents at the next stop, Wickliffe, Kentucky, who will take over the investigation from the Klondike police…." the captain explained.

Martin finished her sentence for her, "and make sure no one disappears off the ship or from one of the tours."

Wow, this was turning into an international incident. Sally had somehow not thought through what it meant to have a diplomat aboard. And she knew the U.S. was usually quite cautious when it came to the Chinese.

Well, that explained why the boat was moving again.

She was continually amazed how the rich and powerful could do whatever they wanted. If they had all been ordinary citizens, they would have been locked down on the ship until someone confessed, or worse all thrown in jail until the investigation was concluded.

Though she wasn't too sure how secret this would all be with them out and about with an escort. Continuing the trip may be only for a few hours, if that, before the ship was put on lockdown.

"Thank you both for being so open and honest. I really appreciate it," Sally replied.

Captain Kramer smiled wanly.

"Please do not tell anyone what I just told you. I would like to explain to the rest of the group at once."

"Of course, thank you again," Sally replied.

They both nodded without saying anything. Then the captain turned away and began checking some gauges in front of her.

This was Sally's signal to exit.

She prayed that she wouldn't meet any of the passengers on her way back to her room, especially Brin. She would immediately know something was going on. Sally wasn't good at keeping a poker face.

As she tiptoed back down the hallway of the passenger cabins luckily there wasn't a peep. She quietly let herself into her room again, the door's card reader giving its tell-tale beep. Shutting the door slowly, she walked over to the couch and dropped onto it.

She checked her phone. It was now almost 7:00 a.m. Sally wondered when the captain would tell everyone what was going on. She assumed it would be at breakfast.

Sally decided the best thing for her was to be as late as possible to breakfast so no one, in particular, Brin could read anything into her expressions.

She made herself a cup of coffee and sat out on the balcony, enjoying the sun and the soothing ripples of the river.

What a trip this had turned into. She hoped no more bodies would be found. One was definitely enough for her on this trip.

Chapter Sixteen

The chattering was deafening. Sally wished she had brought earplugs.

Captain Kramer had just told the rest of the passengers what was going on, including a stipulation that no one was to notify the outside world of what was going on and that their electronic devices would now be confiscated.

Everyone walked over and placed their devices into large plastic bins.

Sally wondered what Brin, the "influencer," was going to do without a phone or connection to her followers.

That got her thinking about the demands of social media that took over people's lives.

Pushing that thought out of her mind, she scanned the room.

Some people had panicked looks on their faces, and she kept hearing snatches of conversation.

FBI

Investigation

Diplomat

Death

Sally noticed that the Wongs stayed quiet. Apparently, being the center of attention was disquieting. Amy Wong was staring at the floor while Jason Wong kept moving in his chair.

Jason Wong finally got up, and the room went quiet.

He coughed.

"Um, I am sorry for this, my dear fellow passengers…" he began, turned red, and sat back down.

Amy huffed and stood up.

"Well, look on the bright side. We can continue the trip," Amy said, her South African accent quite pronounced.

That didn't help anything. The room went ice cold. Aharon and Niv walked out in silence.

That seemed to break up the gathering, and everyone else stood up and began walking around.

Francesco went over to talk to the captain, perhaps to offer counseling services to the passengers and crew if needed. She saw him coming and smiled.

As he began to speak, she led him out of the restaurant.

Sally watched as Brin made her way over to her.

"Oooh, isn't this exciting?" Brin said, reaching into her bag and showing Sally the top of a smartphone.

"Brin, what are you doing?" Sally hissed.

Obviously, the crew had not been smart enough to go through everyone's belongings but rather rely on the passengers' honesty to give up their phones.

Brin wagged her finger, slipping the phone back into her bag: "Shhh! Don't be such a fuddy-duddy. You sound like my grandmother."

"Whatever. But just be careful. You're the most fun person on this trip. I wouldn't want to see you escorted off the boat and sent back to Canada, or worse," Sally said, patting Brin's shoulder.

"Ooh, isn't that sweet. You're fun too, Sally!"

At that, Brin glanced around to make sure no one was watching them and ran out.

Sally watched her go, assuming she would be surreptitiously taking some photos.

Now that the group had broken up, Sally decided to have a think on the upper deck.

Before she headed upstairs, she went back to her room to get her trusty notebook.

Time to continue her list of suspects and motives.

She wondered what Detective Finnegan would be thinking now. Hopefully that she wouldn't get hurt.

On the deck, Sally settled herself into a lounge chair. The sun was shining, and the Mississippi was glorious.

Something good to go with the bad.

She opened her notebook and got her pen ready.

Suspects, she wrote

She tapped her pen on the page.

This was difficult.

Jim hadn't been so friendly, but who would want to kill him after three days?

Aharon or Niv

She didn't know either of them that well, but they seemed a bit upset about Jim and his reaction to them being a male couple.

But kill him?

And how would they know he was allergic to fish? Lucky guess?

The Wongs

Pinning murder on a Chinese diplomat and his South African famous chef wife seemed to be a long shot, unless you were writing the script for a movie.

Jason Wong really seemed excited about the posting in Washington. Why would he do anything to compromise that? And Sally couldn't see a connection between Jim and the Wongs.

She was just about to continue her list, when there was a cough.

Sally looked up and saw Brother Francesco.

"May I join you?" the monk asked.

"Of course, Brother Francesco," Sally replied, a bit stiffly.

She didn't like getting interrupted while thinking, even if he was a monk.

He obviously understood the tone.

"I'm sorry to bother you, Sally. I just thought you might want some company. And my thoughts on what happened last night."

Another amateur detective? Well, she could certainly use the additional brain power.

Sally pointed to the deckchair next to her.

"Please, sit down. I'm sorry if I was a bit harsh. You startled me," she said.

He planted himself comfortably on the deck chair, swinging his legs up and sighing as he leaned his head back onto the cushion and closed his eyes.

Sally thought he had gone to sleep.

"So, who do you think killed Jim?" he asked, eyes still closed.

Sally laughed.

"Well, isn't that the question of the day. I've just been making some notes. It's all a bit strange considering none of us met Jim until three days ago," Sally said.

"Or so they say," the monk replied.

"True, I guess," Sally said, looking down at her notes.

"Any main suspects, detective?" Francesco asked.

She perused what she had written and read off a bit to him.

"Well, Aharon and Niv, because Jim obviously was uncomfortable with a male couple. That's as far as I've gotten, to be honest."

The monk's eyes were still closed, but he didn't seem to be sleeping.

He opened them and turned to her.

"Well, I have a connection to him, and so do you," he said.

"What?" Sally replied.

"Well. We're all Catholic," and he laughed at his own joke.

She wasn't sure how serious he was being.

"True, but is that a reason to kill someone? Other way around: what if someone hated Catholics?" Sally blurted out, realizing if that were true, she or the monk could be next.

Chapter Seventeen

Sally went back to her cabin for a short nap before lunch. She wanted to be well-rested when the group got together again, and for when the FBI came. She hoped they would welcome her help.

Maybe she was hoping for too much. I mean, come on, it was the FBI, not her local keystone cops.

She had just gotten back to her cabin when there was a knock at the door. *Now what.*

She pushed herself up and padded to the door. Looking through the peephole, she saw Hoppy.

Sally opened the door and smiled wanly.

"Um, hi Hoppy. I was just about to take a short nap."

"So sorry to bother you, but do you have a minute? I really need to talk to someone."

Sally moved into the room, and Hoppy followed her.

They both sat down on the couch.

"Would you like a coffee or tea?" Sally asked.

"Booze would be more my thing at the moment," Hoppy replied.

Sally looked at the clock on the wall.

"Um, Hoppy, it's the middle of the morning."

"Yeah, yeah, I know."

She put her head in her hands and began sobbing.

Sally had an inkling of why, but she was still surprised about the sudden outburst of emotion from the outback doctor. She put an arm on Hoppy's shoulder and squeezed.

"What's wrong, Hoppy?"

"Oh, Sally, I really wish I could have done something for poor Jim. I really wanted to save him," she said.

She stopped crying, wiped her eyes, and looked over at Sally.

"Like I told you before, there was nothing you could have done. If he was allergic to fish that badly…"

"I know, but I'm a doctor. I'm supposed to save people," Hoppy replied. The crying started again.

Maybe what she had told Sally about the reason for coming on the trip was only partially true. Maybe she was burned out, but maybe she had also just lost a patient in Australia.

Sally decided this wasn't the best time to get into the details of that. And Sally realized that it probably had nothing to do with Jim's death anyway.

She needed to get the results of the food tests and the tox screen from the police to know more. Sally was still wondering whether the FBI would let her be involved, so she decided to find Detective Watkins or Officer Burnham quickly to see if those results had come in, before the FBI arrived.

But she couldn't just leave Hoppy there.

"Hoppy, why don't we head to the upper deck. The fresh air will do you good," Sally offered.

Hoppy shook her head.

"No, I just want to be alone now. Thanks for listening to me, Sally. I really appreciate it."

Sally hadn't really been listening that long, but she had an idea.

"Why don't you talk to Francesco. He might be able to help work through your feelings."

Where was that sage advice coming from?

"I'm not religious, but maybe he would be helpful. I'm going to first go back to my cabin for a short nap before the next tour."

"Okay. I'll come by in a bit and pick you up," Sally said, leading Hoppy to the door.

They were due in Wickliffe, Kentucky, soon, and Sally was glad lunch would be included with the tour. They weren't scheduled to disembark until one p.m., so this was extra time to investigate.

"Great, thanks."

They hugged.

Sally watched Hoppy walk to her cabin next door. When the door shut, she slipped on her sneakers and strode down the hall to find the police.

Chapter Eighteen

Sally went to the lounge, the temporary office set up for the police. Just inside the restaurant, she bumped into both Officer Burnham and Aharon, also heading in the same direction.

Burnham gave Sally a once-over quickly, figuring out why she was there.

He was about to speak when Aharon interrupted, "Have you seen Niv? I thought you were interrogating him, but now I find you here."

Burnham shook his head.

"No, we are finished with him. He left a while ago and said he wanted to work on his book."

Aharon shrugged and left the restaurant.

Sally continued walking with Officer Burnham.

He turned to her.

"Um, can I help you?" he asked.

She smiled.

"Just a quick question, Officer."

"Well, we're kind of busy at the moment," he replied, waving what looked like a medical bag.

"What's in that?" she asked, eager to grab it from him and peek inside.

He looked like he wasn't going to tell her.

Then his voice dropped to a whisper, "I know you're supposed to be helping us, but the Detective doesn't want you to know everything."

Sally started running scenarios through her head of how she could change that.

"Oh, um…" she started.

"Yeah," he replied, "But I'm not the detective. Have a look."

He held the bag open for her to peer inside. It was filled with pen-like objects that resembled the anti-allergy pen Hoppy had jabbed into Jim's thigh the night before.

"Whose bag is it?" Sally asked, already knowing the answer to that question.

"Dr. Wilcox's, of course. We found it in her room," he said as if he had just discovered the Holy Grail.

"Well, wouldn't Hoppy have a bag like that with her? She is a doctor, officer," Sally replied.

"Filled with anti-allergy pens?" he countered.

Sally shrugged.

Why would her bag be filled with those pens? Sally would have to talk to Hoppy about that. Delicately, of course.

"We're just about to ask her about this."

They reached the door to the lounge.

"Why don't you wait here. Maybe I can get the Detective to talk to you after we're done with the doctor."

Sally smiled, "Thank you. I'm patient."

He laughed, "Yeah, right."

She took a seat as he walked into the lounge and began thinking.

* * *

After about ten minutes, the door opened and Hoppy slinked out, a look of fear on her face. She was obviously so engrossed in her own thoughts, she hadn't noticed Sally sitting near the lounge.

Detective Watkins came out a few seconds later, frowning.

"Can I help you?" they said a tad harshly.

"Um, sorry, well, I just was wondering..." Sally began.

Watkins took a deep breath and laughed. Apparently, the anger had subsided.

"Wondering if we had gotten the results of the food test or of the tox screen back on Jim. Ms. Witherspoon, this isn't New York, where tons of people are waiting to do tests and other police work. And it's Sunday morning," Detective Watkins explained.

"Yeah, I guess that makes sense," she replied.

Darn. She really wanted to get those results. She quickly debated whether there was a faster way, but she knew there wasn't.

"Well, when you get them, could you share them with me, in confidence, of course," Sally said.

"Let's see what the FBI says," Watkins replied.

As they were talking, Burnham came out of the lounge.

"The captain just called. We're docking soon, and I thought you might want to consolidate our notes before the FBI arrives," he said, looking at his feet.

"Okay, sure," Watkins said.

Sally took this as her cue to get out of there.

"Thanks again, Detective," Sally said as she walked out.

The two Klondike police ignored her as they returned to the lounge.

Sally decided to think some more before she had to pick up Hoppy for their tour and lunch.

The biggest question was how she could slip in questions about all those anti-allergy pens Hoppy apparently had brought with her.

They seemed innocuous, but not in that quantity.

Sally couldn't believe Hoppy had anything to do with Jim's death. She had tried to save him.

When she got upstairs and found an empty deckchair, she dropped into it for a brief moment of relaxation, though her mind was churning.

Until they had the test results, they wouldn't know more about Jim's sudden death.

She also wondered how far the police had gotten in finding Jim's relatives. If they couldn't, the FBI would be able to.

As she was considering this, she scanned the deck to see which other passengers were there and saw Amy Wong sitting by herself.

Hmm, maybe she could tell Sally something.

Her need for relaxation was fighting her need to interrogate.

She only considered it for a few seconds, before her puzzle-solving brain won.

She quietly got up and sauntered over to Amy.

"Hi Amy, mind if I join you?" Sally asked.

Amy had been staring off in the distance and obviously hadn't heard her.

Sally coughed, and Amy turned around.

"Oh, it's you," Amy said.

"Mind if I join you?" Sally repeated the question.

"Whatever, have a seat."

What a friendly offer.

Sally sat down on the chair offered but didn't say anything, hoping Amy would start a conversation.

"What a terrible trip," Amy said, surprising Sally with her candor, "What a shitty idea."

"What a tragedy," Sally added.

"Yes, terrible that Jim passed away."

Amy said all this while looking out onto the river and away from Sally, who wasn't sure what this openness meant. Amy Wong had not exactly been the friendliest the last few days. Maybe it was the shock of a death on board that had shaken her.

"Well, at least we're continuing the trip," Sally added not so helpfully. It felt weird that someone had died, and they all had to pretend that the trip was going on as planned, as if nothing had happened. Having the FBI and police on board added an odd touch to everything.

Sally hoped the killer would be found before they reached New Orleans, and they could finish up the trip with some closure.

As she knew from her previous investigation at home in Berry Springs, finding the killer takes time, something her patience was not cut out for.

"Sally, I'm glad you sat down," Amy said, finally turning to her.

"I want to apologize for my bitchiness. I'm just so stressed about moving to Washington, leaving my restaurant, and starting a new life," Amy explained.

Sally beamed inwardly. She was always astounded at what her bartender demeanor could do to get people to open up.

"Did you even want to come to the U.S.?" Sally asked bluntly.

Amy sighed.

"Well, not really, but I know Jason was so excited about the posting, and it really is a once-in-a-lifetime opportunity for him and his career, Deputy Ambassador. I made the decision to leave the restaurant a bit rashly. And only afterwards realized what I would be giving up."

Wow, Deputy Ambassador. The Wongs hadn't mentioned the exact position up to then, but that would definitely explain the kid gloves the U.S. government seemed to be donning when dealing with them. That would also explain how they were still continuing their trip. If Jason Wong had been about to be just a clerk, the boat wouldn't be going anywhere.

Putting those thoughts aside, Sally touched Amy's arm.

"Well, there are a ton of great restaurants in Washington. Don't you think one of them would love having you as a guest chef?"

"Maybe," Amy replied, looking away again, "But the Chinese government loves to keep a tight rein on its diplomats. I don't think they would like it if the wife of one of them was working at a restaurant in Washington, particularly the wife of the Deputy Ambassador. Too much opportunity to cavort with those evil Americans."

"Well, you could at least try," Sally said encouragingly.

Deciding to change the subject, Sally thought Amy might want to dissect the events of the night before.

"So terrible about Jim. I wonder what happened?" Sally asked, trying to be naive, but it didn't come out that way.

"Oh, Sally, he was poisoned, wasn't he?" Amy replied, looking at her like a schoolmarm.

"Well, we don't know that for sure," Sally said, "Food poisoning perhaps."

"He said he was allergic to fish, but he didn't have the fish," Amy said.

"I know, but could there have been fish in his food anyway?" Sally asked.

"Well, I doubt it. So far, I've been quite impressed by the food preparation and quality on board. It seems excellent. And if so, they would not use a pan for fish to prepare another dish. His carbonara shouldn't have had fish in it," she said, adding, "And Jason was fine."

True, Sally thought, but he had coughed. Though he explained that away, and he definitely didn't collapse on the floor clutching his throat.

As she was thinking about this and him, Jason came up the stairs.

She decided the two needed to be alone, so she got up quickly.

"Oh, Sally, don't go," Amy said.

Sally checked her phone.

"Well, it's already 12:30 p.m., we're leaving at 1:00 p.m.," Sally replied.

Jason came over to them.

"Hi Sally," he said, looking down and smiling at his wife. She looked up and touched his arm.

"Time to go, dear," he added.

"See you two in a bit," Sally said.

She got back to her cabin and stuffed her backpack with sunscreen, sunglasses, the mystery she was reading, her notebook and pen, and a sweater if it got chilly.

I don't think I will need it, but you never know, Sally thought.

It was turning into a warm, sunny day.

She felt the boat slowing and docking. It was almost time to go.

Just before 1:00 p.m., she knocked on Hoppy's door.

The two walked to the gangway together for the start of a new tour. This time with a (hopefully) subtle FBI presence.

When they got to the exit of the ship, the rest of the group was waiting, along with the captain and six official-looking guys. They were all in gray tracksuits, but they screamed "FBI" a mile away.

This should be fun, Sally thought. I'll just pretend they are my personal security detail, which they are.

Chapter Nineteen

"Hi, I'm Special Agent Erik Lazarus," the first guy in an ill-fittingtracksuit explained, "My team and I will be part of your tour from now on. Well, at least until we find who killed your fellow passenger. The rest of my group is now meeting with the Klondike Police. We will be questioning you all again later today or tomorrow."

He was around 5' 5", shiny bald head, grey eyes.

He pointed to his five colleagues, but didn't say their names or introduce them.

"This should be lots of fun," Francesco whispered to Sally, glancing at the captain, Martin, and the FBI officials.

The captain was frowning.

So much for a quiet ride down the Mississippi, Sally thought.

"Yes, well, we signed up for an adventure, didn't we?" Sally replied.

Hoppy jabbed her shoulder.

"Not quite the adventure I signed up for," she said.

Sally wondered how Hoppy could now be so outwardly calm since she had just been questioned by the police. She had looked a lot worse when she had walked out of the lounge.

There was a lot more to Hoppy than met the eye.

"Let's go," Martin said, and they walked off the ship and down the street.

The group followed him out. Most of them looking stoic, staring at their escort.

The Wickliffe Mounds State Historic Site was only a few minutes walk from where their ship was docked.

Sally's first thought as they arrived there was what Jim would have thought of it.

Reading the flyer they all got, Sally thought about all the peoples that were displaced or killed to make way for the settlers. This was just one of numerous locations all over the country.

On the other hand, she thought it was important that this one was preserved. More people in the country needed to see this.

She stopped herself, wondering where this activism was coming from. She was really getting herself worked up.

Looking over at Amy Wong, she could see the South African was disturbed. Jason was pushing his wife forward around the site.

"No subtlety there," Brin said behind her, "Ugh, I hate that woman."

Sally nodded, though she didn't think Brin really hated Amy. Hate was a very strong word, as her mother liked to say.

"Let's go into the exhibit building and get away from them," Brin suggested, who just started walking toward the building as if Sally would blindly follow her.

And Sally did just that, looking back at Hoppy, who was chatting with Francesco.

"Wow, beautiful," Brin said as they entered the building and found the first exhibit on pottery.

Sally just felt sick. So much art and history that was just washed away. She was getting the same feeling she got at the Trail of Tears Park. But maybe this was a sign that she was really trying to process what she was seeing and learning.

They only had been there a few minutes when Sally said, "Brin, can we do the walk outside. I'm not feeling so well."

"Guilty conscience?"

Brin always knew exactly what to say.

They walked outside with their FBI escorts to find Aharon and Niv heading into the building with theirs.

"You must go and see the burial mound. Unbelievable," Aharon said. Niv seemed less enthused about the whole place, but he was following his partner into the building.

Aharon and Niv seemed as complex as Jason and Amy.

Sally and Brin strolled along the signed path to the first mound. In the distance, Sally could see Amy and Jason walking swiftly along the trail. Both were staring at the ground. They walked a few minutes and came upon Brother Francesco on a bench. He seemed to be praying, so they quietly passed him without disturbing him.

Sally looked around, wondering where Hoppy was.

While Brin marveled at the mound, Sally took a more somber stance and read the information board at the edge of the mound.

She spent most of the time spacing out, thinking about what the peoples who had built the mound had lost. Sally knew they would never get it back. She shed a tear.

"Oh, please, Sally. Look forward, not back. If I spent as much time as you worrying about the past and what the world did to people, I would probably go mad," Brin said, staring at Sally, hands on her hips.

Sally didn't respond because she didn't really know what to say at that moment.

Instead, she just started walking toward the next mound. Brin followed her harrumphing behind her.

Sally ignored her.

When they got to the next mound, they heard shouting. Rounding the bend, they found Hoppy and Amy in a shouting match, Jason and their FBI escort trying to pull them apart.

Sally hurried over.

"What's going on?" she asked.

Amy gave her a look of death and walked into the woods, her husband and the FBI agent in tow.

Everyone in the group seemed a bit sensitive. Was it Jim's death that was disturbing them? Or the difficult history they were seeing? Or just the stress of being cooped up together on the boat?

Sally wasn't sure. But maybe someone had snapped and killed Jim. Though she wasn't sure how they would have gotten fish, or something else into his food.

Sally decided to tackle Agent Lazarus about the food results when they got back to the ship. Hopefully, Detective Watkins had told him about her helpfulness in solving the murder. Sally prayed he would be as obliging as the Klondike police had been.

"Hoppy, are you okay?" Sally asked after Amy had gone.

She debated having a conversation off the boat with the FBI agents nearby, but there was no time to lose.

She glanced back and saw the agents sit down on a bench and watch them. A few other guests at the site walked by and stared at the three men in the gray track suits.

She could tell by the looks on their faces that they stood out like a sore thumb.

Hoppy waited until the tourists were past them and into the woods before she replied.

"I don't want to talk about it," she said.

"What's going on with you two?" Brin asked, moving closer to Hoppy, who stepped back.

"I said I don't want to talk about it," Hoppy barked.

"Well, sensitive aren't we?" Brin said, wagging her finger.

"Let's go on the trail into the woods, you two," Sally suggested, "I could use a bit of exercise."

"Already sick of the history, dear?" Brin asked a bit sarcastically.

"No, I think we all need some fresh air," Sally replied.

"Let's go, then," Brin said, and the three women walked in the direction the Wongs had headed.

It didn't take too long for them to catch up with the diplomat and his wife. They were now sitting on a bench in the woods holding hands. Amy was in tears.

Their escort was off to the side, trying to be discreet.

Amy looked up and saw Sally and Brin and quickly wiped her eyes.

Brin had her secret phone in her hand, and Sally was worried she was going to try to get a picture of the famous chef and post it.

Amy saw the phone and snatched it from Brin.

"What the hell are you doing with this? I'm reporting you!" Amy cried as the FBI escorts approached them.

"Whose phone is this?" one of the gray track suits demanded.

Both women pointed to the other.

Sally stepped in, wondering if she should be truthful.

Then again, it could get her in with the FBI, which she was going to need if she wanted to get important information about their investigation from them.

"It's Brin's," Sally replied.

"Sally?!" Brin cried.

Sally shrugged.

Gray tracksuit recognized Amy. His face said it all. Even if it had been her phone, he wasn't going to be arresting her and demanding it back.

"You're coming with me," gray tracksuit said as he led a protesting Brin away.

Amy and Jason looked at each other and followed them back.

Sally glanced around, wondering if any other guests had seen what had just happened.

Luckily, the coast was clear.

"Shouldn't we go with them to help Brin?" Hoppy asked.

"They're just going to be taking her back to the ship for questioning. I'd like to enjoy the fresh air off the ship," Sally replied a bit harshly.

She prayed she would be able to get back on Brin's good side, considering Sally found her to be the best of the bunch.

Hoppy stared at her.

"Well, maybe it is better for the both of us to stay out of the FBI's way for a bit."

"Let's go," Sally said, starting off toward the wooded trail.

Hoppy quickly followed her.

They weren't alone, of course. The crunch of leaves behind them said it all.

Glancing back, Sally remembered they couldn't go anywhere alone. Two of the gray tracksuits were a short distance away.

Hoppy and Sally walked in silence.

Was it one of the passengers or one of the crew? While they had been on the boat for four days of the ten, that still wasn't that much time to get to know people. Someone on the ship may have known Jim before and had a grudge. But who?

Looking at her watch, she saw that they still had an hour or so before she had to get back to the ship.

Turning to Hoppy, she asked, "Hoppy, what was going on with you and Amy back there?"

Hoppy swore.

"She, well, she claimed I should have done more to try and save Jim."

Why would Amy care about saving Jim?

"Well, I'm not a doctor, of course, but you and Martin seemed to be working like mad to save him."

"That's what I told her," Hoppy replied, stamping her foot.

They came upon a bench, and Sally got Hoppy to sit down.

"Don't worry," Sally said, "No one's accusing you of anything."

Sally didn't lie very well, and Hoppy shifted on the bench.

"The police questioned me earlier," Hoppy confessed.

"I know," Sally blurted out.

Hoppy went wide-eyed.

"What?" she yelled.

Sally went red.

"Well, I was sitting next to the door when you came out. You seemed so upset and obviously didn't notice me."

Hoppy laughed.

"Ms. Detective is everywhere," Hoppy said.

Sally chuckled but got right to the point.

"So what were they questioning you about?"

Hoppy sighed.

"My medical bag is filled with anti-allergy pens," Hoppy explained.

Sally tried to look like this was new information to her. Luckily, Hoppy was staring at the ground and not at her.

"Okay, but why?" Sally asked, placing a hand on Hoppy's.

Hoppy looked up at her, her eyes wet.

"I'm obsessed with allergy and allergic reactions."

Sally remained silent and frozen in place. She wasn't going to interrupt.

"Aren't you going to ask me why?" Hoppy asked.

"I want you to tell your story when you're ready. I trust you," Sally replied, though she didn't quite believe her own words.

They sat quietly for a few minutes before Hoppy continued.

"Well, I told you I needed to get away and that I had burnout," Hoppy began.

Sally nodded.

"Well, I lost a patient after a snake bite. We have a lot of poisonous things in Australia, as I mentioned at the botanical garden. I know so much about allergens and snake bites, I was just overconfident. The patient died, and I have felt guilty ever since. That all came back to me when Jim died."

"That's terrible, Hoppy. There was probably nothing you could have done, just like with Jim," Sally replied, not really knowing if that were true.

"Well, there wasn't an official inquiry, thank goodness. We have a lot of snake bite deaths, so this was just one more, but I still feel so guilty. After that, I always kept plenty of anti-allergy pens in my bag. Just in case."

Hoppy stopped talking and spent the next few moments sniffling.

Well, at least that explained the anti-allergy pens in Hoppy's bag, if that's all it was about.

"What do the police and FBI think?" Sally asked.

Hoppy laughed.

"Of course, they think I did it, though I had medication in my bag, not poison. But wouldn't I have gotten rid of all that after Jim's death, if I were smart, which maybe I'm not," Hoppy replied.

Sally had no idea what to believe at this point, but she wanted to give Hoppy the benefit of the doubt.

"Listen, Hoppy. The person responsible for Jim's death is the person that put fish, or poison, in his food," Sally said.

Hoppy looked up, her eyes wide.

"Poison?" she mumbled.

"Until we know the results of the food test, we won't know whether someone put fish in his carbonara, or poison."

"But we were all sitting there at the table. How could someone have slipped poison into his food without someone seeing?" Hoppy wondered, crossing her arms and waiting for Sally to reply.

Sally realized this seemed a challenge.

"Well, Brin and Martin were sitting on either side of him. One could have leaned over and dumped something into the food while he was looking away. You know, a small vial in the palm of their hand," Sally said, thinking aloud more than anything else.

Hoppy laughed.

"Okay, Ms. Detective. And what is their motive for killing Jim?" Hoppy asked, raising her eyebrows, obviously feeling better.

"Well, someone did it. I just have to find the motive. And do we really know that much about each other?" Sally replied.

"Yeah, that's true. Hey, you could be the murderer," Hoppy said, not too convincingly.

They both laughed, though murdering someone wasn't really a laughing matter.

Turning serious, Hoppy got up.

"Shouldn't we go back to the ship now and make sure Brin is okay?" Hoppy asked, starting to walk in that direction.

"I guess you're right," Sally agreed, though she had hoped for more time in the woods to work through everything that had happened so far and any clues she may have missed.

Chapter Twenty

Back on the ship, Sally went straight for the police setup in the lounge to try and talk to Special Agent Lazarus.

She has suggested to Hoppy that it was probably better if only one of them go rather than try to tackle the agent together. They might be able to get more out of him that way.

Hoppy had agreed and gone back to her room for a nap before dinner.

Sally was glad to find the agent alone.

"Um, Special Agent Lazarus?" Sally asked quietly as she stepped into the room.

"Who are you?" he barked.

"Hi, I'm Sally Witherspoon, one of the passengers, and I was wondering about Brin. Your guys took her in for having a phone," she said.

He frowned.

"Oh, the busybody," he said.

Darn. This wasn't going to be easy.

"Well, I like to think of myself as a help to you and the police," she said, smiling widely.

"Listen, Ms. Witherspoon. This is an official investigation. Leave the detecting to the experts. Now get out. I have work to do."

"What about Brin?" Sally demanded.

"She's staying on the ship for now and can't leave. We've confiscated her phone," he replied.

"Is she under arrest?" Sally asked, ready to call her lawyer if needed.

"No, just a warning, but she's now my prime suspect," he barked.

"Brin? She couldn't hurt a fly."

"Well, someone did it, didn't they, Ms. Witherspoon," he said, reeking of sarcasm.

Sally opened her mouth to give him a 'fuck you,' but decidedly that probably wasn't the best course of action.

She contemplated asking him if they had been able to contact Jim's family, but decided against it.

She'd have to get out of there and find Detective Watkins. They may be more helpful.

Walking out of the lounge, she hoped the Klondike police were still on board. Considering Agent Lazarus' demeanor, he may have thrown them off the ship already.

Luckily, she was a passenger and he couldn't do the same with her. Or could he? They had Brin under house arrest.

Somehow, she always had a love/hate relationship with law enforcement. Or was that a hot/cold relationship? She wasn't sure which fit better, thinking back to the investigation of Bill's death months ago, where she was sometimes on Detective Finnegan's good side, and sometimes not. Maybe she really didn't care. Or did she?

Thinking about this took her to the upper deck, where she saw Detective Watkins and Officer Burnham sitting at a table with the captain.

They both frowned as Sally strode over.

"Hey," she said, trying to be as friendly as possible.

"Hello, Ms. Witherspoon. Can we help you?" Detective Watkins said.

"Um, yeah, I just had a question, but I see you're busy," Sally replied. She didn't want them all to hear of her curiosity

"Is it about Brin?" Watkins asked.

Sally shook her head.

"No, Agent Lazarus told me about her situation. I can't believe she was so stupid," Sally blurted out.

That wasn't really helping Brin's cause.

"So what do you want to know?" Watkins asked.

"Um, well, um…" Sally began looking at the captain, "It can wait. I don't want to interrupt your work."

Watkins sighed.

"Well, why don't I come to your cabin when we are done talking to the Lazarus. After that, we are off the ship. It's now an FBI investigation," Watkins explained.

Sally responded, "Sounds good, thanks."

She turned and headed over to the stairs and her cabin.

* * *

Sally sat on her balcony sipping an herbal tea. She wondered how long she would have to wait for the Klondike police to pay her a visit.

She put her mug down and stared off in the distance. The ship wasn't moving yet, but she had a great view of the woods across the river. The sun was shining, and it really was a beautiful day. The only shadow that day was Jim's death and the FBI presence. Sally tried to put that out of her mind.

As she looked across the mighty Mississippi, she began to nod off.

Just as her eyes closed, there was a knock at the door.

This snapped her out of her dreamy state, and she practically ran to the cabin door.

She looked through the peephole and saw Detective Watkins, alone.

Opening the door, she stood aside to let them in.

"Thanks so much for coming by, Detective," Sally said, "Would you like something to drink?"

"This isn't a social call, Ms. Witherspoon," Watkins replied.

"Um, well, Detective. I did have a question about Jim's death. Did you get the results of the food test or the tox screen?" she asked.

Watkins stared at her.

"You know I can't really tell you that. Why don't you leave the police work to the experts for once?" Watkins replied, getting louder by the end.

Sally wasn't sure how to respond to that.

Watkins sighed.

"I'm sorry, that was rude," they admitted.

"I am so sorry what happened to Jim, and I just want to do whatever I can to help," Sally explained, hoping that would help pacify the situation.

"Well, your Detective Finnegan did say, reluctantly I might add, that you were a bit of help during that last murder investigation…well, all right, we did get the results of the food/drink test."

"And…?" Sally asked, rocking nervously on her toes.

"Shouldn't you ask Agent Lazarus about this? I could lose my job for telling you, and as I told you on the deck, Burnham and I are out of this, unless Lazarus changes his mind. The death did occur in our jurisdiction."

"Well, I did ask him and he was less than helpful," Sally replied.

"That's not surprising," Watkins replied.

Sally waited to see whether there was more forthcoming.

"Okay, I'll tell you, but you didn't hear this from me. There was no fish or poison in the carbonara or in his drink," Watkins clarified.

Sally's mouth went wide with surprise.

"But how did he die, then?" she asked, incredulous.

"That's a damn good question, Ms. Witherspoon," Watkins replied.

"Well, something killed him," Sally said.

"Really?! That's quite smart of you," Watkins retorted.

Sally raised her palms.

"Sorry, I know. I just don't understand it," she said.

"Neither do we," Watkins admitted.

"What are you going to do now?" Sally asked.

"We've ordered a full autopsy. And the FBI is sending in their best medical examiner to assist," Watkins explained.

"How long will that take?" Sally asked, hoping it would be sooner than later. There was no use investigating unless the cause of death was determined. That might help narrow the list of suspects.

"Hopefully not more than a day or two," Watkins replied, "I'm as eager as you to figure out who did this. Well, that's all I have for now."

Watkins turned to go.

"Oh, wait, Detective, one more question," Sally pleaded.

Watkins stopped but didn't turn back.

"Yes," they replied impatiently.

"What about Jim's family?" Sally asked.

"Nothing yet, I'm afraid, which I have to admit is puzzling. Now I really have to go," they said.

"Thanks, Detective. I really appreciate it," Sally replied.

Watkins left, and Sally headed back to the balcony and a snooze. Maybe she would dream up the solution to Jim's murder. Dinner that night wasn't until eight.

Chapter Twenty-One

Sally decided to be ultracasual for dinner, putting on jeans and a sweatshirt. It seemed the proper antidote to the festivity of the night before that ended in tragedy.

She walked into the restaurant to find most of the group already there.

Niv and Aharon were sitting at one table at the window. Next to them were Brin and Hoppy. Then Jason and Amy Wong took the third.

She walked toward Brin and Hoppy's table to see how Brin was doing. The look on Brin's face as Sally approached made her steer clear of that table.

Sally noticed Brother Francesco sitting alone, so she decided to sit with him. Across the room, she saw Agent Lazarus huddled with the Klondike police. Martin Sandworth was sitting with them as well.

She didn't see Captain Kramer, but she guessed someone would have to be in charge on the bridge.

"May I join you?" Sally asked as she slid into the seat next to Francesco without waiting for an answer.

He replied, "Of course."

"Thanks. What a day," she said as Kwame came over. She definitely needed a drink.

She saw the monk was sipping a soda.

"What can I get you, Ms. Witherspoon?" Kwame asked as he approached the table.

"So formal this evening?" she replied.

"Showing off for the FBI," he said and laughed loudly.

Everyone's head turned. He coughed, looked at them, and then turned back to Sally.

"I'll have a glass of white wine tonight and some sparkling water," she ordered, leaning back into her chair.

Kwame left to get her drinks.

"Have you heard about Brin?" Sally whispered.

The monk nodded.

"I don't know what she was thinking," he responded just as quietly.

"She does love her influencing," Sally said.

The monk shook his head.

"Addicted to it, methinks," he replied.

"Yeah," Sally agreed.

The drinks came, and they sat in silence for a few minutes, staring out the window.

Her first thought was that this was the least relaxing vacation she'd ever been on. So much for trying to get away from it all.

The monk broke the silence finally.

"What did you think of today's location, Sally?"

She shrugged.

"Well, it was another difficult spot for me. I took a walk in the woods with Hoppy to try and process it. I never really dealt with this part of our country's history before as intensely as I am now. Somehow it's getting to me," she explained, keeping her hands squeezed together in her lap.

She decided not to mention to the monk about Hoppy's confession and the questioning she had gotten from the police. Though Francesco would probably be able to get that out of Hoppy without even trying.

"Your country, as many countries, have done some terrible things to get where they are today. It's important to never forget. I can understand how difficult this might be for you. But confronting things often helps one move on."

Sally felt like she entered the confessional whenever she was in the monk's presence.

"Brother Francesco, I have to admit to myself that I'm glad I chose this trip. I needed rest and relaxation, but something about the history did call to me. Or maybe it was a premonition that a murder would happen. They seem to be following me around recently."

Sally looked at the monk. She couldn't tell whether he was about to grin or frown. His lips trembled, but he showed neither one nor the other.

"I doubt it was a premonition, Sally. Do you really believe that?" he asked.

"Well, um, not really. But it does seem strange that I go on my first trip after having helped to solve three murders in my town, and someone dies on the trip."

The monk shrugged.

"Coincidence. Or the hand of God telling you what your calling should be."

At this, Sally laughed.

"A bar-owning detective. Cool," she said a bit sarcastically, even though that is exactly what she seemed to be turning into.

"You told me how difficult the time was those months ago. However, I got the sense that you really enjoyed it. The investigating part, I mean," he said.

The first course came, and that gave Sally time to think about what the monk just said.

She didn't like talking too much about her personal feelings at the moment, even with a monk, so she decided to change the subject.

She dipped into her cold gazpacho, which was gloriously spicy, and spent a few moments in silence. The only sound coming from the table was slurping.

"This is delicious," she finally said.

"Wonderful, yes," the monk added.

"That's the best part of this trip, I think, the great food and drink," Sally said.

The monk agreed.

"We seem to be going from sleep, to food, to tours, to food, to sleep.

"It's a tough life, but someone's got to live it," the monk blurted out.

Both laughed.

"Speaking of food and drink," Sally began.

Francesco put down his spoon.

Sally lowered her voice to a whisper and confessed to the monk what Detective Watkins had told her. She was going to need all the help she could get to find the killer, so she let her sense of duty, and any legal requirements, fly out the window.

The monk's eyes widened as she talked.

"But how did he die then? Maybe it was just a heart attack. He wasn't the fittest person," the monk said, as softly as Sally had spoken. Luckily, the room was quite lively with conversation, otherwise even their whispers might have been overheard.

Sally kept glancing over to the police table, hoping no one was listening or coming over to talk to them.

But they were engrossed in their own conversation with Martin Sandworth. He looked up at one point and winked at Sally.

She shivered, but she could feel her cheeks reddening. That British accent and muscled fit body was too much for her.

Focus, Sally.

Turning back to the monk, she said, "Well, a very good question. But I don't think it was a heart attack. Hoppy is sure his throat was closed, and he was grasping at his throat, not his chest."

The monk touched her hand. "Maybe we will never know."

Sally pulled her hand away.

"No, we'll know. I know I will solve it."

At this, everyone stopped talking and stared at her. She got quite a glare from Special Agent Lazarus.

Oops, was she that loud?

"Be careful, Sally," Francesco said, looking solemn and tapping her hand.

Kwame came over to take their plates.

"Would you excuse me? I'd like to go chat with Brin and Hoppy."

"Enjoy," he said, smiling as she got up.

* * *

"Hey, mind if I join you for the main course?" Sally asked, starting to sit

121

down before Brin or Hoppy had time to respond.

"Of course, Ms. Detective," Brin said, shrieking with laughter.

Well, that was a change of attitude from when Sally walked into the room.

There were several glasses of wine in front of Brin.

That might explain it.

"Are you drunk?" Sally asked.

Sally planted herself between Brin and Hoppy.

"I'm so sorry, Brin, for today. I just, well, my truth obsession made me blurt out that it was your phone."

Brin waved it away.

"Water under the bridge. Hoppy has talked me down from throwing you overboard. I know you were just trying to do the right thing. I don't forgive you, but let's all try to make the most of this trip," Brin explained more calmly than she had ever been up to now.

That's something Sally was never going to get used to. It was kind of endearing. Sally wondered if she would ever get the opportunity to visit Brin in Valencia or perhaps see Hoppy in Australia.

"So what do you want to interrogate us about?" Hoppy said, cracking a smile.

Sally grinned.

"Is it that obvious?" Sally asked.

"You are definitely determined. I have to give you that," Hoppy replied.

Sally felt the rush of adrenaline or a rush of something. It was like after Bill and the others had been killed. Something in her was pushing her to solve Jim's murder. And her competitive spirit meant she wanted to solve it before the police or FBI did.

As a member of the tourist group, she could get more out of the people than someone with a badge or a uniform.

Leaning down and dropping her voice to a whisper (this was getting to be a habit of hers on the ship), she explained what she had learned from Detective Watkins.

"So, how did he die?" Brin asked.

The question on Sally's mind as well. It made no sense.

"Well, I know his throat was closed. His body reacted to something in the food or drink. There's no other way," Hoppy said.

"Well, either the results are wrong or maybe Watkins is not telling me everything," Sally said.

"I wish I could do an autopsy on Jim," Hoppy replied.

The main course arrived just then, and they spent the rest of the meal enjoying each other's company, trying not to think about the job ahead. Or the fact that one of their tour group had already been murdered.

They were just enjoying a coffee at the end of the meal when Agent Lazarus came over to their table.

He went right for Sally.

"Ms. Witherspoon. I want to see you at ten tomorrow morning in the lounge. I think we have a lot to discuss, don't you?" he said, turning around and walking away before she had a chance to respond.

"Now what was that about?" Hoppy asked.

Sally shook her head.

It could be good or bad. She would just have to wait and see.

Chapter Twenty-Two

Sally lay awake in bed, the sun streaming in her window.

She was glad that it was a day on the river as they headed further south towards Memphis. She somehow hoped the murder would be solved by then, but since it was only a day away, that wasn't very realistic, she knew.

Looking at her phone, she saw it was already eight am. Time to order breakfast. And then get ready for her meeting with Agent Lazarus. Sally couldn't figure him out. Was he interested in her thoughts, or did he just want to warn her off again?

Somehow, she would have to weave the events of the months before and Detective Finnegan into her conversation.

But first breakfast. She grabbed the phone and placed her order. Kwame had said it would be about twenty minutes. Time enough to head out on the balcony with her notebook and her thoughts.

Sally cracked open the book to the last page she had written. All it said was *Niv, Aharon,* and *the Wongs.* She hadn't gotten very far.

Tapping her pen on the arm of the chair, her eyes focused on *the Wongs.* Maybe it seemed too obvious, because Amy Wong was a famous chef, but she could certainly know about ways to doctor food, Sally figured.

Then there was Hoppy's medical bag full of anti-allergy pens.

She had to admit that at the moment, though, there was no cause of death. As she had learned from Detective Watkins, there was no fish or poison in Jim Sullivan's food or drink Saturday night.

Sally, you need to think bigger, she told herself.

She ran through the rest of the people on board in her head.

And what about Jim's relatives?

She made a mental note to question Lazarus about any contact they had so far with his relatives in Boston. There must be someone there with such a big family as he claimed, even if he had told her he didn't see them that much.

These thoughts had taken longer than she thought when there was a knock at the door. Must be Kwame or Mary with her breakfast.

She padded over to the door and found Mary standing there with a cart and her breakfast.

"Good morning, Sally," she said, pushing the cart into the room.

Sally followed her.

"Could you push it out onto the balcony. I was just sitting there enjoying the sun."

Mary arranged the cart in front of the chair on the balcony.

"Everything to your liking?" Mary asked.

Sally thought something was off. Mary was always so perky and cheery. This morning, she seemed more robotic than Sally would have expected.

"Is everything okay, Mary?" Sally asked, getting right to the point.

Mary looked at her.

"Of course, why wouldn't there be?"

While Sally was trying to figure out what was bothering Mary, she was also enjoying the Irish lilt in Mary's voice. Sally could listen to that every day. Maybe that's why she had sort of gotten along with Jim. Well, they had had that nice chat in the café in Cape Girardeau. Well, sort of nice.

Sally snapped back to the moment, and Mary, who was staring at her.

"Well, you usually are so cheery and smiling. You aren't today. What's wrong? I'd like to help if I can."

Mary burst into tears. Sally had her sit in a chair on the balcony.

She let Mary cry it out before trying to get more out of her.

"I'm sorry. I shouldn't be burdening you with my problems. And you're a passenger. Oh, I'm going to be fired," Mary cried.

Sally hoped no one else had their windows open on that side or was sitting on the balcony. But they were already sitting there, so if someone overheard, that was that.

"Well, like I said. I'm here to help, Mary. Please tell me what's bothering you. I can help," she encouraged.

Mary looked at her as if she were about to speak, but kept her mouth shut. Sally decided to try a hunch.

"It's about Jim's death, isn't it. It was just terrible. I can imagine you are upset about that," Sally began.

"But it has nothing to do with you, Mary. It will all be forgotten when the next tour group comes aboard."

Sally knew what she was saying was bullshit, but maybe it would help comfort Mary, at least for the moment.

"Oh no, it won't be forgotten," Mary said, starting to cry again.

"Why won't it be?" Sally asked.

"Well, I...well...I...we..."

"Take deep breaths and tell me. Don't be worried," Sally said, rubbing Mary's shoulder.

"Well, Jim and I discovered we were distant cousins. So I've lost a relative," Mary explained, a bit more calmly.

Wow, that was news. But is that a motive? Sally's detective brain went into overdrive.

"When did you two find this out?" Sally asked, wanting to grab her notebook and make notes. But she knew that would kill the moment, and she probably wouldn't get as much out of Mary.

"Saturday. Just after you all got back from your tour, I was cleaning his room when he came in, and somehow we got talking about Ireland. We had a common ancestor, it seems, in the 19th century. My family stayed in Ireland in spite of the potato famine, and his part went to America. I don't have many friends here, so it was great to find someone I could talk to about the old country. And then he ended up dead that very night."

Mary's words were just pouring out. Sally let her talk.

"Wow, what a coincidence," Sally said.

"Yes, it was. And I was so glad to find him. And now he's dead," Mary said, and with that, she put her head in her hands and cried. Sally pulled her in for a hug, which was a bit awkward.

A part of Sally felt this all might be an act, the crying, etc. But if it were, why would Mary tell her this story? It would implicate her more than it would exonerate her. She had just told Sally that she was excited to find Jim. Why would she then murder him a few hours later Saturday night?

Mary got up, rubbing the tears from her eyes, and cleared her nose with a tissue she pulled out of her pocket.

"I'm sorry for this. I have to get on. Enjoy your breakfast."

As she turned to leave, Sally grabbed her arm.

"Mary, I'm glad you were able to talk to me. Please, if there is anything I can do for you, just let me know."

Mary left the cabin without saying another word.

Sally looked down at her breakfast and decided she wasn't hungry.

She poured herself a fresh cup of coffee and sat back to consider what she had just heard.

It was just past nine, and she still had time before she had to shower and get dressed to meet Agent Lazarus at ten. Sally was definitely not looking forward to that conversation.

Chapter Twenty-Three

Sally took deep breaths as she slowly walked to the lounge to meet Agent Lazarus. She wasn't easily scared at any rate, but she knew she had to put on a good face.

Strolling into the restaurant, she walked over to the lounge and saw the door open.

She found Agent Lazarus shuffling through papers and hacking away at a laptop.

She knocked on the door frame.

"Good morning," Sally said as she walked toward him.

"Oh, good morning, Ms. Witherspoon. Sorry for the mess," he said, standing up and shaking her hand.

He motioned to the empty seat next to him, and Sally planted herself, a bit hard.

She winced.

Lazarus didn't seem to notice and sat back down.

He pulled out a notepad from his shirt pocket and uncapped a fountain pen.

Oh, how quaint, she thought.

Or hoity-toity.

"Thanks for coming in this morning," he began.

Coming in? Well, she just walked down the hall, but whatever.

"Glad to help in any way I can," Sally replied, trying to put on her friendliest demeanor.

"Let's get right to the point. I learned from Detective Watkins that you offered your help with the investigation. She also told me about your Detective Finnegan."

Uh oh, she gulped, waiting for what she was sure was to come.

"I don't like busybodies, Ms. Witherspoon. But I do admit that you might be able to help, being a passenger and all."

Sally breathed a silent sigh of relief.

"Like I said, Special Agent Lazarus, I want to help in any way I can."

"Just call me Lazarus," he replied a bit gruffly.

"Now, let me see," he said as he rifled through the papers.

For all his gruff "I'm the boss" manner, he didn't seem very organized.

"Well, we got the results from the food and drink test. I understand Watkins shared that with you already. They really shouldn't have, but whatever," he said.

Lazarus turned the paper over.

"But the medical examiner did find evidence of an allergic reaction in the victim. And found some fish protein in his lungs and throat."

"What? How is that possible?" Sally said, immediately leaning forward to try and peer at the document. Lazarus quickly moved it away from her.

Sally believed him, but maybe he wasn't telling her everything.

"Anything else, Lazarus?" she asked, still leaning forward, trying to read the paper.

"Well, we don't know how the fish protein got in his lungs and throat. That's for sure. But that looks like it was cause of death. A severe allergic reaction."

Sally's head was spinning. So it was fish. But how? Nothing in the food.

Her brain came up with two possibilities: either the food that was tested was NOT the food on his plate, or someone had somehow slipped him fish protein during the meal or into his drink. But how was that possible? He wouldn't have let anyone shove anything in his mouth. And that would have been quite obvious to everyone else at the table. As would have someone tapping a powder or such into his food or drink.

And then how did it get in his lungs?

Her first thought went to Amy Wong. Not that she had done it, but maybe

Amy had an idea of how the fish protein could have been prepared to give to him without anyone noticing.

Thinking back to the dinner Saturday night, the only two people sitting near Jim were Brin and Martin Sandworth.

The only other person with access to both his food and drink was Kwame.

With this investigation, friends could be enemies, and enemies could be friends over and over again. She just needed to get to the bottom of it all.

"Do you have a theory, Lazarus?" she asked.

He shook his head.

"It just doesn't make any sense."

No, it didn't.

"Who do you think did it?" he asked Sally.

"To be honest, I have no idea at this point. Well, there are a couple people that might not have liked his bigoted attitude, but if you don't like someone do you necessarily go and kill them? And we had only been on the ship for a couple days. That seems a lot of planning and not a lot of time to do it. If there was no fish in the food or drink, or poison for that matter, it would take a lot to manage to get it in his throat and lungs," the words were spilling out.

As she spoke, Lazarus neither smiled nor frowned.

Sally really had no idea what she was saying, but she thought if she threw out information, it might make Lazarus think she could perhaps be helpful. Though he, and she, needed more than theories. They needed facts.

"Okay, so who were the people who were annoyed by him the most?" Lazarus said.

She didn't really want to tell him. One, so she could investigate on her own. And two, because she didn't want to rat on her fellow passengers.

But she realized she needed to stay on his good side.

She repeated what she had told the Klondike police.

"Okay, Lazarus. First, Niv and Aharon. Jim made disparaging remarks about them being gay. And um..."

Here she was debating whether she should tell Lazarus about Mary Roger's relation to Jim.

Lazarus waited, tapping his fingers on the table.

"Okay, and maybe Mary Rogers, the maid on board."

"The maid?" Lazarus said, his fingers no longer tapping.

"Well, yeah. She, um, came to serve me breakfast this morning in my cabin, and somehow she told me that she had discovered Jim was a distant cousin. They just learned about each other Saturday afternoon. I just can't believe that she would then kill him a few hours later. And why? She seemed so happy and excited about finding a relative on board."

Her stomach was twisting in knots as she spoke. Why did she tell him that story about Mary? She would probably regret it.

His bossy manner seemed to be getting to her, making her spill everything she knew.

Pull yourself together, Sally!

Lazarus was scribbling furiously with his fountain pen. As Sally looked over, she saw the ink was running every which way.

"Anyone else?" Lazarus said, putting down the pen. It hit the table hard, and a small jet of ink spat out. Luckily, it just missed her arm. She pulled it away and put both hands in her lap.

Lazarus didn't seem to notice.

Sally contemplated for a moment.

"Well, maybe Brin Clarkson," Sally began slowly. She liked Brin, but she had the feeling Brin was turned off by Jim's ancient and discriminatory attitude.

"Why is that?" he asked.

Sally explained her thinking.

Lazarus noted that down and got up.

Sally remained seated.

"Um, before I go, I do have one last question?" Sally began.

"Yes," Lazarus replied gruffly.

"Have you been able to contact Jim's relatives?" she asked.

Lazarus shook his head.

"There don't seem to be any relatives to contact," Lazarus replied.

Sally frowned.

"But he said he had a big family," Sally explained.

Lazarus shrugged.

"Who knows? If we don't find anyone, we're going to have to consider what to do with his body when we're done with the investigation," Lazarus replied.

Sally shuddered. That was not something she wanted to be thinking about. She got up and shook Lazarus' hand.

"Thanks for coming in, Ms. Witherspoon. As I mentioned before, I want your help, but don't interfere. And last of all, don't do any detecting on your own," he ordered.

Sally nodded and headed back to her cabin to plan her next move. Of course, she would do some detecting on her own. She just wasn't sure if she could ask any of the other passengers to help her. They were all suspects.

Chapter Twenty-Four

Back in her cabin, Sally decided she had to share the fish protein in the lungs information with Hoppy. There was nothing she could have done.

She got ready for lunch and headed down the hall to the other end of the ship.

Sally arrived in the restaurant right on time, but no one was there.

That's strange, she thought.

A door creaked, and she saw Kwame emerging from the kitchen.

"Looking for everyone?" he asked.

A fairly obvious question, as she was standing there looking around at the empty room.

"Uh, yeah," she replied.

"Lunch today is upstairs on deck," he explained.

That must have been in the itinerary somewhere, but she hadn't really looked at it much since the first day she arrived in Hannibal and sat on the bench, starting this long-awaited vacation.

"Oh great, thanks, Kwame," she said as she headed out and up the stairs.

As she climbed the steps, she heard a lot of noise. Apparently, everyone was in a good mood.

She emerged onto the deck and saw something completely different than she had expected.

Mary Rogers and Amy Wong were standing near each other, screaming, both red in the face. It looked like one might hit the other at any moment.

Brother Francesco stood near them.

"Please, just calm down. Let's all have a seat," the monk said.

To Sally, his voice seemed so calming, but then Amy pushed him out of the way. He fell hard.

Niv ran over to help him up.

That was it. Sally had seen enough.

She rushed over and stood between the two ladies.

"What the hell is going on?" Sally yelled, pushing both women further apart.

"Let me at her," Amy Wong screamed.

Jason Wong was standing far away from the crowd, trying to ignore the incident.

As Sally was about to ask again what was going on, Agent Lazarus came bolting up the stairs with Captain Kramer right behind them.

Someone must have called the captain.

"Okay, everyone, calm down," Captain Kramer and Agent Lazarus ordered simultaneously.

They had better luck than Sally. It must be the police badge and tall Germanic presence that did it.

Lazarus and Kramer walked over to where Sally was standing and glared at everyone.

"I was just trying to break this up," Sally explained.

"I don't want anything broken up. I want her dead," Mary screamed, "She killed my cousin Jim!"

That got everyone to stop talking and exchange glances. Amy Wong killed Jim?

Jim was her cousin? Only a few people had known that up to that point.

"Calm down, everyone," Lazarus yelled again in a very not-calm manner.

Captain Kramer grabbed Mary and started to pull her roughly down the stairs.

Lazarus turned to them, "Wait! I want to hear what Mary has to say."

Sally thought it might have been better to take Mary to the lounge to talk to her, but apparently, Lazarus wanted it all to be heard by the group.

Well, good thinking, Mr. FBI agent. It might bring out the killer.

Or get someone else killed.

Captain Kramer reluctantly brought Mary Rogers back, Francesco helping.

The captain and maid took seats away from the rest of the group while Francesco took his seat near Aharon.

Sally somehow hoped Kwame would show up with lunch and a pitcher of alcohol-laden cocktails to lighten the atmosphere.

Lazarus strode around between the tables looking as menacing as possible, Sally thought.

"What is going on?" they asked, looking directly at Amy.

"She started it," Amy and Mary screamed, pointing their fingers at each other.

"Now, why would she do that?" Lazarus asked.

"Oh, please, Agent Lazarus. Mary thinks Amy killed Jim. Didn't you hear that?" Brin said semi-sarcastically.

"Why would you think that?" Lazarus asked, now as calmly as possible, looking directly at Mary.

Captain Kramer had to hold her down as she tried to lunge toward Amy.

Amy didn't move a muscle. But just glared at Mary.

Mary sat back down and huffed.

"Amy Wong's a chef. She knows food, and she could somehow get something into his meal to kill him," Mary explained.

"Now, why would I do that?" Amy Wong asked.

"Also a good question," Lazarus said.

"Listen. You can't go around accusing people of a crime. If you have information, if any of you have information," with that Lazarus eyes swept the group, "You come to me first before accusing someone. Got it?"

"Okay, I do have something on her," Mary screamed.

Jason looked like he was going to tackle the maid.

"What have you seen?" Lazarus asked.

"Do you think I'm an idiot to put myself in danger and tell everyone here?"

Though if she was smart she wouldn't have blurted out, she knew something in front of the passengers and crew.

"Let's go," Lazarus said, turning and leaving, and indicating that Mary Rogers follow him.

"Geez, that was fun," Hoppy said once they had left.

Everyone else ignored her.

Sally sat back and was lost in thought.

What had Mary seen? Perhaps she could get it out of her after the FBI were done with her, if she were still on board when they finished lunch.

A big part of Sally was ready to head downstairs, but she didn't think Lazarus would let her sit in, and anyway, she noticed Kwame standing at the edge of the group. Her stomach was telling her to stay put.

Kwame must have come up the stairs while the screaming had been going on. As everyone was now seated, he walked over to the dumb waiter at the edge of the deck and began unloading lunch items as if nothing had happened to stir up the vacation atmosphere.

The first course was a cold salad plate with fresh fruit.

And Kwame had brought up a variety of alcoholic and non-alcoholic drinks.

Sally grabbed a glass of wine. The rest of the guests did as well.

That fight had shaken everyone's nerves.

Once everyone had a plate of food and drink, they dug in quickly.

No one said a word during lunch, least of all Amy Wong.

Chapter Twenty-Five

L unch ended much more quietly than it started.

Kwame had cleared the food away, and Brin, Amy, and Jason had gone back to their cabins for a post-lunch snooze.

Sally, Aharon, Niv, Hoppy, and Francesco were still upstairs.

Sally had moved to the edge of the deck for a quiet spot to think.

She saw Hoppy and the monk deep in conversation at the other end of the deck, and they somehow looked cute together.

Aharon and Niv were sitting in the center. Aharon was lost in a book, and Niv was banging away at his keyboard.

She opened her notebook and reviewed her list of suspects.

None of this made sense. Maybe there was a psychopathic killer on board. How else could someone plan and execute a murder after knowing someone just three days? There needed to be some history behind Jim's killing.

Particularly because someone had somehow gotten fish protein into Jim's food or drink.

The only connection to the past Sally had discovered so far, was that Mary was Jim's cousin.

She decided to have a chat with the two gentlemen.

She thought they might want to pick over the carcass of the lunch. So she got up and chanced it.

"Mind if I join you?" Sally asked, sitting down before they had a chance to answer.

Both men looked up at her. She couldn't tell if Aharon was frowning, but she ignored it.

"One more paragraph, Sally," Niv called, staring back down at his laptop.

Aharon smiled, "He does love his work."

"And it pays a lot," Niv added from the peanut gallery.

Aharon laughed, "That too."

"What a lunch," she began.

Aharon agreed, "Oh yes. I haven't had so much fun since my father took me to London as a child to see a murder mystery play."

That's a thought.

"You think this is part of the shipboard entertainment?" Sally asked, realizing this probably wasn't a great joke to use.

Niv stopped typing and turned to them.

"I don't think so, but the screaming at lunch certainly helped people blow off some steam."

"Do you think Amy Wong did it?" Sally asked directly.

"You don't waste any time, Ms. Detective," Aharon replied.

Everyone was calling her that. She hoped they meant that in a good way. She thought for a moment.

"I do agree with Mary. If someone knew how to kill someone with food, it would be Amy," Niv admitted.

Sally decided to tell them what she had learned from Watkins and Lazarus. Her first thought was whether Lazarus would consider this "interfering with the investigation" if she revealed some details.

"Wow, that is crazy," Niv said.

Sally replied, "That's what I thought. But someone got fish protein into him. We just don't know how."

"Amy wasn't even seated next to Jim," Aharon said.

"And neither was Hoppy," Niv added.

Sally scrunched her brow.

"Hoppy?"

"Yeah, I've read of cases where doctors make someone sick and then play hero to save them."

Sally looked across the deck, hoping Hoppy wasn't listening in. She was relieved to see that she and the monk must have gone below deck, as she was now alone with the Israeli couple.

"You've read way too many murder mysteries, my dear," Aharon said, patting his hand.

"Well, there have been real cases like that, Aharon."

Sally thought back to that night. Then remembered she had noted the seating arrangement in her notebook. She opened it to check

"Right. Jim was sitting between Brin and Martin Sandworth, with Amy Wong next to Martin," Sally read out.

"Well, unless Martin was involved," Aharon offered.

"That would be a lot of planning needed," Sally replied.

Niv shrugged.

"Like Aharon said, I've read a lot of murder mysteries. Anything is possible."

"In fiction," Aharon teased.

Niv continued: "Well, someone on board did it. And it seems most likely they slipped something into his food or drink."

"Yeah, but the police found nothing in the food or drink," Sally reminded her.

"I know, but it got into his throat and lungs somehow. Maybe one of the police is involved. Or they aren't telling you the truth about the food test," Niv said.

Sally threw up her arms.

"That is a lot of conspiracy theory."

Both men laughed.

"Yeah, I guess you're right," Niv replied.

That had given Sally a lot to think about, but she decided to concentrate on one thing at a time.

"I'm going to go find Mary to talk to her," Sally said.

Chapter Twenty-Six

Mary turned around and screamed.

The scream made Sally jump.

"Oh, you startled me," Mary said, planting her hand on her chest.

She placed a hand on Mary's shoulder.

"So sorry. I didn't mean to. The FBI let you go?"

Mary tutted.

"Can I just do my job and not have you harassing me?" Mary replied, moving to open the small closet in the hall.

She began pulling out the small cart with cleaning supplies.

Seeing the cart made Sally realize what Mary was talking about.

"Did you find something in someone's room? Is that what you are talking about upstairs?"

Mary ignored her and began pushing the cart down the hallway to the first room on the left, which belonged to Niv and Aharon.

"Mary?" Sally said, coming up behind her.

"Please leave me alone," Mary pleaded.

Sally put a hand on her shoulder.

"Mary, I'm just trying to help."

That brought out a laugh.

"Help? You are a busybody who is going to get someone else killed," Mary replied, holding her key card to the door.

It beeped, and she pushed the door open.

"That's harsh," Sally replied.

Mary stopped moving into the room.

"I'm sorry. I don't know where that came from," she said, turning toward Sally, "I know you're just trying to help."

Sally let her calm down and just offered a smile.

Mary wheeled the cart into the room and motioned for Sally to follow.

Sally glanced around to make sure none of the guests saw her go in.

Mary stood with her cart in the middle of the room, while Sally stood just inside the door, which she had just closed.

"Could you tell me what happened at lunch today?" Sally began.

"That bitch," Mary yelled.

"So why were you two arguing?" Sally asked matter-of-factly.

"We weren't arguing. I was accusing her of killing Jim."

"But why would you accuse her of murder?" Sally asked, not understanding the connection.

Mary stood silent for what seemed like forever before speaking.

Sally wasn't sure she was going to get anything out of her.

"I've seen Amy go into other cabins," Mary said finally.

Now she was getting somewhere.

"Doing what?" Sally asked.

Mary shook her head.

"I have no idea, but I saw her go into your cabin, Hoppy's, and the Wongs'."

"My cabin," Sally replied as if that was the only thing that mattered.

"Was she carrying something or taking something out as far as you could tell?"

"She had a large handbag with her, so I couldn't really tell."

"Did she see you?" Sally asked.

"I don't think so, I was peering around the corner each time, though once I coughed."

Sally couldn't tell if she was making this all up, but at least she was getting somewhere.

"Did you tell the FBI when they were questioning you just now?"

Mary nodded, "Of course. I have nothing to hide, and I want the murderer brought to justice."

There was a beep at the door.

Ugh, she shouldn't be in here.

"Quick, hide in the bathroom, I'll distract them," Mary urged in a stage whisper.

Sally slipped into the bathroom and pulled the door almost closed but left it open a crack.

The cabin door opened and through the slit she saw Aharon.

Luckily, he walked right past, and Mary pulled him into a short conversation out on the balcony.

She chuckled silently when Mary began by apologizing for the incident at lunch.

Perfect, that should distract him, she thought.

She slipped out and sprinted across the hall to her own cabin.

After that close call, she decided it was time for a nap, which might also help her process all that she had seen and heard.

Chapter Twenty-Seven

Sally woke refreshed.

She crossed the room, pulled out a chilled soda from the fridge, and sat out on the balcony.

The best thing to come out of her nap was that she had clarity that she was getting somewhere.

And she had decided on her next move.

It was time to talk to the captain, though she probably wouldn't be too happy to see Sally on the bridge again, but then again, she was semi-officially helping the police investigation. So Sally did have an excuse to be there.

Sally climbed the stairs and as she turned the corner toward the bridge, she heard the captain's voice yelling.

"What were you doing leaving your post?" Captain Kramer was yelling.

Sally could easily guess whom she was yelling at.

"I uh, I…" the voice responded.

Yup, it was Martin Sandworth.

Sally debated turning around and heading down to her cabin to update her notes, but decided to just risk it by continuing down the gangway and turning into the bridge.

"Hey," Sally said.

Both captain and first officer glared at her.

"Ms. Witherspoon, what the hell are you doing here again? Can we not run this ship on our own?" the captain yelled, pushing Sally out of the bridge and slamming the door.

Boy, there was a lot of aggression and door slamming going on this afternoon.

Sally headed back to her cabin to get her notebook. It was just coming on six p.m. and dinner wasn't until eight.

Tomorrow, they would be in Memphis on a whirlwind tour, hoping to take all their minds off Saturday evening's "incident."

Maybe she could use that time to check in with the other guests. After talking to Mary, she definitely wanted to talk to Amy Wong. And perhaps she would be a bit more relaxed if Sally "happened" to chat with her on their tour the next day, rather than confront her now on the boat.

As she walked down the hallway to her cabin, Brin came out of hers across the hall.

"Hey, Ms. Sleuth. Any luck?" Brin asked, bouncing over to Sally, her red hair gleaming.

Geez, how could Brin always be in such a good mood? Nothing seemed to get her down. Even after she had been led away by the gray tracksuit after he discovered she had a hidden phone. Brin seemed to have put that completely behind her.

"It's getting a bit frustrating. I feel like I have a lot of clues that don't all fit together, a plethora of international characters that have never met before, and one dead Irishman."

Brin gave her a big hug.

"Oh, you are so smart. You're going to figure it out. And someone did give him the fish somehow. Or some other substance. He's dead. We definitely know that," Brin offered.

Sally grinned in spite of herself.

"Yeah, I guess you're right. What frustrates me the most, I guess, is that we have only been on the ship a few days. How could someone want to kill him after that short time and be able to plan it all? It doesn't seem spontaneous."

"See, you're already thinking smartly," Brin replied, bounding down the hall.

So much for the long pep talk.

"Where are you off to in such a hurry?" Sally asked.

Brin stopped, turned around, and sauntered back to Sally.

In a loud whisper, she explained, "I'm off to the gym. Francesco said he would help me get fit. And we thought we'd rehash the trip," Brin told her.

Ah, that would explain her sweatpants and t-shirt. Sally was just about to ask her about it.

And apparently, Niv wasn't the only fitness freak on board

At that, Brin headed for the gym. Sally went in her room, grabbed her notebook and pen, and headed up to the sunny deck. Hopefully, everyone else was in their cabin. So she could be alone with her thoughts.

As she climbed the stairs to the deck, there was a cough behind her. She looked down and saw the captain.

"Ms. Witherspoon, may I have a word with you?" Captain Kramer asked. Witherspoon came out like Vitherspoon.

Gosh, Sally loved that Germanic accent.

"Uh, sure. Now?" Sally asked.

The captain nodded and followed Sally up the stairs.

Sally didn't think talking on deck was very private, but oh well.

Come to think of it, there weren't that many private places on the ship anyway.

As Sally got to the top of the stairs and scanned the deck, she was glad to see no one else there.

Sally and Captain Kramer sat down at a table under an umbrella. The sun was still quite powerful. Sally was glad she was just wearing shorts and a t-shirt. She'd have to be quick about showering and changing before dinner.

Sally looked at the captain and waited for her to speak first.

They looked at each other for several minutes before the captain finally spoke.

During this time, Kwame came up the stairs and came over to see if they wanted anything to drink. Both women shook their heads.

He turned and left. Sally heard his loud footsteps on the stairs. Boy he must have to put up with a lot of shit on this ship.

Sally looked at the captain, who was now staring down at her hands.

She kept her head down before speaking.

"Um, I vould like to apologize for my outburst. You are a guest on my ship.

I shouldn't have treated you that vay," Captain Kramer began, her Germanic accent a bit stronger than usual, Sally thought.

"Thank you, Captain. I'm sorry, I barged in on you like that, but I just wanted a chat," Sally replied.

"About Jim O'Sullivan's death, I imagine."

"How did you guess?" Sally asked.

Both laughed.

"What did you want to know?" the captain asked.

"Well, what do you think happened Saturday night?"

The captain shrugged.

"I have no idea. We have strict procedures in the kitchen. From what I gather from the police and Agent Lazarus, somehow a fish got into his food, and he had an allergic shock. I just don't know how that would be possible. No one has access to the kitchen except the kitchen crew, and the food is prepared under strict observation by the chef."

"Could one of the other crew have gotten into the kitchen?" Sally asked.

"No. I rarely even go in there. We have strict sanitary procedures we must adhere to," the captain explained.

Of course, the kitchen crew. Could one of them gotten fish somehow into Jim's food? If caught, that would leave them without a job. If they did do it, they must have hated Jim a lot. Or gotten paid to do it.

Sally dismissed that thought, for now.

"Did you see anything at dinner that night?" Sally continued.

The captain looked out at the riverbank.

"No, I don't think so. You all, we all, seemed in such a fun mood with the night club atmosphere."

Yes, it had been a wonderful atmosphere. Well, until Jim grabbed his throat.

"Have you heard any of the passengers talking about Jim? You know, as if they didn't like him?"

Sally was throwing the questions at the captain, but Kramer didn't seem to mind.

"Well, Mary has it in for Amy Wong, of course. I joined Lazarus' questioning of her."

Sally leaned forward.

"Did she say anything about Jim's death beyond accusing Amy?" Sally asked.

The captain shook her head.

"No, just that she knows Amy did it. But has no proof to back it up. He thinks the familial connection between Mary and Jim may have to do with it. Thought what that means, I don't know," Kramer explained.

It looked like Mary didn't tell them what she had seen, or the captain was being cautious about the interrogation.

Yes, Mary was related to Jim, but that seemed to make Mary want to protect him rather than kill him. But then again, she really knew nothing about Jim O'Sullivan's past. Or Mary's, for that matter.

Or the captain's.

"Ever been to Boston, captain?" Sally asked, throwing out another question.

Kramer looked at her, "Um, no. Why do you ask?"

"Jim's from Boston. Just wondering."

"Ah, I see. Yes, good point. But no, I've never been to Boston. I've heard it's lovely. And I never met any of you until you came on board my ship. I'm sorry I can't be of more help."

The captain stood up, indicating the discussion was over. She walked away and down the stairs, leaving Sally to contemplate everyone's past.

Chapter Twenty-Eight

Sally got to the restaurant early to get the best table with the best view. She also wanted to be alone with her thoughts, and maybe pick up a vibe as she watched everyone come in for dinner.

Jason and Amy Wong were the first to arrive. Sally was quite impressed to see them both in quite formal attire. Maybe they were starting to get ready for their diplomatic life. They were walking hand in hand, which also surprised Sally. As they walked by her table to get to the second-best one, Sally even got a nod and partial smile from Amy.

She wondered when she would get a chance to ask Amy about what Mary had told her. Though Sally wasn't really sure how to slip that into a conversation without sounding accusatory, which it was.

The next group somehow did not surprise her. It was Aharon and Niv, with Brin in tow. She wondered what happened to Francesco, if Brin was supposed to be meeting him in the gym. Though she was probably playing the field as it were to get all the juicy details out of everybody. Not that Brin had a phone at the moment. Though she probably had another stashed away somewhere.

It was now already past eight, but no monk or doctor in sight.

Kwame came over to Sally's table first. Maybe it was her sort of close connection to the police that got her first service. Speaking of police, where were the cops and the FBI agent?

Sally looked over to the lounge and saw the door was closed. Maybe they were in conference there.

"Hello, Sally. How are you this evening?" Kwame asked, greeting her.

"Hi, Kwame. I'm doing well. Hope you are too," Sally replied.

"Oh yes, ma'am. All is great. I'm trying to make the most of the situation. Definitely the weirdest voyage I've been on."

"Yes, I can believe that," Sally replied.

"Now what would you like to drink before dinner?" he asked, quickly changing the subject.

Sally guessed he already knew what her answer would be.

"I would love a glass of chilled chardonnay, that Californian one. And a big bottle of fizzy water."

"Yes, ma'am," he replied, turning to leave.

Sally put a hand on his arm. He stopped.

"One question, Kwame. Where is our law enforcement this evening? Are they still on the ship?" Sally asked.

She saw Kwame roll his eyes but quickly catch himself.

"Yes, they are here, but with the captain and Martin below deck in conference."

With that, Kwame bowed and went to take the rest of the drink orders.

Shouldn't she be with them, Sally thought.

Oh, Sally, sometimes you really are a busybody.

Sally pushed aside the details she was probably missing and scanned the room.

Still no sign of Brother Francesco or Hoppy.

She chuckled silently. Wouldn't it be amusing if they somehow got together? The monk had said he was thinking of leaving the order.

Just as she was considering this, the doors to the restaurant opened, and there the two of them were. Sally was worried by the look on Hoppy's face.

Francesco and Hoppy walked slowly over to Sally's table and sat down with her.

"What's going on? Where have you two been?" Sally asked accusingly.

"Well, we haven't been snogging, if you must know," Hoppy replied, smiling.

Brother Francesco went beet-red.

"Um, no, um, well..." he began.

"Oh, please, Francesco, we all know you're gay. That's why you're leaving the order," Hoppy said a bit too loudly.

Francesco went even redder as the conversation in the room stopped and everyone's head whipped around.

"You go, girl!" Niv cried, and Francesco looked like he would now melt onto the floor and under the table.

"Nothing here, kids," Hoppy said, waving them all away and back to their own conversations.

"Okay, now that that is settled. Where have you two been?" Sally demanded, wagging her finger.

"Oh, puhlease. What are you, the nursemaid?" Hoppy asked.

"Sorry, just a bit on edge, I guess," Sally admitted.

"Solved the crime yet?" Hoppy asked.

"No, that's the problem. And now I just found out the cops and Lazarus are meeting with the captain and Martin now, without me. Ugh. I wish I had a spy inside that room."

"Oh, forget about that. You'll be able to talk to one of them after. We have something juicy to tell you. And no one knows except the monk and me," Hoppy explained in a low voice.

Sally leaned forward as all three heads came together.

Then Sally leaned back and tried to subtly point in Brin's direction.

All three shifted themselves into a comfortable dinner position rather a in a conspiratorial huddle.

Hoppy was about to speak again when Kwame came over with Sally's drinks.

"Oh, are you joining Ms. Witherspoon this evening?" Kwame asked.

"Obviously," Hoppy replied, laughing. "I'll have a beer, as cold as you have it."

"Just water, please, Kwame," Francesco said, smiling at the waiter.

Kwame walked away to get the rest of the drinks.

"Cheers," Sally said, not waiting for the others. She needed a sip of water and a glug of white wine. Both felt glorious and refreshing going down her throat.

"Okay, what did you see?" Sally asked, putting down her water glass, debating whether she should share what she heard from Mary about Amy going in and out of cabins.

"Well, I was walking down the stairs from the deck this afternoon. Hoppy had already headed to her cabin for a nap, which I guess the other passengers were doing. You were still upstairs talking to the Israelis. I came down the stairs and was just about to turn the corner toward my cabin when I saw a dark figure climb out of the ventilator shaft. They glanced around and assumed the coast was clear. I was mostly hidden by the wall, so they didn't know I was there."

"Out of the ventilator shaft?" Sally repeated questioningly.

"Yeah. It was weird. I couldn't see who it was, but it was a tall person dressed in black. They hurried away and disappeared. I tried to follow, but no sign of the person," the monk explained.

"What were they doing in the ventilator shaft?" Sally asked.

"How would he know?" Hoppy interjected, perhaps a bit too loudly.

Sally shushed her up, glancing over at Brin. She still seemed engrossed in conversation and was laughing at something.

Turning back, she saw the monk brush back his hair and wipe the sweat from his brow.

The air conditioning was on full blast. Sally wondered why he was sweating.

"Are you okay?" Sally asked.

"Yes, I'm fine, just nervous that the person is in this room and might know I saw them."

"Maybe it was just a maintenance person?" Sally asked, a bit naively.

"Dressed in black and sneaking out of the ventilator shaft in a ninja outfit? Come on, Sally," Hoppy said.

Sally was still processing the ventilator shaft clue when the monk continued.

"I saw that the person was carrying a canister of some kind. I have no idea what was in it," the monk explained.

"Why didn't they wait until the middle of the night? Wouldn't that have been safer and quieter?" Sally asked the two, more thinking aloud than anything else.

"Well, the police and the FBI are here, so maybe they decided to take a chance and get it out of there when there was no one around rather than wait any later," Hoppy proposed.

"Hmm, but they could have pulled it out earlier, right? Jim has been dead for two days," Sally offered.

"Maybe the person is not the smartest," the monk said.

Sally decided to share the Amy information with them.

Both were wide-eyed.

"What does it all mean, Sally?" Hoppy asked, apparently expecting Sally to put the puzzle together in two seconds.

Sally felt like the canister was the key to the whole affair.

Chapter Twenty-Nine

Sally didn't get much sleep Monday night. She kept tossing and turning, trying to figure out what the canister and ventilator shaft meant. And why Amy was apparently in other cabins.

The other main question on her mind was who to talk to next.

She should probably touch base with the police and Agent Lazarus to determine what or who they were looking into at the moment.

Sally had hoped they might pop in for dinner after their conference, but she never saw the captain, Martin, or the FBI agent all evening.

Hoppy had grilled her to come up with an explanation, but she wasn't that fast.

Sally had no idea what was going on there.

So many thoughts, names, and facts swirling around in her mind. She had to put the pieces together. Her notebook would only go so far.

But it was a start.

She pushed herself up and switched on the bedside lamp.

Squinting at her phone in the bright light, she saw 3:23 a.m.

Oh lovely. She would be so awake for the day's tour of Memphis.

The one good thing that came out of the investigation was that the tour program was now flexible. There was so much to see in Memphis, so the captain had told them at dinner the night before that they were free to see what they wanted, rather than follow the planned tour of the city. She had also let slip that the police and Lazarus wanted to keep them on board indefinitely. They didn't want possible suspects leaving the ship and perhaps making a run for it in Memphis.

Luckily, the diplomatic angle was keeping them sort of on the tour. Jason Wong had apparently told the police and Lazarus there would be an international incident if they weren't let out to see Memphis.

Though Sally was surprised there hadn't been rumors in social media or the mainstream media yet.

Diplomatic clout could be helping there, too.

Sally got up from the bed and walked over to the sliding doors to the small balcony. It was still dark out, so she wasn't going to be sitting out there with her notes and her thoughts.

Sighing, she walked over to the coffee machine and made a big, dark cup of coffee. No use waking the staff when she had this glorious machine in her room.

What would she do without coffee?

Perish the thought, Sally.

The coffee went on the coffee table in front of her, while she plopped down on the sofa.

Pulling her notebook out of her bag, she began writing the main clues she had, thinking if she wrote them all down together a pattern would quickly emerge.

- *Fish*
- *Jim*
- *Ventilator Shaft*
- *Canister*
- *Mary*
- *Amy*
- *Martin*

Tapping her pen on the paper, she still didn't see how it all fit together.

She had written down Amy and Mary because she needed to talk to Amy about their "fight" at lunch the day before. And ask her about her cabin visits, if that was really what she was doing.

And she really needed to get some time with Martin. He had been sitting next to Jim at dinner Saturday night, and she hadn't had a chance to talk to him.

Oh, and she almost forgot Brin. How could she forget her?

Brin had hopefully gotten something from the other passengers.

The nagging feeling in her mind wasn't going away, even if she connected the ventilator shaft clue to Jim's death.

She wasn't any closer to figuring out who did it.

Not too many interconnected people on this ship, as far as she knew, though who knows what she might uncover yet.

Putting pen and notepad down, she did make one decision.

She would start with Martin, because he was right there next to Jim Saturday night.

But before that, she would try to get some shuteye before breakfast. She didn't want to nod off during the tour. There was too much to see and do. And too many people to question.

She did love investigating. Even if this was now only her second investigation.

That thought put her right to sleep, and in spite of the coffee, she didn't wake until her alarm blared at 7:30.

* * *

Sally had learned that Martin was taking part of the group to the Civil Rights Museum. This included Amy and Jason, Hoppy and the monk while Aharon and Niv had decided to stay on the ship. And Brin, of course, was still under house arrest.

Martin had told them that the museum was exclusive for them today. He told them quite openly that was to keep their visit under wraps as far as possible. This had been arranged by the State Department on their behalf.

Walking behind the group down the street to the museum gave her time to watch everyone. Though it was a bit difficult in the pouring rain. Luckily, they had planned something indoors. There wouldn't be much strolling around Memphis today. Sally looked up at the dark clouds. They didn't look like they were going anywhere.

She had brought a mini-umbrella which was only partially covering her.

Sally decided it was time to talk, so she sped up to overtake the group and walk next to Martin. He was a few feet in front, leading the way.

"Hi Sally, enjoying Memphis so far?" he asked, laughing. His umbrella swayed as he laughed, and water dropped onto Sally's raincoat.

"Oops, sorry," he said, grinning.

Well, wasn't he in a fun mood?

"No worries, it's just water," she replied, "It's so nice to be walking around again after a day on the river. My head is still spinning from what happened Saturday night."

"Definitely the weirdest and saddest trip I've been on. And with our escort, definitely the one I will never forget."

He pointed not so subtly at the several plainclothes FBI nearby.

"I bet. That must have been awful for you sitting next to Jim that night," Sally began her questioning cautiously.

"So sad," Martin said.

"Did Jim seem okay to you?" Sally asked.

"Well, yeah, chatting a bit with me and Brin. He seemed to like the ship part of the tour but not the offshore bits," Martin explained, rubbing water off his strong forehead.

Sally was having a bit of difficulty keeping up with his pace. His long legs went a lot faster than hers did.

She kept glancing back to see if anyone was listening, but the heavy rain made a lot of noise, and the rest of the group with them just looked around at the sights, as far as one could see them in the downpour.

"Yes, he seemed very uncomfortable with the history of America that many don't know or don't want to know. He didn't seem to want to admit these things actually happened," Sally agreed.

"He was kind of annoying about that wasn't he? Oops, I know I'm not supposed to talk to one guest about another, but I had wished he had been more open about everything. To be honest, I don't even know why he booked the tour in the first place if he didn't want to hear the history,"

Martin confessed.

"Don't worry. Your secret is safe with me."

"Thanks, Sally. I do feel bad about his death, of course. I hope the police and FBI can find out who did it. Or maybe you will solve it before them. Any luck with your investigation?" Martin asked, turning toward her and dumping more water on her. This time her hair was drenched.

Sally decided to be open with him.

"It seems strange that someone would dislike him on our trip and decide to kill him after a couple of days. Who would do that? And how did the fish get in the food?" she said.

"True. He told Kwame he was allergic to fish, and he did get the spaghetti dish. It certainly smelled like carbonara when it arrived, not fish," Martin replied, "And he really seemed to be enjoying it, digging in right when the plate was set before him."

"Did he seem to cough or something right away?" Sally asked, not really knowing how long an allergic reaction would take.

"Well, he did cough after the first bite, but told me something had gone down the wrong way, like Jason did. He took a swig of water and said he was fine. It was only after a few more bites that his face went red, and then he jumped up, clutching at his throat. I'm sorry to say that I was shoveling in my fish, not really paying attention to what he was doing. I didn't know something was wrong until he jumped up and I saw him grabbing his throat."

So much for people paying attention, Sally thought. No one would have been expecting a death at dinner.

That's for sure. Except the murderer, of course.

Chapter Thirty

By the time the group got to the Civil Rights Museum, the rain had stopped, of course. Now that they would be inside for a while, the sun was, of course, shining gloriously through the museum's atrium.

Maybe this was a good sign, Sally thought.

She was ready to learn as much as she could. Both from the museum's exhibits and stories, and from the people in this mini group from The River Queen.

Sally stayed at the back of the line watching Hoppy chat with the monk (were they doing more than chatting? Sally wondered, but wait he's gay, isn't he?), Amy and Jason standing near each other holding hands. At the front, Martin was talking to the ticket seller, pulling out his phone to show him the reservation.

After only a minute or so, Martin turned and motioned them to follow him. He stopped at the entrance to the museum.

"We're getting a special tour guide today. She should be here any minute," he explained.

They all stood around a bit awkwardly, waiting for the tour guide to appear.

The FBI agents were so obvious, but maybe that was just her.

She was still amazed they were continuing the tour, though it wasn't quite the same with an official presence keeping them in line. VIP status really got you everywhere in the world, didn't it.

And they were better at their jobs than they looked. No one had bolted yet.

Sally debated having a chat with Amy here, but thought it would be better to wait until their tour started. She could quietly chat with her more discreetly inside the museum. And pull her aside for a private chat if needed. Sally hoped Amy would be helpful for once.

And she kept glancing over the FBI agents. Their looks told her she better not even think about asking them anything.

If Sally was going to get to the bottom of Jim's murder, she probably had to get more out of the people on the boat. Even the ones she didn't take a liking to.

A tall, thin woman with a name tag came over to the group.

"Hi, I'm Amanda. I'll be your guide today. Welcome to Memphis and welcome to the Civil Rights Museum. We're so glad you took the time to come here today," Amanda said with a lot of enthusiasm.

Sally thought she was amazing.

This was going to be a fun tour. Well, maybe fun wasn't the right word. Serious, thinking, words like that probably fit better.

Amanda led them through the tall double doors into the first room of the museum.

She explained the history of the museum and what they would see throughout the ninety-minute tour. At the end of it, they would be served some snacks and light refreshments in the museum's café at the center of the massive stone structure.

"Now that the sun's shining, you can really enjoy our Atrium Café," Amanda beamed.

She was very bubbly. She immediately reminded Sally of a taller version of Brin.

Sally watched the others as they followed Amanda into the first exhibit. They all seemed to be in a great mood. Maybe it was the sun. Maybe it was the fact that they were off the ship. Or maybe it was because this was a smaller, more intimate group. Sally wasn't sure. But she was going to enjoy herself as much as possible. And learn a ton in the process. Everyone seemed to be forgetting the fact that one of theirs had died, probably murdered. It was amazing what the human brain could do, Sally thought.

Coming back to the tour, Sally heard Amanda going into great detail about Martin Luther King, Jr, the first person to be featured in this first exhibit.

Sally saw Amy standing away from the group and off to a corner, and let her eyes wander around the room.

Sally decided this was her chance.

"A great museum so far, isn't it?" Sally asked.

"A difficult part of your nation's history, don't you think?" Amy replied a bit caustically.

Sally made a conscious decision not to bring up Apartheid here.

"Sorry, I didn't mean that to come out like that," Amy said apologetically.

"No worries. These tours have been difficult for me, too. I know my family owned a plantation in Georgia and kept slaves in the 1800s. Being confronted with it on this trip has made me more upset, well, it made me feel more guilty than I thought it would. But I am glad I picked this tour, rather than just a plain boat ride down the Mississippi," Sally confessed, partly because it was true, partly to try to get on Amy's good side.

Amy turned toward Sally.

What came out of her mouth next shocked Sally.

"You know, I've been a real bitch on this tour," Amy said.

Sally didn't know how to respond to this, so she only nodded slightly.

"Really. A real bitch," Amy said more loudly.

The group turned to look at her.

Jason looked like he was going to hit her.

"Yes, I've been one. Please, all just admit it," she continued.

Sally had no idea where this was coming from.

Jason began to walk toward them. Amy put up her hand and shook her head.

He turned red and returned to the group.

Amy put her hand on Sally's shoulder.

"I'm sorry," she said, more quietly. "It's just been so stressful with the move to the U.S., giving up my restaurant..." Amy's voice trailed off.

Sally took her hand.

"Why don't we leave the tour and get a drink in the café. That is if you want to talk privately," Sally suggested.

Well as privately they could with an FBI escort.

Amy replied, "Oh yes, please."

The group was listening to Amanda and didn't notice them leave.

Sally didn't think they really cared. And Amanda was probably happy to not have any outbursts in the museum.

They followed the signs to the café and walked out of the hallway into bright sunlight. The atrium was full of cozy tables and plants.

"How lovely," Amy exclaimed.

They found a table in the corner. The FBI agents sitting not too subtly at the next table.

Sally glanced over and actually got a slight smile from one of them.

Amy got up.

"Oh, let me get you a coffee or something," Amy offered.

"A strong black coffee would be great. And maybe a croissant to go with it."

"Sure," Amy replied and headed over to the counter.

Sally wondered how to slip in what Mary had told her into the conversation. She would have to if she was going to find out what that was all about.

Amy returned with two coffees and two croissants.

"Wow, museum prices. This cost thirty dollars," Amy said.

Sally sipped her still hot coffee and broke off a piece of croissant to dip in it. That was one of her favorite taste combinations. The croissant sucked up the delicious coffee and just melted in her mouth.

This gave Amy a chance to settle in and begin talking.

"So you're enjoying the trip?" Sally asked, breaking her own rule of letting the other person start first when she wanted to get something out of them.

"Well, actually, yes. It's been so relaxing not to have to plan a menu, run a restaurant, or pack up our apartment. I guess my little outbursts have been more about the stress I'm feeling about moving to Washington. It's been Jason's dream all his diplomatic life, but I'm not sure it's going to be as great as he thinks. It's not like we'll be invited to the White House every night," Amy said, laughing quietly.

It was a weird laugh, with snorts every other beat.

Sally was going to ask another question, but decided to just let her keep talking.

"So yes, I've been a bitch this trip," Amy confessed, again.

Sally wasn't sure if she preferred nice Amy or bitchy Amy. Maybe there were only two Amy modes. Oh well.

"Um, you've had a couple of heated exchanges with Jason. Was it about your move? Or is there something else bothering you?" Sally asked, breaking her code of silence. She wanted to give Amy time to warm up, but she also wanted to solve Jim's murder.

She wasn't a very patient detective.

Sally hoped she hadn't pushed Amy too hard with that question.

"Um, well, sort of," Amy began.

Sally looked at her as she rubbed her temples and smoothed her hair, like she was preparing to admit to something terrible or just have a breakdown. Sally wasn't sure.

"Well, Jason is more a traditional man. While he supported me and my restaurant back home in China, he now thinks that I should play the traditional diplomat's wife while we are in DC. Apparently, it's what the Chinese government expects. Well, fuck that," Amy explained, yelling the last words.

Amy ate her croissant, washed it down with coffee, then sat back with a sigh.

"Sorry," Amy said.

"Don't worry. I would be pissed to. So you have plans for D.C.?" Sally said as calmly as possible.

"Yes, I want to open a branch of my restaurant there but Jason is dead set against it. And he is panicked the Chinese government will not be happy and make us move back to China. Which, to be honest, wouldn't be a bad thing. Well, hopefully I'd be able to continue with my restaurant back there, but then again, they could send Jason, I mean, send us, to the far reaches of

China near the North Korean border."

Sally was really warming to Amy. She was actually beginning to like her. Which if you had asked Sally a few days ago, Sally would have denied ever being able to.

Maybe it was time to pounce.

"Well, as you know, I've been helping a bit with the investigation," Sally began.

"Yes, you seem to be really enthusiastic about it," Amy replied.

Sally beamed.

"Well, yes, I, um, well, I do have a question for you," Sally explained.

She was worried this would mean Amy would clam up, but she just looked at her with what Sally could only term a neutral look.

"Oh, yes, and what is that?" Amy asked, sipping her coffee but keeping her eyes on Sally.

Sally needed to be delicate.

"Well, you and Mary…"

"Uh, I don't know what that girl was getting on about. Why would I kill Jim?"

"I think she was concluding that from something in addition to your knowledge about food."

Now Amy put her cup down, but said nothing, waiting for Sally to continue.

Sally shifted in her seat, feeling the heat from Amy's glare.

Amy broke the silence. "Now what would that be?"

"Well, she claims you've visiting other cabins then your own," Sally explained in a whisper, thinking of the FBI agents nearby.

Amy belted out a laugh.

"That is ridiculous, why would I be doing that? I have enough to worry about in my own cabin to be snooping around in others. She's lying for some reason, obviously."

While Sally was processing this, Amy got up.

"I'm going to see what Jason is up to. Thanks for the chat," Amy said with little warmth in her voice, Sally felt.

"Sure, I'm just going to sit here and enjoy the rest of my coffee."

Amy headed out of the café with an FBI agent in tow.

Sally watched her go, her gut telling her that she didn't kill Jim, no matter what Mary Rogers thought. She saw Amy was going through a life crisis. Sally doubted she had the room in her head to plan a murder. And what was the motive anyway?

Chapter Thirty-One

Back on the ship, Sally went to find Brin to see if she had gotten anything out of one of the other passengers over the past day. And also how she was doing, cooped up on the ship the whole time.

Sally first checked the upper deck, but no Brin.

She was probably in her cabin using another phone she had hidden, or maybe she was just napping.

Sally headed back downstairs and over to Brin's cabin just across from hers.

She knocked softly, not sure if Brin was sleeping.

Sally waited a few seconds and heard a sound.

"Yes," Brin said.

"It's me, Sally," she replied.

The door quickly opened.

Brin pulled her into a hug.

"Oh, Sally, I'm so glad to see you. I'm going crazy on this ship," Brin said, pulling Sally in and shutting the door.

"Don't you have another phone stashed somewhere?" Sally asked.

Brin laughed.

"No, I'm not that smart, and I don't want to be thrown in jail. I'm going nuts without my fans."

Sally patted her shoulder.

"Well, hopefully we will all be out of here soon…" Sally began.

"…after you've solved the crime," Brin replied.

Yes, Sally knew she would do it.

They walked through the cabin to sit on the balcony. It was another glorious day, almost making Sally forget about the tragedy that had occurred on board. Well, almost.

"Would you like something to drink?" Brin asked, starting to head back inside.

"Something cool and refreshing would be lovely," Sally replied, leaning back in the lounge chair, soaking up the sun.

She really should have booked a room on the other side of the boat. Oh well, next time, if she could bring herself to do another cruise, river or otherwise.

Brin returned with two cold beers and handed one to Sally.

She sat up and took a glug.

Brin did the same before sitting down herself.

"So any gossip to share?" Sally asked, getting right to the point.

Brin gave her a look, but didn't say anything immediately.

"I love your enthusiasm for detecting, Sally," Brin said finally.

Sally smiled, "I could say the same for your influencing my dear."

Brin frowned.

Oops, Sally had stepped in it again.

"Sorry, you know what I mean, I hope," Sally replied, hoping she had the most soothing voice at the moment as possible.

"Yes, sorry, Sally, I appreciate that I really do. I wish I could be doing it now."

"I get that," Sally responded, wanting to quickly get back to the subject at hand.

Brin did it for her.

"Well, let's see. Aharon and Niv are so cool!" Brin replied, "They even said they would come to Valencia to stay at my quaint hotel," Brin explained.

"But what did they say about Saturday night?" Sally asked, a bit impatiently.

"Well, they didn't really see anything. They told me they were chatting to Hoppy about Australia, their next trip, they were planning apparently. You know I'd love to go there too. Maybe I could join them," Brin said, shooting out the words.

"Three's a crowd," Sally blurted out.

"Spoil sport," Brin retorted.

Both women laughed.

Brin took another sip of her beer and looked over at Sally.

Was there something more interesting coming? Sally certainly hoped so.

"I was talking to Francesco, and he is really intent on leaving the monastery. He has spent too long in Italy, he said, and the monks are starting to feel like family, which is apparently something that Francesco is allergic to. Well, he told me his father was not a kind man and that was one of the reasons he had joined the order."

Sally listened and let Brin babble. She had learned that was best way to get information out of people. Not that she did that too often at her bar.

Oh, the bar. She hadn't heard from Magda in a while. She hoped that was a good sign, and anyway, they would hopefully be seeing each other soon once her trip was over.

Not before she solved the murder, of course.

Sally decided to change tack.

"And what did you see that night, Ms. Influencer?" Sally asked.

"Little ol' me?" Brin asked.

"Well, yes," Sally replied quite seriously, "You were sitting on the other side of Jim."

"What did Martin say?" Brin asked without responding to Sally's question.

"I want to know what you saw, dear," Sally replied.

"Ugh, are you interrogating me now?" Brin asked.

Sally felt she was being evasive, but why? Brin didn't seem to have any connection to Jim, and she certainly seemed to want to help Sally solve the crime. Why would she do that if she had killed Jim or had something to do with his death?

"You know I just want to help solve Jim's murder," Sally explained, smiling. "And maybe you saw something, or looking back, something seems strange to you?"

"Well, Jim was in a very good mood. He loved to tell stories of his life back in Boston or about his family back in Ireland," Brin began.

"But did he seem okay to you? I mean, healthwise?" Sally asked.

"Well, he was definitely overweight, and he drank too much, but he really seemed in a good mood Saturday night. Though Hoppy is the doctor, of course. Jim did admit to me that he and Mary Rogers had discovered they were related that afternoon. Maybe that's why he was so happy."

Or maybe it was the booze, Sally thought.

"Do you think Mary had anything to do with it?" Sally asked.

"Oh, you think she killed Jim? I doubt it. He seemed so happy about finding her. And from what he told me, she did too," Brin said.

"Did you smell any fish in his food?" Sally decided to ask.

"How would I do that? I didn't stick my nose in his plate. And most people had fish, including me, I could smell it everywhere."

Okay, that had been a stupid question, Sally.

"Did Jim say anything while he was eating?" Sally asked.

Brin shook her head.

"He just shoveled it in. Coughed once but said he had a frog in his throat," Brin explained.

Okay, similar to what Martin had told her.

"And then?" Sally asked.

"Well, I was concentrating on devouring my wonderful fish when I heard a sound. Jim had gotten up, was red in the face, and clutching at his throat. As we all saw," Brin replied.

Oh well, same story as Martin.

Sally had really hoped that talking to the two people sitting on either side of Jim would give her some clue that would solve the mystery, but alas, it was not to be.

"Francesco saw something," Sally blurted out, but in a whisper, just in case Niv or Aharon were sitting on their balcony next door.

Brin shifted in her chair.

"What, saw what?" Brin asked her eyes wide, speaking just as quietly as Sally had.

"Well, not at the dinner directly," Sally replied.

"Ah, okay" Brin said, seemingly relieved.

"Well, last night at dinner, he told me he had seen someone in black climb out of the ventilator shaft near the restaurant," Sally explained.

Brin leaned forward, "When did he see that?" she asked.

"Yesterday afternoon. A tall person is climbing out holding a canister of some sort."

"Probably just a technician," Brin said.

"Well, yeah, but why dress in black? It all seems weird. Do you have any clue what it means?" Sally asked.

Brin shook her head.

"No clue."

Sally checked her watch.

"Wow, time flies when you're having fun. I need a nap before dinner," Sally said, getting up.

Brin stood up as well.

"Sally, thanks so much for stopping by. I really needed that," Brin said, hugging her.

Sally smiled but also thought that Brin loved gossip, so the canister story was perfect to feed into that.

At any rate, interrogation time would have to continue at dinner. Sally hoped the police or Agent Lazarus would show up again. She needed to get an update…and give them an update on the few bits she had found, particularly about the mysterious person in black climbing out of the ventilator shaft with a canister of something.

The murderer seemed to be getting desperate if he, or she, had removed the canister in the middle of the day.

Sally felt she was getting closer to the truth.

Chapter Thirty-Two

Leaving Brin's cabin, Sally bumped into a menacing Agent Lazarus. Was he ever pleasant?

"Ms. Witherspoon, we'd like to have a word with you," he said, motioning for her to follow him down the hallway.

As they walked away, she heard Brin call, "Have fun!"

Yeah, thanks.

Sally glanced at her phone. It was just 4:00 p.m. Hopefully time to get back to her room and relax before dinner. She loved the investigating and the sightseeing and the chatting, but she hadn't had too much time to relax. Wasn't that the main reason she came on the cruise, to get away and relax? Somehow, she had found herself involved in another murder investigation.

As Lazarus led her to the interrogation room, um, the lounge, Sally played the facts through in her mind. She was debating what she should tell him and what she should try to find out more about herself, if that were possible.

By the time they were seated, she had made up her mind. Tell him everything. Sally hoped that would help him see she really wanted to help, and maybe give her more access to his own investigation.

Sally had always thought her Detective Finnegan back home in Berry Springs was gruff, but this guy was much worse.

Sally reached down to open her backpack and take out her notebook and pen.

"What are you doing?" Lazarus asked, turning red.

"Well, I have information for you, but I hope you have some update for me. I want to make sure I get all the facts right," she explained, smiling as kindly as she could, hoping it wasn't a fuck-you look. Giving him grief might endear her to him.

He didn't respond to this, but just opened the folder in front of him.

That was a classic Finnegan move. Open the folder, stare at it as if there is something terrible to say or ask, but just use the time to make the person uncomfortable. Even if she knew the spiel, it still made her shift in her seat. Or maybe it was the fact the chair was very hard. Another interrogation ploy apparently.

"So we learned that Mr. O'Sullivan only had one brother in Boston," Lazarus began.

So much for the big family Jim had told her about.

"Is he coming here?" Sally asked.

"Actually, he told me he hadn't had contact with Jim for years, and while he was sad to hear about his brother's death, he didn't want to have anything to do with him, alive or dead," Lazarus explained.

Wow, Jim seemed to have a lot of people that didn't like him. The most likely person to get killed, Sally thought grimly.

This was going well.

She was waiting for the right moment to tell him about the canister, which must have to do with the fish protein found in Jim's lungs, but a part of her hesitated. She loved being ahead of the game, even if she was sitting across from a federal agent.

He took care of the topic for her.

"I also wanted to tell you that we found traces of fish protein in the ventilation system in the restaurant."

Aha, now we're getting somewhere.

"What?" Sally asked, holding her pen above her notebook, ready to scribble whatever Lazarus was about to tell her.

"Well, you know about the fish protein found in his lungs," Lazarus said, and Sally nodded. "Well, it seems it was being pumped into the restaurant through the ventilation system, meaning it was all over the place. "

Sally was stunned. She put down her pen and couldn't even begin to contemplate writing anything. She'd just have to catch up on her notes later when she was back in her room.

"Wow, how is that possible? Wouldn't Jason Wong have died too? He also said he was allergic to fish," she said.

"Apparently, his allergy isn't that bad, and Jim was sitting slightly closer to the air vent," the agent clarified.

"That explains it," Sally exclaimed.

Lazarus looked up from his folder for once.

"Excuse me?" he said.

Sally explained what Brother Francesco had seen: the tall person in black coming out of the air vent with the canister.

"Well, I guess we know what was in the canister. But we have to find it to get proof," Lazarus said.

"So Agent Lazarus, you're saying someone planted fish protein in the canister, stuck it in the air vent near the restaurant, and that shot out its contents toward Jim, killing him?" Sally was shocked and sickened.

What cruelty that must be to do that to someone. And excellent planning and knowledge.

"Well, that fits all the facts so far, doesn't it?" he replied.

Sally smoothed her jeans to give herself time to contemplate.

"Well, I guess, yes, it does. Any clue who did it?" Sally asked.

"I'm guessing the maid. She found out she was a relative, had some family feud, and decided to get rid of him," Lazarus said quite sure of himself.

"But Francesco said he saw a tall person come out of the vent. Mary Rogers is tiny. And where would she get a canister of fish protein or know about it, for that matter?" Sally asked, laying out the facts that didn't fit his theory very well.

"She had an accomplice on board, of course. I know it's her and I'm going to get her," he said, raising his voice.

Sally took a deep breath to remain calm.

Smiling, she asked, "Shouldn't you talk to Francesco first so you can get his story firsthand?"

"Good point," he replied, laughing.

Sally wasn't sure what was wrong with him. Or he was just trying to test her if she fell apart, or even confessed, if he got a bit rough with his questioning or his attitude.

Oh no, sir, he did not know Sally Witherspoon.

"Is that all, Agent Lazarus?" Sally asked, wanting to get out of there and back to her room. She had thinking to do, and she felt like she should tell Hoppy this news as fast as possible. There really was nothing she could have done to save Jim, especially if the fish was in the air the whole time and continuing to be pumped in even as Hoppy was trying to revive Jim.

Sally started to get up.

"Please sit back down. I have one more question," Lazarus said.

Ugh.

"Yes," she said a bit sharply.

"No need to get snippety, ma'am. I just want to know if you have a theory on who did it."

Sally thought for a minute about what she should say.

"Well, it seems to be well-planned. So, spontaneous killing makes no sense. It could be any of the tour group, as we got the list of passengers a while back. I guess none of us would know for sure who the other people were with just a name and a home city. And of course, it could be a crew member. They would have the same passenger information, well, they would have even more passenger information," Sally replied, watching Lazarus nod as she spoke.

"You're smart, Ms. Witherspoon. I have to give you that," he replied.

Sally wanted to vomit.

"But I don't think it was Mary Rogers, Agent Lazarus. She was so excited to find Jim, her relative. Why would she kill him right after finding him?" she asked.

Now she was staring at him.

"That's a front. She wants us to think she was so excited, but she was actually seething inside. I'm sure of it," he replied.

"Well, don't you need proof for your theory?" Sally reminded him.

Lazarus stood up and leaned over very close to Sally.

"I'll get it. I'll get it."

Chapter Thirty-Three

inner wasn't for another two hours, so she had plenty of time to update Hoppy and have a relaxing shower and cup of tea before heading back to the restaurant.

Knocking on Hoppy's door, she heard voices inside. Sally guessed who the other person might be. And that actually was good, so she could update them both.

"Who is it?" Hoppy's voice called.

"It's Sally. Can I come in?"

She heard scrambling and whispers. Sally debated yelling to Hoppy that she knew she had a visitor, but decided against making a scene in the hallway.

She tapped her foot, anxious to get inside and tell Hoppy what she had just found out.

The door finally opened, and she found Hoppy in a bathrobe, her hair wet.

"Hey Sally. What's up?" Hoppy asked, not moving away from the doorway.

"Hoppy, I know he's in there, so let me in. I guess Francesco isn't gay. I'm not sure why you both told me that."

Hoppy frowned and seemed ready to protest, but Sally quickly added in a whisper, "I've just come from talking to Agent Lazarus, and you will definitely want to hear this."

At that, Hoppy moved away from the door and let Sally in. She closed the door quietly, glancing around the hallway to see if anyone had seen Sally enter. As if that made a difference.

Sally smirked, wondering why the bold Hoppy was nervous all of a sudden.

Hoppy led her into the living area, where they found Francesco lounging on the sofa, also in a bathrobe with wet hair.

"Well, at least someone's getting some," Sally blurted out and immediately turned red.

The monk blushed as well.

"Um, well, um," he began.

"Oh, please, Francesco. I think it's obvious what we have been doing," Hoppy scolded, grinning the whole time.

Turning to Sally, "Okay, he isn't gay. I don't know why we made that up."

Francesco grinned, "Yeah, I would probably be fending off Niv at this point."

All three laughed. That broke any tension in the room.

Sally sat on one of the comfy chairs opposite the couch, while Hoppy took the other.

"So what can we do for you?" Hoppy asked.

Sally pointed to Francesco: "First, you need to go see Agent Lazarus."

Francesco started to tap his fingers on the arm of the couch.

"Um, what, why?" he asked.

"I told him what you saw, and it connects with some information he shared with me. You're not a suspect, but he just wants to hear directly from you about the person climbing out of the ventilator shaft."

Francesco stopped tapping and glared at Sally.

"Don't worry," Sally said, trying to reassure him.

Obviously, even a monk could be nervous.

Sally wondered whether Agent Lazarus was Catholic. Brother Francesco could perhaps use that to his advantage.

He got up and went into the bathroom to change.

"Geez, why did you just throw that on him, Sally?" Hoppy asked.

"Sorry, you know Agent Lazarus. If Francesco didn't show up ASAP, he would be knocking on all our doors," Sally explained not very convincingly.

Francesco didn't need long. He came out of the bathroom in jeans and a t-shirt. Not saying anything, he walked out of the cabin.

"So what was the big rush?" Hoppy asked when the monk had gone.

"Well, I have the latest from Lazarus on Jim's death," Sally began, "As you know, they found fish protein in his lungs, meaning there was fish protein in the air of the restaurant. Now they've discovered fish protein in the ventilation shaft."

"How the hell?" Hoppy replied, eyes wide.

"Yeah, it is weird, but those are the facts. Before you wonder why Jason Wong didn't die, apparently his allergy isn't as severe as Jim's was," Sally explained.

"Ah, I do remember him coughing just before Jim started choking. I guess that was it," Hoppy surmised.

Sally replied, "It seems so. He just kept breathing in the toxin."

"So that's what was in the canister Francesco saw," Hoppy said, shaking her head, sending drops of water Sally's way.

Sally pulled out a tissue to wipe her face dry.

Hoppy just started laughing.

Then Sally joined in.

"Thanks for that. I needed some comic relief," Sally admitted.

"My pleasure, darling," Hoppy said, giving Sally an air kiss.

Then Hoppy went serious.

"So we have to find that canister. It must be somewhere on the ship," Hoppy surmised.

"Well, unless that person in black chucked it overboard," Sally added.

Sally's stomach growled.

"First, let's eat. I'm starved," Sally said, looking at her phone, "I'm going to head next door to shower and get ready."

She got up and began walking toward the door.

"Thanks for stopping by, Sally. Why don't we have a search for the canister after dinner?" Hoppy suggested.

Sally replied, "Sounds like a plan."

Chapter Thirty-Four

Dinner Tuesday evening was mostly uneventful for once.

Sally and Hoppy sat together, keeping a seat free for Francesco. Apparently, the guests and crew had become a bit too nosy about the questioning, so Agent Lazarus had requisitioned a small storeroom in the crew area below deck and had freed the lounge.

Sally was sad they couldn't be closer to the questioning, but it did mean they could now use the lounge again for its original use.

She knew she needed a drink with Hoppy after they finished their search. She was thinking about the timing of that while they ate dessert.

"Hoppy, maybe we should search for the canister in the middle of the night and not right now just after dinner," Sally suggested.

Hoppy looked up from the chocolate mousse she was spooning into her mouth. Bits of it covered her face.

"Gosh, I do love chocolate anything. Thanks for interrupting," Hoppy teased, "What were you saying?"

She really loved Hoppy and her way. Actually, Brin too. Both did or said whatever they wanted. It was a breath of fresh air.

"Well, that it would make more sense to wait until everyone is asleep before searching for the canister, don't you think?" Sally repeated.

Hoppy shrugged.

"Well, I guess, I was really looking forward to the evening search. But I guess you're right. Fewer people who could catch us snooping around," Hoppy replied.

Sally responded, "Exactly! Why don't we have a drink in the lounge, get a couple hours of sleep, then meet back here at one a.m.?"

"Sounds like a plan. Now let me finish my dessert," Hoppy said. She dove back in with a relish Sally had rarely ever seen with a dessert. Though she herself also loved chocolate, she didn't quite get as enthusiastic with it.

Sally had a sip of the red wine in front of her when Francesco came into the dining room. Kwame saw him and followed him to their table.

Francesco planted himself squarely in his chair, and Sally couldn't wait to hear what he had to say.

"Brother Francesco. Hello. Would you like some dinner? The main course was a choice of ribeye steak with potatoes or pasta primavera," Kwame explained, smiling broadly as always.

Francesco took a deep breath.

"The steak, please, medium. And a large beer," Francesco ordered.

Kwame left to get the food and drink.

Francesco then dropped his head onto the table with a sigh.

"So, how did it go?" Hoppy asked.

"How do you think?" Francesco responded, "I feel like I've just been through a day-long interrogation. That Agent Lazarus is a bastard."

The last word came out like "bastard-e" as his Italian accent cranked up, due to the stress, Sally guessed.

The last word also came out loudly, and there were a couple of gasps in the room, one of them from Sally.

Francesco stood up.

"Yes, monks are human and sometimes we swear," he yelled to the room.

Hoppy pulled him back down, waving an apology to the rest of the guests.

"So what happened?" Hoppy asked again, more forcefully this time.

"Ugh, of course he thinks I made up what I saw and that I was the one getting the canister out of the ventilator shaft. Lazarus seems upset that he hasn't solved the crime yet. Though it has only been three days since Jim left us," the monk explained, pulling the crucifix around his neck out of his t-shirt and running it through his fingers.

His eyes closed, and Sally assumed he was in prayer.

"Anything else?" Hoppy asked, ignoring the closed eyes.

"Oh, sorry, I feel like I could fall asleep at any minute," he explained.

"I repeated what I had seen. Told him it was not me, that I was just trying to help. And asked him why I would bring up the person I saw coming out of the ventilator shaft if it had been me. Wouldn't that be stupid? I asked him. He didn't like that at all. Thought I was calling him stupid. That's when he turned on me and demanded I confess. Of course I didn't. I reminded him I'm a monk, and that got him to quiet down. Luckily, he is Catholic. I threatened to tell his parish priest about how he was treating me. That got him to finally shut up and let me have some dinner."

Francesco was really getting himself worked up. Sally thought he might stand up again and swear.

Sally watched as Hoppy stroked his arm, and that calmed him. Kwame came over with the large beer, and Francesco took a huge gulp, put the glass down, and sighed.

"Ah, that's just what I needed," the monk said.

"So, does Agent Lazarus have an idea of who the person could have been with the canister?" Sally asked, regretting she had left her backpack with her notebook in her cabin.

"He wants to get the height of everyone on the ship and somehow compare that to what I told him. Which is ridiculous. I said a tall person. He just needs to look at the tall people on the ship," Francesco said.

Sally began scanning the room, estimating heights. Of the people in the room, there were only five who could match that: Martin, the captain, Kwame, Niv, and the monk.

"So you think it was a man?" Sally asked, trying to match her mental list against what Francesco saw.

"I think so, but I wasn't that close to be sure," he replied.

Kwame brought his steak, and Francesco didn't say anything after that as he shoveled the food in.

Boy, Sally could see what Hoppy and the monk had in common. They both loved to eat. She enjoyed their enthusiasm.

A cough next to their table made them all look up. The monk rolled his eyes when he saw who it was.

Agent Lazarus pointed at Sally, "Can I have a word?" he barked.

Sally quickly downed the last of her wine and followed Lazarus out of the room.

* * *

Down in the storage room cum interrogation room, Sally sat across from Lazarus.

"What can I do for you, Agent?" Sally asked as nicely as she could. While she had been done with dinner, she didn't like the interruption, particularly as she thought she might be able to get something else out of Francesco about the questioning. And she hoped there would still be time for that drink with Hoppy before they had a short nap and began their search for the canister.

"I need your help," Lazarus said quietly.

"Excuse me?" Sally asked, not believing her ears.

Lazarus went red.

"I said I need your help, Ms. Witherspoon," Lazarus said loudly.

Sally laughed.

"What's so funny?" he asked.

"Yelling at me is really going to make me want to help you," Sally explained.

"True," Lazarus replied, now laughing himself.

Wow, there was a human side to this FBI agent. Sally thought she might even get to like him. And she definitely wanted to help him. Even if it had only been three days since Jim's death, so much had happened, though sadly she wasn't much closer to figuring out who did it. The only clue at the moment was the mysterious tall person with the canister, which apparently contained fish protein.

"So what do you need help with, Agent?" Sally asked.

Lazarus got serious.

"We need to figure out who had the canister with the fish protein in it. It must be here on the ship. I wanted to talk to the captain now to figure out who the monk may have seen coming out of the ventilator shaft," he explained.

Sally briefly debated telling him about her and Hoppy's plan to search for the canister later, but she decided to keep her mouth shut. That is, unless they actually found it.

"Okay, and how can I help?" Sally asked.

"The captain likes you, I gather, so I thought you could help me talk to her. She isn't too happy about my presence on the ship. She should be glad I've allowed your trip to continue. Neither the captain nor the company she works for would be happy if the boat tour stopped and created buzz in the press. From what I gather, it's the presence of Mr. Wong on this ship that is keeping everything quiet," Lazarus said.

Sally nodded as he spoke. The only reason Lazarus was there was due to Jason Wong, but he seemed to forget that without Jason, there would be no Lazarus to show up and try to solve the murder of Jim O'Sullivan.

The other thought she had was what he said about the captain. Sally hadn't talked to her that much, but apparently Sally had made a good impression. That seemed to be a good thing.

"Sure, Agent Lazarus, I can help. Did you want to go now?" Sally asked.

Lazarus shook his head and looked at his watch.

"We don't have to go anywhere. The captain should be here any minute."

As if on cue, there was a knock at the door.

"Come in," Lazarus called, and the door opened.

Captain Kramer walked in and stopped when she saw Sally.

"Vat is she doink here?" the captain asked.

Sally smiled as brightly as she could.

"I've asked Ms. Witherspoon to be here. She's got quite an eye for detective work, it seems."

Sally wasn't sure where these compliments were coming from all of a sudden, but maybe Agent Lazarus was getting desperate for a solution.

"So vat do you need, Agent Lazarus?" the captain asked, her Germanic accent thicker than ever.

Maybe it's a nervous tic, Sally thought, or a fake accent.

That idea suddenly came to Sally. The captain had explained about coming from Vienna in Austria, and the family having the old restaurant. But anyone could say anything. There really wasn't a way to check that her story was true, even if Sally had found the Vienna restaurant online. There was no picture of the owners, so the captain could be lying.

"We have a lead. Someone saw a tall person dressed in black climbing out of one of your ventilator shafts near the dining room. They were carrying some kind of canister," he began.

The captain suddenly barked out a laugh, making both Sally and Lazarus jump.

"That sounds like something from a bad movie, Agent Lazarus. What the hell does that mean?"

Lazarus explained about the fish protein found in Jim's lungs and the canister they needed to find.

"Which of your crew would be working on the ventilation?" Lazarus asked when he had finished giving the captain the overall details.

"One of the cook's assistants is also our maintenance person. But none of the cooks are tall, and they certainly wouldn't be dressed in all black like spies in the night," Captain Kramer replied matter-of-factly.

She placed her hands on the table.

"Well, we'll have to talk to him next," Lazarus said.

"Talk to *her*. Our maintenance person and assistant cook is a woman," Captain Kramer explained, her voice rising a notch.

"Okay, whatever. Have her come here now," Lazarus said.

The captain pulled out a walkie-talkie and contacted Martin. He said he was in his cabin and would go to the kitchen and bring the maintenance person to the interrogation room.

Sally was antsy to get out of there and have that drink with Hoppy, or at least have enough time to have a short nap before meeting Hoppy for the canister search.

The three sat in silence, waiting for the assistant chef/maintenance person. Sally's mind was awash with possibilities.

After only a few moments, Martin came rushing in, his face ashen.

"Cook. Maintenance. Dead."

Chapter Thirty-Five

Sally hurried with Agent Lazarus, Captain Kramer, and Martin to the kitchen. There, they found the head chef in tears, holding a steak knife, standing next to a wash basin.

Lazarus quickly pulled out a latex glove from his pocket, put it on, and strode over to grab the knife from the chef.

The chef released the knife easily and didn't even look at Lazarus.

That's when they all saw the body. Sally took a glance and had to look away. The blue lips told her all she needed to know. There was no blood, so she was probably strangled.

So much for the knife Lazarus had just grabbed. He seemed to be more reactive than anything else.

Lazarus pulled out his phone and called his colleagues. The boat was still docked at Memphis, which luckily made it easy for the local FBI office to send over a forensics team.

After finishing his call, he pulled the captain aside in a stage whisper, which Sally got all of.

"I'm sorry, Captain. With two deaths, I'm shutting down this trip. I don't care what Mr. Wong or his embassy thinks. I now have two murders to solve. The boat is staying at Memphis, and I will have armed guards make sure no one gets on or off without my permission.

"Oh vell. And I was so looking forward to an uneventful trip," Kramer said only slightly sarcastically.

Oh, Sally did love her Germanic "humor."

"Okay, I want you to get the crew and guests into the restaurant. We need to let them know what's going on. And that we will be searching everywhere. I'm not going to tell anyone about the canister, and I expect you both to keep quiet about it," Lazarus said, pointing to Sally and the captain.

Both nodded in obedience.

Sally had debated trying to get Hoppy on one of the ship phones in the kitchen to tell her what was going on, but now that Lazarus had ordered them all to the restaurant, Hoppy would be finding out soon enough.

Turning to Lazarus, she said, "Um, should I help get the guests up?"

"That would be great. Captain Kramer here can take care of the crew," Lazarus replied, "While I talk to the chef here."

"*Jawohl!*" the captain said, marching out.

The chef was still bawling his eyes out. "I didn't do it. I found her here. Oh geez," he said, tears dripping down his face.

Sally wanted to hear more, but she could catch up with Lazarus later. She now had a mission.

Sally slipped out more quietly than the captain and headed to the guest area. Though not the first door she reached, she walked to the end of the cabin area to get Hoppy first. It was only 10:30 p.m., so she assumed Hoppy and most of the other guests would still be awake.

Sally knocked quietly, and the door opened immediately.

"Oh, there you are. I thought you had fallen asleep somewhere or jumped into bed with Agent Lazarus," Hoppy said, chuckling.

The thought turned Sally's stomach. He was someone she definitely did NOT want to sleep with.

Pushing Hoppy in and shutting the door, Sally turned serious.

"What's going on, Sally?" Hoppy asked, looking excited and scared at the same time.

"There's been another murder," Sally explained, falling into one of the armchairs.

"What?!" Hoppy yelled.

"Shhh," Sally called, "I have to inform the other guests, but not by yelling through the walls."

Having said that, she remembered her own cabin was next to Hoppy's and there was none on the other side, so hopefully no one heard Hoppy cry out.

"You?" Hoppy said.

"Yes, Lazarus asked me to get all the guests up if they weren't already up. We're to go to the restaurant, with the crew, where Lazarus will tell everyone what happened," Sally said.

"Who was murdered?" Hoppy asked.

"The assistant cook, who apparently is also the maintenance person on board. Lazarus wanted to talk to her about what Francesco saw to learn more about maintenance on the ship and the ventilator shafts. Martin went to get her and came rushing in to tell us she was dead. The four of us went to the kitchen, and that's where she was apparently killed. We found the chef crying with a knife in his hand," Sally explained.

"The chef did it?" Hoppy asked wide-eyed.

"No, no. There was no blood. Looks like she was strangled."

"Ugh, that is terrible," Hoppy replied, finally sitting down in the other armchair.

At that, Sally jumped up.

"Let's go, we have to be in the restaurant as soon as possible," Sally commanded, her graying ponytail swishing every which way. It was as excited about what was going on as Sally was.

Hoppy grinned and stood up.

"Aye, aye, captain," Hoppy said, making Sally laugh.

They headed out of Hoppy's cabin to get the other guests into the restaurant with as little commotion as possible.

Sally wondered what Jason Wong would think of this all.

* * *

The sound in the room from the guests and crew was deafening.

Sally looked around, wondering when Agent Lazarus and the captain would be showing up.

When she had knocked on the other doors, she had just said there had been an incident, and they were requested to proceed to the restaurant.

185

Hoppy did a great job of pretending to have no idea what was going on.

As expected, the most belligerent was Jason Wong, whom Sally had to persuade to come to the restaurant and not call his embassy like he did after Jim's death.

Then Sally remembered no one had a phone.

He had acquiesced, and now Sally was seated with a very reluctant Jason and Amy Wong, just to make sure he didn't run to the bridge to make a call.

"This is absolutely ridiculous," Jason said.

"Oh, shut up, you fool," Amy replied, slapping his hand.

"Agent Lazarus and the captain should be here any minute. Just be patient," Sally explained, not too convincingly.

She wondered what was keeping them. Maybe Lazarus was still waiting for his colleagues with the forensic team to arrive. Maybe the cook had confessed, though she didn't think he did it. Those tears he shed in the kitchen seemed far too real.

The sounds in the room stopped as Agent Lazarus strode into the room with the captain. She was a few steps behind him. Sally didn't see the Viennese Captain Kramer as someone to kowtow to, but somehow Lazarus had bettered even her. Or so it seemed.

Lazarus stood in the middle of the restaurant and coughed.

All eyes were on him.

"Well, ladies and gentlemen," he began as if he were giving an Oscar acceptance speech, "I'm sorry to tell you there's been another death."

Everyone looked around the room.

"But we're all here, Agent Lazarus," Niv said, totally seriously.

"It was not one of the guests, Mr. Peretz," he replied, looking down at his notebook, "The assistant cook has been strangled."

"This means your trip is now officially over," he said with groans and moans reaching his ears.

Jason looked like he was about to stand up, but Amy held him down.

"I have armed guards at the entrance to the ship. We will stay docked in Memphis until the crimes have been solved. No one gets on or off the ship without my permission," Lazarus explained with some glee, Sally felt.

She wasn't sure of the law, but she didn't think he could keep them there for days without concrete evidence against one of them. She also knew that if one or more left, that could easily be the killer or killers, and then maybe neither murder would ever be solved.

Just like months ago in her adopted town of Berry Springs, she was determined to help solve the crimes as quickly as possible. She gave herself until Saturday to do it, which was the regular end of the river tour anyway.

She just needed to find the canister with the fish protein, hope there were good fingerprints on it, find the person, then get them to confess.

Yeah, Sally, that's really going to work.

She realized she was daydreaming when Amy tapped her hand.

"He's talking about you?" Amy said, pointing to Agent Lazarus.

"…and Ms. Witherspoon will be assisting with the investigation, so please give her your full cooperation," Lazarus was saying.

Sally couldn't believe her ears, but she also got applause from Brin and Hoppy. Jason sent daggers across the table.

For some reason, Brother Francesco didn't look so happy.

Or maybe it was indigestion.

"Glad to help," Sally said in reply, smiling awkwardly.

"You can all go back to your rooms. We will be searching each of them now and then, questioning you tomorrow. Any questions?" Lazarus ended his speech with a question.

Aharon raised his hand.

"Yes," Lazarus said, seemingly annoyed that someone actually took him up on his offer.

"Why would someone kill the assistant cook? Can you give us any information about how this connects to Jim's death? What are you looking for in our rooms? And what right do you have to keep us here until you solve the crimes?" he asked, rapid-firing questions and accusations at Lazarus.

"Oh right, you're the lawyer," Lazarus said with a sigh, his face going red.

"The ship is an active crime scene. Two people have been murdered, and I am an agent of the FBI. If you have a problem with that, call your embassy. I will be confiscating all your passports so you can't leave the country. Is that definitive enough for you?" Lazarus barked.

Aharon didn't reply.

Boy, Sally wanted to make sure she stayed on the agent's good side.

"All right, no more questions?" Lazarus asked, not waiting for a reply, "Back to your rooms. My agents will be coming by now to do our search. Oh, and the way, here is the search warrant I obtained to search your rooms. That was the reason for my delay," Lazarus said, winking at Aharon.

Aharon muttered something under his breath, which Sally thought Lazarus probably didn't want to hear.

The guests stood up and shuffled out.

Sally was last, and Lazarus called her over. Brin stood at the doorway to the restaurant obviously anxious to gossip with Sally.

"Brin, let's chat later," she said.

Brin stomped off.

"Thanks, Agent Lazarus. I'm glad to help," Sally said.

"I realized I need someone on the inside. You have helped the police before and are one of the guests. It should help us get to the bottom of the two murders faster," he replied, smiling for once.

Sally looked back flirtatiously, smoothing her ponytail.

"Any idea why the assistant cook was killed?" she asked, kind of guessing the answer but wanting to suck up to the agent a bit.

"Well, she planted the canister for the murderer or saw something," he replied.

Sally thought that was obvious, but didn't say anything.

"Do you think it was one of the crew or one of the guests?" Sally asked the question on her own mind.

Lazarus shrugged.

"No idea, but I'm keeping an open mind. It was somebody on the ship," he replied.

Sally had a thought.

"We're docked at Memphis. Couldn't someone have gotten aboard, strangled the assistant cook, and then hopped off the ship and disappeared into town?" she said, not really liking the sound of that.

"Yes, sure, but then who knows who the person is. I'm convinced it's someone on the ship. Jim's murder happened while you were all traveling on the river, so it's very unlikely someone was able to get aboard then and then disappear without being seen."

She agreed it made more sense that it was someone on the ship, whether crew or guest. But who?

"Okay, I'm heading back to my room, Agent Lazarus, if that's okay. I guess your team will be searching my room too," Sally said.

"Of course. It could be anyone on board," Lazarus replied.

Maybe that's why he wanted Sally's help. Thinking she might know something that she wasn't telling him.

In spite of his seemingly friendly demeanor, Sally decided to remain wary of the agent. His main goal seemed to be just to further his own career by solving the crime, even if solving it meant arresting an innocent person.

Sally felt like a double agent as she walked out of the restaurant and back to her cabin.

Chapter Thirty-Six

"We found this in your cabin, Brother Francesco," Agent Lazarus said, placing the canister on the table. He dropped it just before it touched the table, and there was a loud thud as it hit the metal.

Sally jumped in her seat.

Brother Francesco sat with his arms crossed, staring at the FBI agent.

There was an air of calm around him that Sally had seen before in her church. Priests, monks, rabbis, and the like gave off a sense of being in another world of peace and calm.

She wished she had the willpower to be as calm as the monk was at that moment, though he was the one being questioned, not her.

"Agent Lazarus, I don't know where this came from," Francesco finally replied, "Remember, I'm the one who told you yesterday about seeing someone remove something like this from the ventilator shaft. Why would I tell you that if I had been the person? And why would I then leave it in my room?"

She looked up at Lazarus, who had yet to respond to the monk.

"Are you playing a game with me?" Lazarus said, leaning over closer to the monk.

Sally expected him to move back to his seat, but Francesco just stood his ground. Their faces were only inches apart.

"I tell you, I have no idea where this came from. I can tell you that the canister looks similar to the one I saw that person carrying," Francesco responded, this time raising his voice slightly. It trembled toward the end as well.

Had he really been that close to see a black canister in the dark? Sally wasn't too sure, but she still didn't think the monk killed either Jim or the assistant cook. He was definitely starting to get a bit nervous, but that would probably happen to most innocent people questioned by the FBI.

"Why did you kill those people? Was it revenge? Was it a sick game? Tell me why you did it?" Lazarus said, almost yelling.

At this, Francesco jumped up, but Agent Lazarus pushed him down hard. The monk fell into the metal chair and began crying.

"Agent Lazarus. Do you mind if I have a go?" Sally asked, trying to defuse the situation.

The FBI agent fell into his own chair.

"Fine. Whatever," he replied.

Sally moved her chair closer to the monk's.

"Now, Francesco. The FBI agent is just doing his job. The canister was found in your room, and he needs to find out how that might have happened. And of course, he will suspect you. Doesn't that make sense?" Sally said in the most soothing voice she could find in herself.

She touched the monk's arm.

He stopped crying and looked at her.

"I'm just so scared," he replied, his Italian accent stronger than ever. 'Scared' came out like 'scared-e.'

"Look, I'm just trying to find out what happened. How could the canister have gotten into your room?" Lazarus interjected with a much more normal voice.

The monk thought for a moment.

"Well, maybe the person saw me, so they planted it in my room to point the finger at me for some reason," Francesco replied.

"Or maybe it was random. The killer looked for a cabin to plant it in, and it just happened to be Francesco's. His cabin is the first one on the left in the guest area," Sally offered, trying to be helpful and broaden Agent Lazarus's view of the situation.

Lazarus kept nodding. He seemed to actually be considering what they were both saying.

"Okay, we're going to test for fingerprints on the canister. But for now, you can go," Lazarus said, motioning them both out while he pulled out his phone.

Sally and Francesco jumped up from their chairs and bolted from the room before the FBI agent could change his mind.

Outside the crew mess, Francesco grabbed Sally in a bear hug.

"Grazie. Grazie. Mille Grazie," he said over and over.

Sally's Italian was definitely sufficient to know that he was thanking her for getting him out of that interrogation, at least for now.

"Glad to help, Francesco. Why don't we go up to the deck for some fresh air and a coffee?" she suggested, already leading him in that direction.

"Oh yes. Let's get Hoppy to join us," he replied, smiling broadly.

* * *

"Well, this isn't the relaxing trip I thought I booked," Hoppy remarked, sipping her cappuccino, getting chocolate powder on her upper lip.

"Nice moustache," Sally said, pointing to her own lip.

"Funny," Hoppy replied, smiling.

"Yeah, this isn't exactly what I thought would be happening now either," Sally said.

They should be cruising down the Mississippi toward Arkansas by this point, their seventh day of the tour. Instead, they were stuck at Memphis until the murders were solved, or maybe they would be released before then and could just head home. Sally wasn't really feeling like vacation now, and she was starting to get anxious to get back to her bar, Sally's Smasher, in the Arkansas Ozarks. Her bartender, Magda, whom she had left in charge, still hadn't sent a text in a while. Hopefully, that meant all was well.

Sally had thought of calling Magda to tell her what was going on, but decided against it. After what they had all gone through a few months before, Sally knew it would just panic Magda. And that was the last thing Sally needed.

"I just hope they find the killer soon," Francesco said, sipping a cold beer. After the discussion with the FBI, he had decided to order something a bit stiffer than a coffee.

Hoppy had been glad when they had asked her to join them. And she was even more relieved to see Francesco not in handcuffs.

They were holding hands, and Sally thought that was so cute. Maybe something good would come out of this trip, she thought.

Her mind wandered to the men in her life. She kept wavering between getting to know Martin Sandworth, the first officer, and trying to see about getting a coffee with Mark Soder, the police officer at home. He was married, but Sally had never been one to let that stop her.

"Sally, Sally," Hoppy was saying.

She snapped out of her fantasy.

"Sorry, daydreaming," Sally said.

Hoppy laughed, "You were licking your lips, so it was probably more than that."

All three laughed. It was good to break the tension of the last few days.

"So, who do you think did it, Sally?" Hoppy asked, changing the subject, which Sally most appreciated.

"Well, I think it's definitely a person on board, crew, or guest. I guess the fact that the canister was planted in Francesco's room points to one of the crew," Sally said more or less thinking aloud.

And in all honesty, just regurgitating what she had just talked about with Agent Lazarus. Her mind was wandering and she needed to come to some conclusions, stat!

She had to get back to her room and put her thoughts down in her notebook. That always helped to sort the facts and try and get a realistic picture of what happened.

"Maybe I'm too optimistic, but I just can't believe someone on board did this," Hoppy said quite definitively.

Francesco removed his hand from hers and wagged his finger.

"Someone died, and I agree it has to be a guest or crew member," Francesco replied.

"Yes, Father," Hoppy said, doing the sign of the cross.

Francesco looked hurt, but then burst out laughing.

It was the beer or the company or both, but he was finally relaxing after the Lazarus ordeal earlier that morning.

"We just don't have too many facts at the moment. We have the canister with the fish protein, and we know that is what killed Jim. We now have a dead assistant cook who was also the maintenance person. That person may or may not have known who was in the ventilator shaft. The assistant cook is much too small to be the person you saw Francesco," Sally recounted out loud what she was thinking.

"But what's the motive?" Francesco asked.

Sally slapped her hand on the table.

"Exactly. Who wanted to kill Jim and the assistant cook and why?" asked Sally taking another sip of coffee.

All three sat back in their chairs contemplating the question.

Chapter Thirty-Seven

Sally sat in a corner on the upper deck early Wednesday afternoon. She had taken lunch there to think by herself. Hoppy and Francesco had gone back to Hoppy's cabin for some rest and relaxation. There wasn't much else to do now that they were stuck docked in Memphis and weren't allowed to leave the ship.

She sipped her beer and watched as the water beaded on the cold glass. It was a gorgeous sunny day on the river. She sat back and let the sun hit her face. She tanned easily. Sighing deeply, she sat up.

Sally's notebook lay open in front of her with a pen. When Hoppy and Francesco had left, she had nipped to her cabin to get her backpack. She always worked better when she had something to write on to sort her thoughts.

At the other end of the deck, Jason and Amy Wong were lounging. Aharon was sitting with them.

Sally guessed Niv was in the gym or working. He had mentioned his writing a few times and that he was trying to finish his latest biography. Though he wouldn't tell her who it was about.

She scribbled two columns in the notebook.

One was headed 'Guests', the other 'Crew'.

Under 'Guests', she wrote

- *Jason and Amy Wong*
- *Hoppy*
- *Aharon and Niv*

- *Brin*
- *Brother Francesco*

Sally had just finished this list when Brin came bounding up the stairs. Spotting Sally, she bounced over.

"Whatcha up to?" Brin asked, planting herself in a seat before Sally could object.

Sally thought for a minute before answering. She had really hoped to be alone with her cold beer, her notebook, and her thoughts to be able to sort this mess out.

On the other hand, Brin was a lot of fun. And really smart.

"Trying to sort all the facts and names and information about this case. I feel like the answer is right in front of me, but I can't figure it out. The biggest question I have is why someone would kill Jim and the assistant cook," Sally explained.

"Oooh, detective stuck?" Brin needled.

Sally winced. That hurt. She hated not knowing the answer to something. And she was pushing herself to figure it all out before Agent Lazarus, who seemed to be pushing his weight around but not getting very far.

She knew she had to stay on his good side, particularly if she was going to get any more information out of him, like the results of the fingerprint test on the canister.

Brin apparently noticed that her comment had perhaps not been so diplomatic because she added, "What does your instinct tell you?"

Sally sipped her beer and thought about the question.

"Well, the two deaths are related. I'm sure of that. It seems too much of a coincidence that Jim was killed with a device hidden in the ventilation, and that just as we want to question the maintenance person, who also happens to be the assistant cook, that person is killed."

Brin encouraged, "Go on."

Sally looked out on the river as if the flow of water would give her the strength or an insight into the rest.

"I'm still wavering on whether the killer is a guest or a member of the crew. It has to be one or the other. But none of us or the crew met each other until this cruise," Sally continued.

"…as far as you know," Brin said, grinning.

Sally sat stunned. Of course. Why hadn't she thought of that? She kicked herself for not coming to that conclusion herself.

"Wow, yeah, sure. But how will I figure that out?" Sally asked, leaning over as if she were grilling Brin.

"How do I know. You're the detective, sweetie," Brin said, squealing.

"Brin, you are amazing," Sally replied, reaching across to give her a hug.

"What was that for?" she asked.

"I was feeling like I was at a dead end, and you gave me a great idea to follow through. And as always, you brighten my mood with your presence," Sally said.

Brin laughed, "That's what an influencer is supposed to do, honey," snapping her fingers.

If nothing else came out of the cruise, she was glad to have met Brin. And hoped they would stay in touch.

"Ugh, I wish I had a phone. My social media followers probably think I'm dead," Brin said.

"You'll be back online soon," Sally replied, smiling.

"I guess I'll try to sleep," Brin said, leaning back and closing her eyes.

Sally didn't think she was the type to relax, but then she could be wrong.

The sound of the water lapping the boat was good, thinking background noise.

She looked down at her notebook and finished the second column.

Under *'Crew,'* she wrote:

- *Captain Matilda Kramer*
- *First Officer Martin Sandworth*
- *Steward Kwame Jones*
- *Maid Mary Rogers*
- *Chef (need to get his full name)*
- *Pilot (need to get her full name)*

Beneath this list, she wrote

- *Murdered*
- *Jim O'Sullivan-fish protein*
- *Assistant Cook/maintenance person-strangled*

As she wrote the second death, she realized she didn't even have a name. Did it matter? It might if that would give her a connection to one of the crew or the guests. Unless the maintenance person was killed because of something they saw tied to Jim's death.

She completed her summary of the cast of characters with…

- *Suspicious persons*
- *Tall person in black climbing out of ventilator shaft*

Thinking about suspicious, she decided to add beneath that:

- *Mary Rogers and Amy Wong fighting; Mary discovered she was related to Jim (good or bad for Jim?)*
- *Mary claims Amy Wong was in and out of other cabins.*

Sally raised her head and looked across at Amy Wong, seemingly lost in a book. She was actually smiling.

Looking down, she made one final note in her notebook:

- *Motive/Opportunity?*

She then put her pen down, leaned back, and closed her eyes.

Chapter Thirty-Eight

Sally woke with a start.

She stretched and yawned, wondering where she was. It slowly came back to her. She looked around and saw she had fallen asleep on the deck. The Wongs were still reading at the other end, while Aharon and Brin had left.

"Have a good nap?" Amy Wong called.

Sally smiled.

Looking at her watch, she saw she had been asleep for two hours.

She kicked herself, seeing the two hours as wasted time when she should be getting on with the investigation.

Sally picked up the open notebook in front of her and read the latest entries.

Thinking back to what Brin had said, she quickly came up with a plan.

The first thing to do was see Agent Lazarus to find out if he had gotten any fingerprint results from the canister and if there was a match to someone on board. Sally thought it was odd that he hadn't asked everyone to be fingerprinted, but maybe he wanted to first check if there was a match in his system before he alarmed anyone, or give the murderer a chance to escape, come up with a story, or worst of all, murder someone else.

While she did love investigating, she didn't like the fact that someone had to die for the investigation to take place.

Sally grabbed her notebook and pen, stuffed them in her bag, and headed back to her cabin.

She called to the Wongs as she reached the stairs.

"See you at dinner, Sally," Amy responded.

Sally shook her head. She didn't think she would ever understand Amy Wong, but then maybe she wasn't meant to.

As she approached her room in the guest area, she saw the door was slightly ajar. Her heart raced thinking someone was searching it, though she wasn't sure what for. Then she remembered her notebook, which was safely tucked away in her backpack.

Sally slowed down and stopped next to the door and peered in.

She breathed a sigh of relief when she saw Mary Rogers making the bed. Sally strode in.

Mary Rogers screamed.

Sally laughed in spite of herself.

"I'm so sorry. When I came down the hallway and saw the door open, I was wondering who was inside," Sally replied.

"Just me cleaning," Mary said, slowly catching her breath, grabbing the pillow, and continuing to change the sheets.

"I'm almost done," Mary added.

"No worries, I'm going to have a cold drink and sit out on the balcony."

She went over to the fridge, got out a cold bottle of water, and headed outside, planting herself in a lounge chair.

She had just had a nap upstairs, so there was no time or need for sleep now, but she wanted to let Mary work.

And stay there while she was in her cabin. Of course, Mary could come and go as she pleased with her staff keycard.

She bolted upright.

The staff all had all-access cards.

Did that mean something? It must.

That was another thing to discuss with the FBI agent.

But she did have another question for Mary, and she headed back inside.

As she did, she saw Mary moving the cart toward the door.

"Do you have a moment?" Sally asked.

"Well, I...I guess so," Mary said, leaving the cart near the door and seating herself on the couch, her hands in her lap, looking down at the floor.

Sally dropped her backpack on the floor and slid into one of the armchairs across from her.

Sally decided to get right to the point.

"I'm at a dead end here with trying to find Jim's killer. Now your colleague is dead," Sally began not too diplomatically.

Mary began to cry.

Sally, you really need to activate comforting bartender mode stat, she told herself.

"I'm sorry," Sally continued, "I didn't mean to upset you."

Mary pulled a tissue out of her maid's uniform and blew her nose loudly.

"I…I…I know you're just trying to find the truth," Mary finally said.

"Sorry, yeah, um…" Sally said, realizing her note to herself to activate comforting bartender mode had not quite worked.

"I want to help, I do. I feel terrible about what happened to Jim. We had talked of my traveling to Boston to meet the family. Now that's never going to happen," Mary said, bursting into tears again but quickly stopping, drying her eyes.

Sally was wondering what that was all about. According to the FBI, there was no family that wanted to talk to Jim, so who would he want Mary to meet? Maybe he was just being polite.

Sally replied, "Yes, and I need your help."

Mary looked across at Sally.

"My help?" Mary asked.

"You told me you saw Amy going in and out of cabins."

Mary nodded.

"Anything else you can tell me about the passengers, or even the crew?"

Taking a deep breath, Mary spoke, "Well, I've only worked on the ship for about a year, but I know the rest of the crew has been here much longer. People worship Captain Kramer even if they're often a bit scared of her. She loves to talk about her apparently aristocratic Austrian family, but no one really knows how she ended up as captain of the River Queen. I don't really like her, but I just do my job and get on with it. She is very protective of her crew, so I guess I appreciate that. I know she's very upset about the continued police presence on board. The last thing she wants is for her reputation to suffer."

Sally jotted down a few notes in her notebook.

"How does she get along with Martin Sandworth?" Sally asked.

"Sometimes I think they're sleeping together, though, from what I can gather, he prefers the company of men to women," Mary said, shaking her head.

"But is Martin loyal?" Sally asked.

Mary nodded, "Oh yes, he would do anything for the captain."

Would he kill for her? Sally thought. She wasn't sure how that fit into it all.

"What about the kitchen staff?" Sally asked.

"Oh, they pretty much stick to themselves. I liked the assistant cook but didn't know her that well," Mary replied, not seeming as upset about that death as she had been a few moments ago.

"Any connection between Jim and the assistant cook?" Sally inquired.

"No idea," Mary answered, "As I said, I didn't know her, or actually Jim for that matter, that well."

Sally continued writing even if it was gibberish. She wanted time to think about what Mary had just told her.

After a few moments, she put down her pen and looked Mary straight in the eyes.

"Who do you think did it?" Sally asked, almost anticipating what Mary would say.

With that, she got up.

The interrogation, um, conversation was over, apparently.

"I need to get back to work," Mary said, heading toward the door and opening it.

Sally watched as she pushed the cart out and let the door slam shut.

Sally sat back on the couch and wondered whether she had gotten anything interesting out of that conversation. There seemed to be so many secrets on board. And a web of connections that Sally was only beginning to unravel.

Connections! That's it. Sally threw her notebook back in her bag and ran out of the cabin.

Chapter Thirty-Nine

Sally bounded across the hall and banged on Brin's door, hoping she was there. Where else would she be? It wasn't a very big ship. And Sally didn't think Brin seemed like the workout type, except for that one time with Francesco. But that was probably more to pump him for information than anything else.

No answer.

Sally banged even louder, realizing this could bring other passengers out of their cabins. She glanced around the hall, but just heard silence.

"Hang on a minute," Brin finally called.

A few seconds later, the door opened.

Brin's red hair went every which way, and she was frowning.

"What the hell is going on, Sally? I was trying to get a nap before dinner."

"Sorry, Brin. I need your help."

This shook the sleep off Brin.

"Wow, yes, come on in," Brin said, walking inside with Sally following close behind her.

Brin walked to the minibar and got out a beer.

"Wanna drink?" she asked.

Sally looked at her watch. Dinner was only an hour away.

"Sure, a glass of wine would be great."

Brin reached in and pulled out a small bottle of chilled white wine. She opened her beer, opened the wine, and poured it into a glass, then brought both drinks over to the sofa. Sally had already planted herself in a corner of the couch.

Brin put both drinks down on coasters on the small table.

Sally picked up her glass of wine and downed a big gulp.

"Well, well, what is going on?" Brin asked, picking up her beer and taking a swig of her own.

"I need your social media expertise," Sally began.

"But I don't have my phone, my phones," Brin replied.

"I don't believe you," Sally said.

"The FBI took my extra phone, and I almost got thrown in jail, Sally," sounding not too upset about that.

Gotcha.

"Come on, Brin, you are smart. You must have hidden another phone somewhere or somehow gotten your hands on one," Sally replied, wagging her finger at Brin, "You are obsessed with influencing."

Brin looked like she was going to yell at Sally, but she just laughed.

"Yes, I'm like a functioning alcoholic. I pretend not to be too addicted, but boy, I am," Brin admitted, jumping up.

Now what.

Sally watched in amazement as she began pulling the sofa apart, taking out a nail file and cutting into the fabric at the seam.

Brin reached in and pulled out a phone.

"I knew it," Sally exclaimed.

"Yeah, I complained to you upstairs before that my influencers might think I was dead. To be honest, I haven't been posting because Lazarus could find out, and then I'd be in real trouble. But at least I could look at some social media and news while I'm waiting to get off this damn ship."

Both laughed.

Brin sat down next to Sally, her fingers hovering above the screen.

"Yay, I love social media," Brin yelled, shrieking.

Sally explained about her talk just then with Mary Rogers and her thoughts on connections.

"Ooh, you want to see if there is any connection between a crew member and a guest or whatever. Sure, where else to start but social media? Most people post stuff and have no clue about privacy settings. We should be able to see everything," Brin was really getting worked up.

"Am I now your deputy, Sally?" Brin asked.

"We may just be sitting here at the dock, but this is definitely going to be fun," Brin exclaimed.

Brin tapped her screen a few times while Sally watched. She pulled up the first social media app, a very popular photo platform.

"Okay, who should we search for?" Brin asked.

"Let's start with Mary Rogers," Sally replied, "Somehow I doubt Jim was on any social media, but then I may be wrong."

Brin tapped on her screen and started scrolling. She stopped at a name and opened the profile.

"Well, this looks like Mary Rogers, but there are only a few posts," Brin said, turning her phone toward Sally.

Sally leaned over and looked at the few pictures. Mary, on the ship smiling; Mary in a town; then she saw one with Jim. The last couple of pictures were of Martin Sandworth and the captain, but they looked like they were taken from a distance. Sally peered closer to the screen. It looked like they were discussing something. In one of the photos, the captain was stabbing her finger in Martin's direction.

Geez, Sally didn't think she would want to work for her.

"Is this account new?" Sally asked.

Brin turned the phone back to herself and reviewed Mary's profile.

"Looks like she created it about a month ago, but that doesn't tell us anything," Brin explained.

"She probably doesn't have too much time to be an influencer if the ship is running all the time," Sally said, looking back at the picture of Mary and Jim.

"Hey, being an influencer is hard work," Brin said.

Sally wasn't sure if she was joking, but she needed Brin's help, so she wasn't going to make any jokes about it now.

"Who else?" Brin asked.

Sally thought for a second.

"How about Martin Sandworth?" Sally said.

"Ooh, I'm hoping we find some shirtless pictures of him," Brin squealed, and Sally was definitely not going to argue with that.

Brin searched for his name and found a profile on the same platform as Mary's.

"Wow, he has tons of pictures," Brin said.

"Any with Jim?" Sally asked.

Brin stared back down at the phone.

"That's strange," Brin said.

Now Sally was curious.

"What is it?" she asked.

"It looks like Martin was posting pictures of people on board, though that probably isn't a good idea if you want to keep your job," Brin said, scrolling through pictures.

"Well, on second thought, he could claim other people just happened to be in the pictures he was taking of the boat or river. Hard to tell really," Brin continued.

She tapped again.

"Oh, Mary seems to have been doing the same thing. What a crew," Brin said, shaking her head.

"Anything on either of their profiles?" Sally asked, leaning forward.

"Oooh, here's a juicy one," Brin said finally.

"Who's in the picture?" Sally asked, leaning further toward Brin and the phone.

Brin pulled the phone away.

"I'm getting to that," she said, enlarging the photo.

She turned the phone toward Sally.

It was a photo of the captain and Jim. This time, Jim was the one stabbing his finger at the captain.

Chapter Forty

That night's dinner was oddly enough set up as one big table, just like last Saturday when Jim had been killed.

Sally wondered why, though maybe she was reading too much into it. It could have been part of the dinner plans for that night already in the books.

As Sally glanced around the table, she shivered slightly. The seating arrangement was also the same as Saturday, except, of course, no Jim O'Sullivan.

She had sat down at one of the open spots and hadn't even thought of trying to mix things up.

To her left was Aharon, and to her right was Brother Francesco, just like Saturday.

Brin was between the monk and Martin Sandworth.

Across from Sally, next to Martin, were Amy, then Jason Wong, then the captain, Hoppy, and Niv, who completed the circle next to his partner Aharon.

Out of the corner of her eye, she caught Brin winking at her.

Turning to her, Brin made a circle sign with her hand and mouthed 'Saturday'.

Sally grimaced.

She decided to make the most of it while she contemplated what to do with the picture that Brin had found on Martin's social media account.

She was still surprised a picture like that was public, but then Brin had explained again that most people had no clue about privacy settings and just posted away as if no one in the world would notice, except their close friends and family they were connected to on the platform.

Just to be on the safe side, Brin had taken a screenshot of the photo, so if Martin decided to delete it, they would still have it to use or perhaps show Agent Lazarus. And Brin had sent the photo to Sally's phone so she would have it as well, though this was probably a stupid thing as the FBI had taken all their phones. Sally wondered where the phones were at the moment. She was desperate to get her hands on hers.

And wouldn't the FBI have done this kind of check already? Maybe they had. Agent Lazarus hadn't exactly been keeping her fully up to date. But then neither had she. It was already Wednesday evening, and there were theoretically only two more evenings on the boat before the tour was supposed to end. Well, it kind of already had ended now that they were stuck docked at Memphis.

So much for cruising into New Orleans, Sally thought.

She pushed that thought out of her mind and looked across at Martin Sandworth, who was chatting with Amy Wong.

Sally then looked over at Captain Kramer, who smiled at her. Well, half-smiled in her grim Teutonic manner.

Captain Kramer. She wondered why Jim had been stabbing his finger at her. Maybe they had a past, though she couldn't imagine either being with the other. If so, it must have been years ago. But how would she figure this out? She could get Brin to do some digging.

Or take a chance and confront the Captain herself.

That made her stop and really think. Confronting the captain on her own might be dangerous. Her stomach jumped as she thought back to her stupid lone trip to see Margaret Jackson a few months ago while she was investigating the death of her best friend and business partner, Bill Arnold. That visit had gotten her kidnapped and almost killed.

She wanted to solve the two murders on board herself, but she also wanted to make it off the boat and back to Berry Springs alive.

Sally decided the best thing to do would be to see Agent Lazarus, if he was on board. He had been leaving off and on to consult with the FBI team in

Memphis. Even if he was off the boat, it didn't mean they could leave. The four guards posted at the entrance to the ship made sure of that. They also made sure to scan the water regularly, so slipping into the water wasn't a good idea either.

Well, Sally wasn't going to be slipping away. She wanted to stay, solve the crime, or at least be there when the murderer or murderers were arrested.

Kwame arrived with the first course, and Sally tried to put all of this out of her mind and concentrate on the food. That was what everyone else was doing as they all tried to pretend this was still a normal evening on the boat and they weren't stuck there while two murders were being investigated.

The conversation was quiet, and no one seemed to be smiling too much. Oh, except Brin, who was apparently telling a funny story to Martin Sandworth as both burst into laughter. This brought dirty looks from the rest of the table.

"Please, two people have been murdered," Hoppy cried, slamming down her fork, sending salad and dressing flying every which way.

Typical Brin. She didn't say anything, just flipped Hoppy the bird. Hoppy began to stand up, but the captain pulled her back down and whispered something to her.

She slammed her fist on the table, grabbed her fork, and leaned over her plate to shovel in more salad.

Brin muttered "bitch" under breath.

Kwame knew just when to appear as he asked people if they wanted drink refills. Everyone raised their hands in unison.

Laughter broke the tension.

Francesco turned to her.

"How are you, Sally?" he asked as if she had just entered the confessional, which, being around him, she often felt like.

She almost automatically responded that she was 'fine,' but a part of her brain put a stop to that.

"I don't know, to be honest. This isn't quite the relaxing trip I thought it would be."

Francesco smiled, "No, not really. But at least we are both still alive," he said, winking.

Her stomach lurched.

"This is true. I just hope they find out who did it," she responded.

He winked again and turned back to his food.

Sally took the chance to look across at the captain again, well, more stare at her, trying to figure out her connection to Jim. The captain had been grabbing some salad with her fork, but when she felt the glare of Sally's stare, she looked up.

She stared back at Sally and grinned.

The grin lasted a second, and the captain went back to her salad.

Sally grabbed her wine glass and took a sip while letting her eyes follow everything that was going on.

What was actually going on?

Sally needed first to find out if this seating arrangement was planned in advance. She could probably ask Martin about that. Then she needed to find Agent Lazarus and get Brin to show him the photo of Jim and the captain.

Did that discussion have something to do with Jim's death? Sally was determined to find out.

* * *

The rest of dinner went quietly, which Sally was happy about. It gave her time to think.

She ran through scenarios in her mind and solidified her next steps. She would definitely try to have a quick word with Martin after dinner and ask him about the seating arrangement.

Then she would go find Agent Lazarus. Sally hoped he would be in his "office" on the ship rather than in Memphis. She wanted to notify him about the picture of Jim and the captain, and find out if he had finally gotten the fingerprint evidence from the canister.

Finally, she would plan a quiet chat with the captain, but not without warning Hoppy or Brin beforehand.

At that moment, Kwame came over.

"Anyone want coffee?" he asked as he began clearing the dessert plates.

The table remained silent as it was clear they all just wanted the dinner to be over as quickly as possible.

When Kwame had removed the last dessert plate, they all stood up at once.

Sally quickly went to the other side of the table to catch Martin. The rest slinked away.

"Hi, Martin. Do you have a second?" Sally asked.

"Sure, but then I need to get to the bridge. What is it?" he said, turning to her.

"I was just wondering if the dinner arrangement tonight was part of your original plan. It just seemed odd to me that it was just like Saturday night when Jim…um…left us," Sally explained, wondering she hadn't been able to say 'died' or 'passed away.'

"Sure, yeah, we do a couple nights like that during this cruise," he replied, only half listening to her, "Is that it?"

"That's it. Thanks," she said.

He didn't hear her as he strode toward the door.

Sally sat back down at the table.

Martin's answer had been quick, maybe too quick, though he seemed sincere.

She would just have to go with that answer for now. The dinner that night, though almost identical in table setup to Saturday, had already been planned before any of them stepped on board.

Sally pushed herself to go look for Agent Lazarus and hopefully an answer to the canister fingerprint question.

* * *

As Sally left the restaurant, the hallway was clear. They had all left the restaurant quickly; no one had bothered to head to the lounge for a drink.

As she thought about it, she also wished she could just head back to her cabin, pour herself a glass of wine, and sit and sip it on her balcony.

But there was work to do.

She headed down the stairs and found Lazarus in his makeshift office at the beginning of the crew area. He was alone, shifting papers and tapping away at his laptop.

Sally walked in and coughed.

"Oh, it's you," he said as he looked up.

Some greeting.

"What can I do for you, Ms. Witherspoon?" he asked quite formally.

Sally grabbed a chair and sat down without asking him for permission.

She leaned across the table.

"Just wondering if you have any fingerprints you may have pulled from the fish canister," she stated just as formally.

Two can play at that game.

"No, still waiting on the results from the lab. No matches so far, but we were able to pull a couple of good prints," he explained, looking down at his laptop as he talked.

Sally didn't believe him. He had the power of the FBI behind him. How could they not have a match yet? She debated whether she should call him out on this.

It was already Wednesday, she was getting impatient, so she let him have it.

"Agent Lazarus, with all due respect," she began.

He stopped typing, looked up, and glared.

"Excuse me?" he said, getting up from his chair.

Sally stayed seated and crossed her arms.

"You're giving me the runaround. How can you not have a fingerprint match yet? I have no idea what you've been doing here or in Memphis, but it doesn't look like you are trying to solve the two crimes on board."

By the end of her diatribe, Sally was yelling.

Lazarus looked like he was about to punch her. He took deep breaths. His face was bright red.

Sally tried to remain calm. She was glad she had said what she said. She stared at him, waiting for a response. Then his phone rang.

He looked at Sally, but looking down, he snorted and picked up the phone.

"Just a sec. Don't you go anywhere," he ordered, walking out with his phone to his ear.

"Yeah, what is it?" Lazarus asked, slamming the door behind him.

Then Sally heard a click.

She jumped up and tried the door.

It was locked.

Chapter Forty-One

Sally took deep breaths to calm herself down.

How did she get herself into these messes?

Agent Lazarus must have something to do with the deaths. Otherwise, why would he lock her in?

Or maybe he just had a cruel streak and wanted her to sweat, which worked wonders as her face and armpits were soaked.

She wiped the sweat from her eyes and scanned the room for something to try and get the door open.

She hadn't brought her backpack, which had a multitool she could have used to pick the lock, and her phone. Oh, wait, her phone had been confiscated.

She shook the handle again and again, but it wasn't going to budge. She kicked the door, but it was thick steel.

Which made sense since she was on a ship.

She thought she might scream, but she didn't think anyone would hear her.

She tried it anyway.

"Help me. Please. Help," she yelled at the top of her lungs.

Out of breath, she fell into the chair she had been sitting on and waited for a noise, hoping the door would open and someone would be there to help her.

She hoped it wasn't going to be Agent Lazarus who opened the door.

Sally jumped up and began banging on the door again, screaming.

Nothing.

It had only been a few minutes, but Agent Lazarus might be back at any moment. He had just walked out to take that phone call, whoever it was. Or maybe he would make her wait longer to really get her scared.

Though he didn't know Sally, she wasn't scared, she was pissed.

She ran to the cabinets on the wall and began opening every door and drawer. Everything was empty. The crew must have cleared it out for Lazarus to use as an office. She thought it was weird that there was nothing in the room. There wasn't even a ship phone on the wall or the desk.

Unless that was Lazarus' plan. Lock her in and make sure there was nothing she could use to try and get out.

Then it dawned on her.

What would his explanation be when she got out? And if he killed her, wouldn't the rest of the guests and crew wonder what happened to her? Or maybe he was going to pin the deaths on her?

Anything was possible, though it all seemed very far-fetched.

Then she looked at the table.

Lazarus had left all his documents there.

She rifled through looking for a clue.

Unfortunately, there wasn't much there that she didn't know.

Then she saw a page marked "Fingerprint Analysis."

So he did have the information on this.

Sally glanced at the sheet and found they had made a match to the fingerprints.

Captain Matilda Kramer

Sally dropped into the nearest chair.

The captain had planted the canister? But why?

Then Sally thought back to the photo Brin had found on Martin's social media account of Jim stabbing a finger in the captain's direction.

Ugh, what was going on here?

She dropped the sheet of paper and saw a paperclip in the folder next to it.

Unfolding it, she tried to jimmy the lock to get it open.

She had never picked a lock before, but it looked so easy on TV.

Unfortunately, nothing happened. She slid it out before it broke off, and then who knows when she would be free.

Looking up, she saw a vent. Good, she wasn't going to suffocate.

Finding the paper and trying to open the lock had pumped adrenaline into her system.

Now that that was gone, she started to hyperventilate.

Sally tried to calm herself, telling herself everything would be okay. She would get out of there in one piece. She wouldn't die.

Her breathing slowly returned to normal, at least for a bit, but she was still wondering how the hell she was going to get out of there before Lazarus came back.

Would anyone believe her that he locked her in?

Who knows.

Taking a deep breath, she stared at the door and the lock, thinking the power of her mind would get it open.

As she was staring, the lock clicked.

She put her hand to her mouth to not scream.

Grabbing a chair to bash Lazarus over the head, she stood away from the door to give herself leverage.

The handle turned, and the door flew open.

Sally began to bring the chair down on the person entering when there was a scream.

A female voice.

Sally looked over.

It was Brin!

"Oh, Sally, thank god," Brin said, giving her a big hug.

"How did you find me?" Sally asked, hugging her back.

"I've been following you. I thought I could help you investigate. I didn't know I would have to get you out of a locked room," Brin explained.

Sally shook.

"Lazarus locked me in. He has something to do with the murders, I know it. And look at this," Sally said.

She reached across the table and pulled out the paper she had just been looking at.

Brin stared down at it.

"What the fuck?!" she barked.

Then they heard steps in the hallway.

How would they get away from Lazarus now?

Sally and Brin looked at each other and ran out.

They surprised Agent Lazarus, pushed him hard, and he fell. They ran past him and up the stairs.

At the top, they managed to push the door to the crew area closed and bolt it before he got to them.

Of course, they had just locked him in with the crew.

Sally's first thought after that was to find the captain and confront her.

She never took the safe way out, she managed to tell herself. But she shook that off and grabbed Brin to head to the bridge.

Chapter Forty-Two

"Sally, slow down," Brin panted.

"Pipe-smoking making it difficult to run?" Sally blurted out, unintentionally.

It was Brin who had just saved her from certain death.

Brin frowned.

"Sorry, you are literally my lifesaver," Sally replied, smiling, "But we have to get to the bridge to find

Captain Kramer."

Brin grabbed her arm to stop her. She yanked so hard, Sally's shirt ripped.

They both glanced around, hoping no one heard the commotion, but the hallway was clear.

Sally checked her watch. It was already 11:00 p.m. Most of the guests would be asleep.

"What are you doing?" Brin yelled in a loud whisper, "You can't just go up and confront her. If she did kill Jim and her assistant cook, what do you think she will do to you?"

Sally tried to catch her breath from running up the stairs and down the hallway. As she did, she knew Brin was right.

Getting herself killed was probably not a great way to end this trip, or this investigation, which would then be her last.

Sally grabbed Brin in a bear hug.

"You're right. I'm sorry. I just have to do something," Sally said, while Brin tried to push herself away.

"What are you trying to do, strangle me?" Brin asked only half-smiling.

Sally looked at her with sorry in her eyes.

"Well, what do you want to do, Detective Witherspoon?" Brin asked, backing away from Sally a few steps.

Sally thought for a minute, though they really couldn't waste time. They heard a faint pounding on the crew door and a voice.

Agent Lazarus wouldn't be in there long, considering some of the crew was down there.

"Let's go grab the armed guards at the ship entrance for some backup. We can quickly explain what's going on and then head up to the bridge," Sally decided.

"What if they are in on it with Lazarus?" Brin asked, pleading "Or maybe it would be smarter to just call the police. We can use my hidden phone."

Brin patted her pocket.

Sally shook her head hard, "They wouldn't get here in time. Everything is happening at lightning speed."

Brin shrugged, and they headed toward the gangway.

Just as they had started, they heard footsteps behind them.

"What's going on?" Martin Sandworth called.

Sally whipped around and ran to him. Brin, close behind her.

Sally quickly explained what was going on, that they could use his help, and that they wanted to get the guards to help confront the captain. The thought never crossed her mind that he also might be involved.

As she spoke, Brin whipped out the stolen phone and showed Martin the picture they had found on his account.

"How the hell?…" he said, "That was my blackmail picture," he then blurted out.

The pounding and yelling at the crew door had stopped, and the door sounded like it was about to open.

Sally pleaded with her eyes for Martin to do something.

He ran to the crew door and wrenched it open. He almost fell backward as Lazarus came charging out.

Luckily, Martin had the advantage as Lazarus was at the top of the stairs. Martin grabbed his arms and pushed.

Lazarus yelled and went tumbling down the metal stairs.

Sally wondered why the guards at the gangway hadn't already heard the commotion and come running to see what was going on.

Unless Lazarus had killed them. But why?

At that point, Sally turned to look down where Brin was pointing.

There was a pool of blood collecting, and Lazarus wasn't moving.

The crew was collecting behind his body. Apparently, they had thought it wiser to stay in their rooms while the shouting and pounding were going on. Sally would have done the same, considering two people had been killed on board.

They looked at Lazarus and all the blood. Then they looked up and saw Martin.

Still no guards.

Martin held his finger to his lips.

He was their superior officer, so they said nothing.

He motioned them back to their rooms. They turned and walked away.

Sally, Brin, and Martin stood there for a minute, making sure no one was coming either from the bridge or the guest area.

"Where are the guards?" Sally finally asked.

"I'll check," Brin cried, running off.

The corridors were silent, telling no tale.

Martin pushed the door shut, turned the lock, and then held his crew card to a panel on the wall. It went red.

"That locks the mechanism so no one can turn it to open the door. That will keep the crew inside while we figure out what to do," he said.

Sally felt he had a masochistic streak in him that she definitely wanted to stay on the right side of.

Brin came back.

She said nothing but just shook her head.

Sally began shaking.

"Um, shouldn't we see if he needs medical attention before we do anything else?" Sally asked.

Martin looked at her.

"You're right. I'm not sure what I was thinking."

"And check the guards too, though I didn't find a pulse," Brin explained, tears threatening to roll down her face, but she just sniffled and mumbled "allergies."

Martin held his pass against the pad until it went green, opened the door, and slowly padded down the stairs.

Sally and Brin watched him lean down and check for a pulse.

Martin turned his head, looking up at them, and shook it.

Well, it was an accident, sort of, Sally thought.

Martin walked back up the stairs, shut and bolted the door, and turned the pad red again with his pass.

"Let's check the guards and then go get the captain," he said, walking toward the bridge.

Sally stopped him.

"We need backup. Are you kidding? I want to get everyone else to help, if they will," she said, tugging harder as he tried to get away from her.

Sally wasn't that strong, but when she had something on her mind, she was determined to get it done. He was not going to get away from her.

Martin stopped pulling and finally said, "Okay."

The three walked in the opposite direction toward the guest quarters.

"Stop right there or you all die," a voice with a distinctive Germanic lilt to it bellowed.

The three froze.

"You think I don't know what's going on. I was the one who called Lazarus, you idiots," the captain said, her demeanor turned even colder than Sally had seen it up to now.

Sally, Brin, and Martin now slowly turned around and found themselves at the end of a shotgun barrel.

The captain's eyes were blazing.

Sally thought they were all going to die right there and then.

She watched as the captain's finger went toward the trigger.

Then she heard sobbing from next to her. It was Brin.

"Please, please don't kill us," Brin pleaded.

Sally hadn't known Brin could cry; just shriek, yell 'fuck you' and give people the finger. Maybe it was just a tough girl routine she had been playing.

The captain laughed at her, but turned the gun toward the crew door.

"Open it," she barked at Martin, "Let's get Lazarus out of there."

"Um, well," Martin began, not moving.

"I said open the fucking door," Captain Kramer screamed.

Martin glared at her and looked like he might try to grab the gun.

Instead, he shrugged his shoulders, walked over to the door, and opened it.

He stood aside to let the captain discover the gruesome mess inside.

The captain walked over, screamed, and dropped the gun.

Martin quickly picked it up and trained it on her.

Whipping around, she shrieked, "You've killed my son."

Chapter Forty-Three

"Your son?" Sally said, the first to respond to this startling revelation. Captain Kramer looked at Sally, then back down the stairs to Lazarus' motionless body.

Martin kept the gun on Kramer.

"Now, move…" Martin began.

Captain Kramer lunged at him, grabbing the shotgun from Martin.

He tried to get it back, tugging away.

Brin and Sally stood frozen in place.

Every time the barrel pointed in their direction, they ducked.

The captain's anger gave her incredible strength.

Martin was full of muscles, but he couldn't get the gun away from her.

Sally watched as the barrel went up again and a shot was fired into the ceiling.

The bullet made a huge hole in the ceiling and went off like a firecracker.

Considering it was around midnight, there shouldn't be someone above them on the upper deck to get shot.

But it did bring all the other guests out of their cabins, and the crew, flying up the stairs from the crew area.

There was a lot of screaming and shouting as Hoppy, Aharon & Niv, Brother Francesco, and the Wongs appeared.

Then Kwame, Mary, and the cook saw the captain and Martin.

When they all noticed the shotgun, they froze.

Luckily, Martin had just managed to finally wrestle it back from the captain.

Hoppy ran forward and grabbed the captain in a power hold.

"What the hell is going on here?" Brother Francesco yelled.

Ah, monks can swear too, Sally thought.

"They killed my son," Captain Kramer yelled, pointing at Martin, Sally, and Brin.

When she heard this, Hoppy dropped her hold and stared at the captain.

"Your son?" she yelled.

That seemed to be the shocking question on everyone's mind.

Sally walked over to the captain, who now burst into tears and fell to the ground.

Martin kept the gun trained on her.

"Martin, did you know about this?" Sally asked.

Martin shook his head.

"No way. I just thought he was the FBI agent," he replied.

"Well, now we know what happened," Brin said.

Sally turned to her.

"Know what happened? No, we don't. All we know is that Lazarus was her son," Sally replied.

"This is just fucking great," Amy Wong cried. She started punching her husband.

"You wanted to come on this fucking trip. Made me leave my great restaurant and come to this crazy country. Now we're all fucked."

By now, she was screaming.

Brother Francesco went over to her and pulled her off her husband. She tried to punch the monk, but he yelled, "Stop now, Amy!" and she dropped her hands and collapsed on the floor.

Sally knew what had to be done.

She stood next to Martin and whispered in his ear. He nodded and handed her his pass card.

She turned to the rest of the guests.

"I'm going to the bridge to call for help. We need someone here from Memphis police now."

She started to walk away when there was another scream.

"You're not going anywhere. Get back here now!" Captain Kramer called.

Captain Kramer?

Sally spun around and saw Kramer had a pistol in her hand pointed at her.

"What the hell?" Sally said.

"Drop the shotgun now asshole or I kill her," the captain yelled at Martin.

Martin didn't hesitate. He placed the shotgun gingerly on the floor and walked over to the group of guests.

Sally walked back toward the captain.

"Stop where you are," Kramer cried.

Sally had had enough of this bullshit.

She walked right up to the captain.

"Okay, we are docked in Memphis. You can't kill us all at once. How do you think you're going to get away with it?"

The captain laughed.

"Well, you have killed my son. I'll see you all fry."

She did have a point. Martin had done it. Okay, maybe it was an accident. But they were accessories to murder.

"Stop it, I order you," the captain said as she turned to her crew members, who looked like they were about to tackle her, Kwame at the fore.

They froze.

"Get down the fucking stairs," she said pointing the gun toward the open crew door.

Mary and the cook walked toward it while Kwame hesitated.

"I said move. Now!" she screamed.

"Fuck you," Kwame said and he followed the others down the stairs.

The captain walked over and looked down. They gingerly stepped over the body.

Sally saw a tear in her eye, but then anger took over again.

Captain Kramer slammed the door shut, turned the lock, and held her pass against the pad on the wall. It went red.

"You will be here to witness my triumph. You are still my guests, remember," the captain explained why they were still upstairs.

She cackled.

CHAPTER FORTY-THREE

Sally shivered, but knew she had to do something.

Maybe if she kept the captain talking long enough, one of the crew or guests could radio for help. She wasn't sure if the crew had access to any radio below deck. But maybe cell phones they could make a call with. She hoped they were doing that right now. Oh, wait, they had probably all been confiscated by the FBI.

Sally didn't want to see anyone else die on this ship, and she was not going to let some Germanic murderess tell her what to do.

"I think the police and FBI will be more interested in the deaths here on board that involved you. Jim and your assistant cook didn't deserve to die. Your son's death was an accident. You know it. Why don't you tell us all about your smarts and why there were two murders on this trip?"

Sally was rambling, and she knew it, but maybe she could stroke the captain's ego and get some truth out of her.

Out of the corner of her eye, she saw Hoppy begin to move away toward the bridge.

"Stop right there," the captain yelled, now pointing the gun at Hoppy, who stopped walking.

"Okay, okay, we get it," Hoppy replied, returning to the group.

"I'm not telling you anything," the captain said. She began backing away from the group, the gun pointed at all of them.

Sally froze but saw Martin beginning to move.

The captain fired a shot, which just missed his leg.

"Stop this," Martin screamed.

The captain ignored him.

By this point, she had reached the hallway toward the bridge and turned the corner.

Martin dashed after her, with Sally close behind.

They both sped down the hallway, taking the corner at breakneck speed.

Sally's sneaker slipped slightly, and she almost went down. She managed to right herself but groaned, realizing her ankle was sprained. Falling against the wall, she slid toward the floor.

She listened to Martin gallop up the stairs toward the bridge.

She heard a door slam and something clicked and beeped.

"Fuck," she heard Martin yell, pounding on the door to the bridge.

Martin came down the stairs and around the corner.

He was panting and red in the face.

Then he saw her sitting on the ground.

The rest of the guests came running.

"What happened to you?" Brin asked.

Sally grimaced and rubbed her ankle.

Hoppy dropped to the floor and began examining her.

"I think I sprained my ankle," Sally replied.

"You could have been killed," Brother Francesco said as he knelt down to give her a hug.

Then Martin spoke between still heaving breaths.

"She…has…locked…herself…on the bridge," he finally managed to get out.

"What's going to happen now?" Amy Wong said quietly, tears in her eyes.

Jason touched her arm.

"No idea," Martin said.

Then they all heard what sounded like a gunshot.

Then another sound, and the boat shifted.

"Shit," Martin muttered.

"What is it?" Sally asked.

"She must have remotely unlocked the clamp from the dock. We're moving down the river," he answered as they all looked out the small porthole in the door at the end of the corridor and saw buildings and trees moving by.

"But the gunshot?" Francesco said.

"She must have shot the pilot," Martin replied a bit too matter-of-factly for Sally's taste.

"We have to call someone for help," Sally said, stating the obvious.

"How? We don't have a phone," Martin declared.

Sally looked at Brin, who shook her head.

When had she hidden the stolen phone?

They were stuck on the boat with a mad captain with a gun while they careened down the Mississippi.

Sally hoped the captain wasn't going to do something too dramatic.

229

Chapter Forty-Four

To consider their next move, they had all walked to the restaurant and sat around the tables.

Well, Sally had hobbled with Martin's help.

His strong arms gave her comfort, and he had helped her into a chair near the restaurant entrance so she wouldn't have to move too far.

Everyone was sitting except Martin.

"Okay, I think we should storm the bridge," he suggested.

"Does the crew below have a radio?" Brin asked.

But Martin shook his head.

"No, the only radio is on the bridge," he replied.

Martin looked around the room.

"Any other ideas?" he asked.

Jason Wong stood up.

"I demand to call my embassy. This is now an international incident and you will all pay," he said, shaking, red in the face.

Amy pulled him down and whispered in his ear. He remained silent after that.

Sally noticed Amy had his hand in a death grip.

Martin looked out the window.

"We're heading toward New Orleans and open sea. We're not going that fast, but the boat isn't made for ocean currents. We need to get back control before we hit New Orleans," Martin said a bit too calmly, Sally thought.

"How long will it take us to get to New Orleans?" Brin asked.

"Well, it should take about twenty hours, but if she speeds us up, maybe less," Martin replied.

"Well, that gives us a lot of time to get control of the boat, doesn't it?" Sally offered.

Everyone nodded except Martin.

"Sure, but she could also decide to run us aground or worse, smash the boat into the shore. We could break up in minutes," he replied.

No one moved as that notion sank in.

Amy Wong stood up.

"Then let's fucking do it," she yelled, her South African accent wound up like Sally had never heard before.

Hoppy jumped up and whooped.

"Fuck yeah," she yelled.

"I'm in too," Brin added.

Sally pushed herself up.

"Let's go, crew," she called, hobbling toward the door.

Martin came over to her.

"You're not going anywhere. None of you," he said, staring at Brin, Hoppy, and Amy.

"I have known her for years. I will go upstairs and try to talk some sense into her."

It sounded like an order, not a request,

Well, he was the first officer on board.

The women hesitated but finally all moved, or hobbled, back to their seats.

"Fine. But be careful," Sally said, as if that was going to make it all better.

Martin strode out of the restaurant.

Sally hoped they would see him alive again.

Once he was gone, everyone turned to Sally as if she were Martin's deputy.

"What do we do now, boss?" Brin asked, echoing what the others were probably thinking.

Sally considered for a moment before answering.

"Brin, you have to go get that phone you took," Sally said, to gasps in the room.

"No can do, honey. I chucked it overboard when I went to check the guards. Didn't want anyone finding it. Which now sounds the dumbest thing I've ever done," Brin said, looking at the floor.

"Yup," Amy replied.

Surprisingly, this didn't get a bird flip from Brin, but then again, Amy was absolutely right.

"Ugh, we should just follow him upstairs and break down the door. I wanna get her," Brin cried like she was readying for battle.

"Okay, I know you are out to get blood, all of you," she said, her eyes sweeping the room, "but the goal is to get off this ship safely. Not end up getting shot, or having the captain lose control of the ship as we're trying to take her down. Then we crash into the shore and bye-bye people."

Sally tried to push herself up to give her words more weight while standing, but she winced and fell back.

"Damn," she yelled out loud, "Fucking ankle."

The room went silent.

They weren't sure it appeared whether to tackle her or listen to her.

Of course, they listened.

Hoppy got up, followed by Francesco. They were holding hands, Sally noticed.

"Alright, boss. We'll go and try to find a cell phone," Hoppy said, dragging the monk along with her.

"Thank you!" she said.

Looking over at Niv and Aharon.

"Could you two try to get the crew out of their quarters. We need all the help we can get," she explained.

"Um, how are we going to break in? That door is steel, and the keypad is locked."

Damn, Sally thought, we should have gotten Martin's crew card before he left.

"Well, try looking for something to break the pad. Maybe that will short out the lock and you can open the door," she offered helpfully.

She didn't think that was really that helpful, but she was trying to stay positive in the light of a difficult situation.

How did she get herself into them?

Well, if she were honest with herself, she loved danger, loved investigating, and somehow couldn't wait for the next exciting turn to take in her life.

She finished that thought, thinking about her bartender, Magda. She would certainly have a story to tell Magda when she got back to Berry Springs!

Aharon shrugged. Niv looked at him and smiled. Both Israelis left the restaurant.

Sally hoped they were successful.

That left her with Brin and the Wongs.

Brin jumped up and ran over to her.

"What can I do?" Brin asked, trembling a bit.

Sally wondered if it was because she didn't have a phone to check at the moment or update her followers on the exciting events she had found herself in.

"We really need to find a phone, so why don't you also search the ship. Maybe Amy can go with you," Sally offered, looking across the room at the Wongs.

Amy got up.

"Let's go, Brin," Amy ordered.

Brin looked down at Sally, who grinned.

"Ugh," Brin said, but walked over to Amy and followed her out of the restaurant.

Sally thought it was a good idea to keep Jason Wong with her. She didn't want him doing anything rash, like starting an international incident by calling his embassy.

Well, actually, he couldn't do that at the moment anyway. No one had a phone.

Sally hoped he didn't have some kind of secret satellite phone in his room.

She glanced across the room. He was just sitting there, staring out the window at the river going by.

"Everything okay, Jason?" Sally asked, not even bothering to try to get up again.

Jason didn't move.

"Jason?" she called, a bit louder.

He shook like a dog ridding itself of water.

"Um, what?" he finally asked.

"Everything okay?" Sally repeated.

He just started to laugh.

"Oh everything is fucking good. Don't you think?" he laughed hysterically.

"My wife is a bitch. This trip is a bitch. And I'm headed to Washington to do a shit job at a shit embassy. Everything's great," Jason said, getting louder with every short sentence.

Sally stayed silent.

He clammed up again after that outburst and turned back to staring out the window.

If he suddenly got up and tried to do something, Sally wouldn't have been able to stop him with her sprained ankle anyway.

Chapter Forty-Five

Sally was kicking herself for slipping while they had been chasing the captain to the bridge. She was not someone to just sit around while everyone else looked for a phone and tried to get the captain in custody.

She looked over at Jason, who was still staring out the window. Sally hoped he wasn't having a breakdown.

A part of her really didn't care about his problems. She just wanted to figure out the murders and get the hell off this ship.

She had thought of calling Mark Soder, the police officer who had been so helpful and comforting months before, as she dealt with her business partner Bill's death and the other murders. Without his help, she probably wouldn't have been able to solve them.

She had not thought of calling his boss, John Finnegan. They had a love-hate relationship and she knew he had probably laughed his ass off when he heard she was involved in another murder. Though he had put in a good word for her with the Klondike police.

Of course, to do that, she needed a working phone. Ugh, technology!

Sally joined Jason, watching the world go by. It looked like the boat was still heading straight down the river, so that was a good thing. It didn't seem to be heading for either of the shores.

Sally breathed a sigh of relief for that.

Then she had a thought.

"Jason, could you help me?" she called.

Jason continued to stare out the window and mumble to himself.

"Jason!" she yelled.

This got his attention.

"What? What?" he screamed as if he had just been woken from a deep sleep.

He jumped up and stared at her.

"Jason, Jason. It's okay. I just need your help," she replied in her most calming voice.

The one she used when a drunk at her biker bar started to get belligerent.

It usually worked.

It did this time as well.

"I'm sorry. You startled me," he said, wiping the sweat off his brow.

"I need your help," Sally repeated.

He ran over to her.

"Yes, yes. Please give me something to do. Otherwise, I will just be sitting here feeling sorry for myself," he said, nodding rapidly.

"Well. There is an infirmary on the ship. I was thinking maybe they have a set of crutches I could use. I can't stay here doing nothing," she explained, slowing down for each word, but raising her voice as she spoke them.

"Got it. I'm on it," and he ran out of the room like a puppy going to catch a stick.

Now Sally was all alone. She wished she had somehow gotten a drink. After hours of drama, still awake in the middle of the night, she was hungry and thirsty.

Luckily, she only had to wait a few minutes before the door to the restaurant opened.

It was Brother Francesco alone.

"Oh, Francesco. Great to see you. I was wondering if you could get me some water. I'm parched," she said.

He kept walking toward her.

"Uh, where's Hoppy? Did you find a phone?" Sally asked, wondering why he had come back by himself.

"Hoppy's safe," he replied.

Sally began to get worried. What was going on?

"Safe? What do you mean Francesco?" Sally asked, trying to push herself up.

Putting pressure on her bad ankle made her scream out in pain, and she fell back into the chair.

"Safe. She is safe," Francesco said as he reached her and put his hands on both arms of the chair, sticking his face directly in hers.

Sally froze.

"Francesco. You're scaring me," she said, trying to push him away.

He grabbed her hand.

"Don't touch me!" he said, pushing her back hard into the chair, knocking the air out of her.

Luckily for Sally, he stepped back to stare at her.

"What is going on, Francesco? What is wrong with you?" she asked, hoping Jason would be back with the crutches or any of the other guests would show up to save her.

Because she was sure she was going to die here.

What had happened to Francesco, the kind monk?

"I'm fine," he replied in a tense whisper, "but I'm not sure about you. Let's see."

Sally was ready to scream, but decided that might only make him angrier.

Francesco walked over to one of the tables and grabbed a chair.

He dragged it over to where Sally was sitting and placed it across from her.

He planted himself in the chair and looked at her with piercing eyes.

"Let me tell you about my life," he began.

Chapter Forty-Six

"I grew up in a small town in northern Italy in the German-speaking South Tyrol region," Francesco began.

Sally couldn't move, though she was glad he hadn't tied her up.

She thought if she stayed still and silent, this nightmare would be over soon. And she would get out of the room and off the ship alive.

With every word, she prayed one of the other guests would show up. Or better yet, Martin, the first officer, who was trying to wrestle control of the ship back from the captain.

Where were they? she screamed silently.

Her sprained ankle was now throbbing, which just added to the torture.

"My mother is Austrian from Vienna. My father is Italian from that German-speaking region," the monk continued.

Sally couldn't quite see him as a gentle monk anymore. Now that he had her captive.

Well, that's how she felt. And his piercing eyes told her that that is what she should be thinking.

What was he doing?

Why did he come in here and begin to tell her his family story? He had mentioned getting away from his family at one of the dinners, but did she need the details?

Well, she didn't have a choice at that point.

Francesco pushed himself up, still staring at Sally.

She gave a start thinking he was going to lunge at her.

Instead, he moved away toward the large windows looking out on the mighty Mississippi.

Sally breathed an audible sigh of relief.

He turned.

"Oh, you think you can get away now? Forget it," he said, his words sharp as a knife.

Francesco turned back to the window and continued his story.

"My father died when I was five. I don't remember him, but he was inconsequential anyway. A poor shepherd from a poor region. My mother, on the other hand, is a proud woman, from a proud family of restaurateurs in the beautiful city of Vienna. You like my mother, don't you?" he said, slowly touching each word like he was gently playing the ivory keys of a grand piano.

Then it dawned on her.

Captain Kramer.

Sally wanted to scream, but she thought if she did, she would die right then and there.

Her fancy, relaxing, luxury trip down the river was now filled with a family drama that was playing out before her eyes.

Captain Kramer's old lover. Dead. Murdered.

Captain Kramer's son, Agent Lazarus. Dead.

Captain Kramer's son, Brother Francesco, unhinged and ready to kill for his mother.

As she was contemplating this, the door of the restaurant opened.

Sally pushed herself up an inch and hoped it was Martin.

Then she saw Jason Wong walk in with crutches.

He moved toward Sally and then noticed Brother Francesco sprinting for him.

Jason swung the crutches just as Francesco was about to pounce.

The monk went down with a grunt, his forehead bleeding from the gash Jason had just caused.

That's when Sally let out a loud scream.

Jason ran to her.

"What's wrong?" he asked.

She wondered if he was kidding.

"Wrong? Francesco was going to kill me," she yelled.

Her scream and loud voice brought Niv, Aharon, Amy, and Brin running in.

They looked at Francesco on the floor, bleeding, Jason holding the crutches over Sally, and Sally looking panicked.

Niv ran and punched Jason, who dropped the crutches and fell to the floor.

"What the hell are you doing?" Sally said, only slightly calmer.

"Jason was after you," Niv replied.

Sally grunted.

"No, you ass. He was saving me from Francesco," she yelled.

Brin came running over and helped Jason up and onto a chair. He pulled out an old-fashioned handkerchief and held it against his bloody nose.

Amy rushed over to her husband, placing a hand gently on his shoulder and squeezing.

"Uh, sorry there, Jason," Niv said, trying to smile.

"Francesco?" Brin asked, looking over.

"Yes, he apparently is also Captain Kramer's son," Sally explained.

"Jesus," was all Brin could say.

Then she glanced around.

"Where's Hoppy?" Brin asked.

Sally began to cry.

"Probably dead. Who knows. Or locked up somewhere. I tried to ask. He wouldn't tell me," she said between sobs.

"You need a drink," Brin cried, sprinting for the lounge.

Aharon had been standing frozen in the corner, but suddenly went into action.

He grabbed one of the tablecloths and bandaged Francesco's forehead. The bleeding had slowed, and Francesco had pushed himself up and was now sitting cross-legged on the floor.

He didn't look like he was going to hurt someone now.

Amy walked over to him.

"Where is Hoppy?" she screamed.

Sally hoped she was still alive.

Francesco didn't speak. He just sat there looking at the floor in front of him.

"Please tie him up, Aharon," Sally ordered.

Aharon looked at her.

"He's not going anywhere," he replied.

"Do it. Please," she said even louder.

Aharon shrugged and grabbed another tablecloth to tie Francesco's hands behind his back. Then he knotted another end to one of the heavy tables.

Brin came out of the lounge with a large glass.

"I poured whatever I could find into the glass. You may want to sip slowly. I didn't really look at the bottle as I poured," Brin said.

Sally didn't think downing a ton of alcohol at three in the morning was really going to help, but Brin looked at her so helpfully that Sally took a sip and almost passed out from it.

She coughed.

"Uh, thanks," Sally gasped, putting the glass down on the table next to her.

Then the door opened again.

Martin had returned…with the captain.

Chapter Forty-Seven

"How did you get onto the bridge?" Sally asked.

"There's a safety mechanism on the door to stop someone from taking full control of the ship, just in situations like this. In her haste and anger and emotion, our smart captain forgot that. It needs two codes to deactivate, for obvious reasons. I was able to wrestle the gun from her," Martin explained.

Sally kept waiting for the captain to struggle free. Instead, she walked slowly next to Martin, her head down. He planted her on a chair and just left her there.

He didn't even bother to tie her hands or tie them to the chair or table.

Francesco, on the other hand, was struggling against the knots Aharon had tied.

"Let me out. I will kill you all," he screamed.

Everyone stared at him. So much for the quiet monk with the calming demeanor.

He was a monster.

Sally looked over at the captain, wondering if she was going to say something about all of this.

She was just looking at the ground, apparently in defeat.

"*Mutti*, do something," Francesco cried, suddenly using the German term for 'Mom.'

Captain Kramer looked up at him but said nothing.

Francesco continued to thrash.

Martin moved over to stand next to him, putting a hand on his shoulder and obviously using some force as the monk stopped moving about.

Sally suddenly had a thought.

"Martin, who's piloting the boat?" Sally wondered.

There was a clamor of noise as everyone else wondered the same thing. Were they headed for disaster?

He laughed and pointed to the windows.

Sally stared out. Even if it were still dark, she looked across at the riverbank and saw lights. But they weren't moving.

Breathing a sigh of relief, she realized the boat had stopped. They were anchored in place.

But where?

"How far have we gone?" Brin asked, obviously realizing the same thing that Sally just had.

"Not too far. I've already put in a call to the Memphis police and the FBI office there. I need to turn the boat around and head back there, but I wanted to bring our wonderful captain here so you can all watch her. I see you've got another prisoner too. One more son on board, captain?" Martin said, looking over to Captain Kramer.

This got a reaction out of her. She bared her teeth and growled.

Sally's first thought then was that this whole episode would make a great murder mystery. If she were only a writer. Nope, just an accountant turned biker-bar owner.

Niv went over to stand over Francesco.

"How long do we have until we're back in Memphis?" Sally asked, thinking of what to do in between. And she definitely had a plan.

"About an hour, maybe slightly longer," he replied.

Hmm, not that much time.

"Okay, thanks. We really appreciate your help," Sally replied.

Martin left.

"But what about Hoppy?" Brin said.

They all suddenly realized someone would have to go and look for her.

Niv grabbed Francesco and shook him.

"Where is she asshole?" Niv yelled.

"Fuck-e you," was the only thing Francesco responded, looking over at his mother, who continued to remain silent, her head bowed.

Then Brin ran over and slapped his face.

"You bastard. What have you done with her?"

Francesco couldn't look at her.

Then the room shifted slightly. They were underway back to Memphis.

And the nightmare would soon be over, Sally thought.

But they still didn't know where Hoppy was.

Sally pushed herself up and hobbled over to Francesco.

She wasn't going to scream, or slap, or punch, or shake.

She just looked down at him.

"Please, Francesco. Just tell us where Hoppy is. Please tell me she is still alive," Sally pleaded.

Francesco said nothing. All Sally could feel was her heart pounding in her chest.

She was also standing on one leg as her ankle was throbbing something awful.

Sally leaned down and gently placed a hand on his shoulder.

"Please…" was all she said.

Sally could feel the tension in the room. They were all probably wondering if Francesco was going to head-butt her or spit on her.

He finally looked up at Sally and smiled.

That was a little weird.

"She is not dead. I could not kill her, even if a part of me wanted to. But the other part of me loves her," he said quietly.

Sally turned and saw Brin shooting darts at Francesco with her eyes.

"Okay. That's good," Sally offered, "So where can we find her?"

Francesco looked over to the door to the hallway.

"I locked her in the cleaning closet. You know, in the guest area," he replied.

Aharon and Niv sprinted out of the room.

Sally hoped Francesco was telling the truth that he had only locked her up and not done something worse to her.

Chapter Forty-Eight

They had only been underway a few minutes when Sally thought she saw a hint of sunlight outside the window. The sky was brighter. What a way to start a day.

They were supposed to be enjoying their last couple of days on board the luxury Mississippi paddleboat The River Queen. Instead, they were now dealing with the aftermath of three deaths: two murders, one accident.

Sally shuddered to think there may be another death if Aharon and Niv found Hoppy, but she was actually dead. Though Francesco (Sally could no longer think of him as a monk) claimed she was just locked up there.

Sally walked over to where Captain Kramer was sitting, hunched over.

She pulled out a chair and fell into it with a sigh.

Her ankle was throbbing so badly that she had tears in her eyes.

She really needed a painkiller, but that would mean sending someone else out of the room, and they couldn't afford that at the moment.

As she sat down, the others came over, took chairs, and sat in a circle with the captain in the middle.

It was Sally, then Amy, Jason, then Brin.

The captain wouldn't look at them.

Sally scanned the circle and just saw hate. Or maybe it was just anger.

Everyone waited for Sally to speak. She kept glancing at the door, wondering when Aharon and Niv would get back.

And what condition Hoppy would be in.

"Captain Kramer. Matilda. Are you with us?" Sally began quietly.

The captain didn't move.

"We just want to understand what happened here," she continued.

Then she heard thrashing behind her.

Francesco was trying to bounce in his chair.

Jason jumped up, grabbed the crutch, and stood over him.

Francesco went silent.

Sally saw him look at the captain, but Sally wasn't sure what the look meant.

"No *mein Sohn*, it is over," Captain Kramer called.

"*Nein!*" he screamed.

Crack!

Everyone jumped in their chairs and spun around.

Jason had just whacked Francesco unconscious. Sally prayed he hadn't just killed him. She really couldn't take any more deaths. Well, this trip anyway.

As they were settling back in their chairs and returning to Sally's attempt to get the story out of Captain Kramer, the doors opened.

Sally held her breath and looked away for a second.

Then she whipped her head around.

Niv and Aharon were helping Hoppy to walk. She looked beaten, but she was alive.

They were followed by Kwame, Mary Rogers, and the chef.

"Thank god," Brin and Amy said, simultaneously jumping up and helping Hoppy into the nearest chair.

"Hi, everyone, I survived," Hoppy said. All that showed on her face was the grimace of pain.

She settled in.

"Boy, I could use a drink," Hoppy said, turning to Brin, who was now apparently the bartender.

Well, Sally could barely walk anyway.

Brin went to get Hoppy a stiff drink while Aharon and Niv grabbed more chairs to add to the merry circle.

"Thank you, sir, for rescuing us," Kwame said.

He turned to the group.

"It was terrible being locked up with dead Agent Lazarus," he said, not smiling.

"Yes, thank you," Mary added.

They both sat there stiffly, looking over at the captain. The cook sat next to them, looking grim.

"What's going on?" Mary asked frowning

"Yes, so what's been happening while I was away?" Hoppy said, making everyone laugh.

"We want to ask you the same question. Are you all okay?" Sally asked, turning to glare at Francesco at the same time.

"Well, I guess the monk and I won't be getting married," Hoppy replied, chuckling.

What she must have gone through, Sally thought.

"I fought him off and got a couple of bruises. I'm okay" Hoppy said, finally sitting back and closing her eyes.

"You bastard," Amy barked at Francesco, but then calmed down when she remembered Francesco wasn't moving or conscious at the moment.

Jason leaned down.

"Okay, I didn't kill him like you probably were just thinking," he said, tapping the crutch in his hand.

"We are okay too. We are just glad to get out of the crew quarters. I don't think I can ever go down there again," Mary said, sniffling and then bursting into tears.

Sally was sitting next to her and took her hand.

Not only had her cousin been murdered, but she had been locked downstairs with Agent Lazarus' dead body.

Kwame was not his usual happy self, but he didn't say anything about their predicament.

The chef was now crying.

Captain Kramer looked up at Sally.

"Let's begin," she said.

Turning to Kwame, Mary, and Hoppy, "Captain Kramer is going to tell us what has been happening on this ship,"

Mary gasped and stared at her captain.

Turning back to the captain, "Let's start with a photo taken by Martin of you and Jim O'Sullivan on board. He looked pretty angry."

The captain sighed.

Chapter Forty-Nine

Captain Kramer sat up straight, took a deep breath, and began her story.

"I want to begin by saying that I did not want any of this to happen. I was angry, yes, I admit, but I did not want to kill or see people killed," the captain said as she looked slowly at each person sitting around her.

"I'm sorry, but I don't think anyone believes that," Brin said, looking around the room at everyone nodding, except Sally.

She always tried to see the best in people, and maybe the captain felt pushed over the edge at some point. She believed the captain that it had all just snowballed.

The captain shrugged her shoulders and appeared to be contemplating what to say next. Everyone was on the edge of their seats as if they were watching a cliffhanger moment in a movie play out before them.

"I believe I told you that I came to America for a man and that I soon found I didn't need him."

"I get that," Hoppy said weakly.

The captain nodded and continued.

"Well, that was only part of my story. I was a wild girl brought up in a very strict Austrian family. For centuries, my family has run a restaurant in Vienna. And I was expected to work in the restaurant until my last dying breath."

"How terrible. That must have been awful," Amy Wong interjected.

Captain Kramer stopped speaking and looked like she was choking.

Hoppy began to rise, but the captain raised a hand, indicating she was okay.

"The idea that I would never leave that restaurant or Vienna made me sick to my stomach. I was too carefree to get stuck somewhere, but I didn't know what to do."

"I know what you mean. I just had to get out of South Africa," Amy revealed.

Sally felt like the entire room had turned into a confessional, though ironically, the one priest on board was still unconscious at their feet.

"Yes, I was too independent to be in Vienna with my family forever. I talked to my friends, but they were no help. They only saw the wealth and prestige of my family and tried to get me to stay."

Brin nodded.

The captain stopped talking and looked out the window, and then at her son.

A tear fell from her eye.

Sally was barely breathing at the suspense of it all.

She didn't want to urge the captain on, but let her tell her tale in her own time, at her own pace.

The captain turned back to them and smiled.

"I finally decided to run away to Italy to South Tyrol when I was sixteen. That is where I met his father," she continued, pointing to the unconscious Francesco.

"They speak German there, but it's another country, and I thought I could easily find a job or someone would take me in."

The captain's words had started quickly but were now coming out one at a time with pauses that seemed like forever. Sally hoped she wasn't going to collapse before she finished her life's story.

"I bought a bus ticket, packed a small suitcase, and slipped out at night. The bus didn't leave until early morning, so I slept at the bus station. It was a long bus ride, but when I got off the bus, I felt freedom for the first time in my life."

Amy nodded, "China."

"The bus had dropped me off in the middle of a small town. As I began walking away from the bus, I saw a young shepherd herding sheep next to the village square. He was young, rugged, and oh so handsome. He smiled at me as I passed, and I decided to get a small snack in the café nearby."

The captain stopped talking, her breaths coming in heaves.

Hoppy began to get up again, but the captain waved her hand.

"I'm fine," she whispered.

The more the captain talked, the more Sally felt sorry for her, no matter what she had done on this boat.

The room was so calm, no one urging her on or asking impatient questions.

"I got a job in that café, which I will be eternally grateful for. I loved my life there in that village, particularly after I got to know his father, the shepherd," she acknowledged, pointing again to Francesco.

He still hadn't stirred, which Sally realized was a good thing. He probably wouldn't want to hear his mother's confession.

"I fell in love with him immediately, I must admit, something I swore I would never do. Worse, I was only there a few months when I discovered I was with child."

At this, she stopped again and her head bent down.

"So shameful," she whispered.

Then her head came up.

"No, not shameful, Matilda," she yelled, slapping her face.

No one moved. The emotion of the story and now her outburst had everyone spellbound.

Hoppy jumped at the slapping sound.

"No, no stop," Hoppy cried.

Niv put his hand on her arm. Hoppy relaxed.

"You've been through so much. Nothing to be sorry about," Sally replied, referring to both Hoppy and the captain.

The captain's voice brought them all back to the moment.

"So, I was going to have a child. I knew I could never go back to Vienna or see my very Catholic family again. My beautiful shepherd was disgusted by my belly, which he had helped produce. So I decided to go away, go far away."

Sally was at odds with herself. A part of her wanted to hate the captain for what she had done. On the other hand, her life story and the way she was telling it, made Sally want to cry. And just give the captain a hug. What she had gone through was horrible.

Captain Kramer paused.

Sally wasn't sure whether it was to let the last information sink in or because the captain needed every ounce of strength to tell her story.

Memories can be terrible things.

"So, my *Oma*, my grandmother, had given me some money when I left Vienna. She had had to make a difficult choice when she was young, and she knew that I wanted to just live and not be forced to labor just because of my family."

As she talked about her grandmother, she beamed and seemed to regain the energy of years past.

Sally looked over and saw Jason and Amy in tears, holding hands. Her cheeks were wet as well.

Looking around, there wasn't a dry face in the room.

The captain took a deep breath before continuing.

"This gave me money to come here. To America. I'm not sure why I chose it. My English was never that good. But I thought putting an ocean between me and my problems would be the answer. I was only partially right."

Brin got up and went into the lounge.

The group turned to follow her walk.

Sally was worried she was looking for a weapon.

Everyone breathed a sigh of relief when she returned a few seconds later with a bottle of water and a cup.

She brought over a small table and set it up next to the captain. Brin poured the water, then removed the bottle and placed it on the floor next to her chair.

Sally noted that it was a plastic cup, not glass.

Brin was smart. Who knows what the captain might do with glass.

The captain took a sip of water and licked her lips.

"So, I came to Boston on the Queen Elizabeth II ship. Maybe that is why I jumped at the chance to be captain of another queen, this ship," she said lovingly.

"Oh, I will miss this ship."

Yes, where she was going, there would be no sailing or water, except in the showers. Sally knew she would never captain a ship again. And depending on which state she was tried for her crimes, the captain might even face the death penalty.

"Maybe this was a warning sign that I did not notice, but just as I came off the boat with my swollen belly, I saw Jim. Yes, Jim O'Sullivan."

There were a couple of gasps in the room. Sally guessed most had figured out what was going on. And the crew probably knew some of this anyway. She looked over at Mary and Kwame, but both were just sitting, mouths shut, staring at the captain.

"He was a dock worker and so rugged, just like my shepherd. May they both rest in pieces," she said, spitting on the ground.

Matilda's eyes went wet as she reminisced.

"I fell in love with Jim immediately. Even though he was also Catholic, he treated me like a queen and didn't ask about my pregnancy. He just helped with it and found me a room to stay while I waited for the birth of my son. The boy you see here," she explained, pointing to the unconscious Francesco.

So this was the child. But what about Agent Lazarus? Sally guessed Captain Kramer would be getting to him at some point. She seemed to want to tell her entire life's story to the group.

"A few months later, with the help of a midwife Jim knew, I produced the man you see here. He was such a beautiful child. I knew one day he would find God. And he didn't let me down. Even if he did go to live with his father when he turned eighteen."

She spit again and took a drink of water.

"I lost touch with him after that. It was only on this trip that I found my son again. I would have recognized him anywhere. He looks exactly like his father," she said, smiling angelically as she stared at her son.

He still wasn't moving. Sally wondered if they should do something about him.

But if she were honest with herself, she wasn't feeling so generous with the evil monk.

"But what about my cousin?" Mary suddenly said.

The captain looked like she was about to tell her crew member to shut up. But then she must have realized she had no power over anything or anyone at the moment, so she just gave her a sharp look.

"Yes, Jim. What about Jim? I would not have recognized him at all. When he came on board, I had seen him staring at me, but I had no idea what that was about. Then he cornered me one afternoon and explained who he was. He was not happy about me leaving Boston when I found out I was pregnant again by another man."

"Slut," Brin blurted out.

"Oh fuck you," the captain retorted.

No one else moved or said anything. They were mesmerized by her story and her honesty.

"But why did you have to kill him?" Mary asked, tears streaming down her face, "What did he do?"

That's what Sally had just been wondering.

"Shame," was all the captain could say.

"The shame of my life came back to haunt me. I know Jim helped me in Boston, but a part of me wanted to punish him for all the shame I felt. I had thought I had put it behind me, found a new life I loved as a sea captain. Tried to forget my past. Tried to forget my sons. But it all came rushing back. I panicked. I found out about his fish allergy from his initial reservation. Used some dried fish on board to create the fish powder. Put the canister in the ventilation shaft. Got everything ready. He died. He died. Oh God, forgive me."

Her words came out rapid fire in between short breaths.

Then the captain collapsed on the floor.

Chapter Fifty

Friday morning, Sally found herself sitting on a bench on the Mississippi in New Orleans.

Rubbing her hands over it, it reminded her an awful lot of the bench she had been sitting on just a few short days ago in Hannibal, Missouri. That was a day she would cherish forever. Free of the bar, free of Berry Springs, awaiting a glorious ten-day paddleboat cruise down the Mississippi.

As with many things in life, it didn't quite turn out the way she had imagined. Though she had made some good friends.

Both Hoppy and Brin had promised to stay in touch, and they had all exchanged contact details.

Sally didn't think she would ever get to Spain or Australia, but a girl can always dream, can't she?

Well, she was living her dream in Berry Springs. That much was certain.

Thursday had been a whirlwind of activity.

Martin Sandworth had docked the boat back in Memphis, meeting a slew of police and FBI. The captain and Francesco, who had now regained consciousness, had been quickly taken off the ship in handcuffs. Sally didn't think anyone on the ship felt bad about that.

The captain's story was certainly a sad one. Did a sad, terrible life justify murders?

No, never.

And she couldn't feel bad for Francesco. He had manipulated them all in the guise of the caring Italian Benedictine monk.

Sally had shed a tear when Agent Lazarus' body was removed. She hadn't liked him, but his death, an accident, was tragic, like the other two.

The guests and crew had been questioned on board the ship. Based on what Lazarus had already provided to his FBI colleagues, the captain's confession, and other evidence, all were let go, except Martin. While Lazarus' death had been an accident, he would still have to face charges, though it looked like he would get off on self-defense.

Another boat was sent by the tour company to take them the rest of the way to New Orleans. Their cars had been transported there on the first day of their cruise.

The River Queen was now a crime scene, and Sally wasn't sure anyone would ever want to take a ride on it again after the coverage that had started to hit the papers.

Sally wondered what Jason's Chinese government thought of all this. Even if he had nothing to do with it, they would probably be keeping extra tabs on him while he was in DC, if he even got to go to DC.

Sally really felt sad for Amy, who had warmed up to her throughout the trip. She had given up her restaurant, which she loved, to follow her man.

Once they reached New Orleans, they all rushed off the boat as quickly as possible, like a dog shaking off water.

Sally looked at the city before her and debated whether she would tack on a day or two and explore it. It had been part of the original plan.

But she quickly knew she had to get back home as soon as possible and try to put this way-too-eventful trip behind her.

Magda, her bartender, would be glad to see her. She had called her on Thursday afternoon and told her everything that had gone on. Magda was shocked, but glad Sally was okay.

She had walked to her car, put her bags in the trunk, and then decided to take a moment of peace before driving the ten hours back to Berry Springs. She loved car trips, but this one was going to be a slog. She couldn't wait to get back to her beloved Ozark Mountains.

Sitting back on the bench, she reached over to pat the hand of the person sitting next to her.

Her friend Sergeant Mark Soder from the Berry Springs police department had surprised her.

He had heard about the murders from Magda and driven all the way to New Orleans to escort her home. One of his colleagues came with him to drive the police car back.

Apparently, his boss, Detective John Finnegan, hadn't had a problem with him taking a couple of days off.

Maybe Finnegan did have a soft spot for Sally.

"Mark, seeing you here is the best way to end my trip. What a nightmare," Sally said.

Soder laughed.

"Oh, come on, you love being an investigator," he replied.

Sally smiled but said nothing.

She had now been a part of two murder investigations. So much for finding people's dogs or ex-lovers. She was really getting used to it, but would never get used to the fear and death.

Whatever the next adventure would bring, she would be ready. And she would love it.

A Note from the Author

I've been overwhelmed by the feedback I've received for the first Sally Witherspoon mystery, *Death in the Ozarks.*

I hope you have enjoyed this second book in the series, *Murder on the Mississippi!*

If you are interested in learning more about me and my writing, please check out my website (https://www.erikmey.com).

Be well!

Acknowledgments

Thank you to Cindy Bullard, my literary agent, and to Shawn Reilly Simmons and everyone at Level Best Books for helping to bring Sally Witherspoon into the wider world. I am eternally grateful!

About the Author

Currently in Austria, Erik S. Meyers is an American abroad for years and years who has lived or worked in six countries on three continents, the longest in Germany. He is an award-winning author and communications professional with over 25 years of expertise in a variety of corporate roles. Reading and writing are his passions, when he is not hiking one of the amazing trails in Austria or elsewhere.

SOCIAL MEDIA HANDLES:
Facebook: https://www.facebook.com/ErikSMeyersAuthor/
Instagram: https://www.instagram.com/erikmeyauthor/

AUTHOR WEBSITE:
https://www.erikmey.com

Also by Erik S. Meyers

Sally Witherspoon Book 1: *Death in the Ozarks* (https://www.amazon.com/dp/B0CKWT4FY2/)

Connections: A Short Story Anthology (https://www.amazon.com/dp/B0DJ7N98R5)

The Accidental Change Agent (https://www.amazon.com/-/en/dp/B08BSR9CDS/)

Caged Time (https://www.amazon.com/Caged-Time-Tarniss-desire-faith-ebook/dp/B08VRCR5FS/)